Take What You Want

BY FAITH BALDWIN

HOLT, RINEHART AND WINSTON

New York *Chicago* *San Francisco*

Published simultaneously in Canada by Holt, Rinehart and Winston of Canada, Limited.

Library of Congress Catalog Card Number: 74-80369

FIRST EDITION

SBN: 03-081839-7

Printed in the United States of America

DESIGNER: MARJORIE J. FLOCK

Dedication

THIS BOOK IS FOR *Jane Rule and Helen Sonthoff, with an apology.*

In dedicating this confection, or meringue, to a couple of eggheads, I realize my temerity. I am also aware that a fairy story in the 1960's is not exactly like those of Perrault. But there are still a few Cinderellas around and even Sleeping Beauties (in some remote hamlet). I had considerable difficulty with it as, while in my youth I had some knowledge of yachts and what one of my minor characters would call "a well-staffed house," that's as far as I went. I also have never set up Corporations or Foundations; nor have I ever had a personal, guardian maid. Actually, this was written in a reactionary spirit because I have so long been reading serious, important literature concerned with Problems, and starred with the now-commonplace four-letter words (the writers have forgotten there are others, such as "love" and "hope").

Therefore, forgive me. This is simply a bread-and-butter letter, sprinkled with a little sugar and cinnamon, to thank you for sharing your view of Spanish Beach, and also George, with me.

With love,
Faith

TAKE WHAT YOU WANT

ONE

❀❀❀

THE FIRST TIME Janice Cooper saw Whitney Dennis, live and in color, was on the autumn morning when he charged through her office, as inconspicuous as a tornado. Half rising, she remonstrated in a sort of contralto squeak, "Where do you think you're going?" But he kept right on, headed for the even more private office of Howard Norton, counselor-at-law.

"Hi, Sweetheart," responded Mr. Dennis without turning; then he swiveled, did a double take, said, "You're new around here," and barreled into Mr. Norton's sacrosanct quarters.

Janice flipped a switch and spoke severely to the receptionist, whose name was Rosalee. "What did you mean," she demanded, "by sending a man in here without notifying me?"

"Oh, him!" said Rosalee inelegantly. "Honey, he's never announced—he's Whitney Dennis." She sighed. "Six years and he doesn't remember my name!"

Well! thought Janice.

She had seen pictures of Mr. Dennis in the press and the weekly magazines, often squinting under an alien sun. She'd read about him—news items, interviews, profiles. He was young, unmarried and had, it was rumored, most of the money in this material world; in a sense, he helped pay her own not-inconsiderable salary as legal and personal secretary to Mr. Norton, senior member of the celebrated firm of Norton, Manly and Sherwood; also Mr. Dennis' personal attorney, advisor to the Dennis Foundation and member of the Board. The corporate section of the law firm handled the business of the Foundation and was occasionally called in on matters pertaining to the Dennis Corporation, although it had its own legal staff.

Once more Janice thought: Well! This was no time for mental rhetoric.

Voices boomed through the private-office door.

". . . something new has been added," Mr. Dennis was remarking. "My reaction is positive and affirmative, but what happened to my dear old doll, Emma?"

"Retired."

"Let me have her address. Does she still like caviar and roses? Who's your new girl? I love Emma dearly, but visually you've improved this magnificent office, with its, and I quote, 'breathtaking view of the river from fifty-six stories up.' "

Mr. Norton said, in the rich, controlled voice which, together with his great size and shock of silver hair so impressed juries—favorably, as a rule—"I'll introduce you to Janice. You'll be seeing a good deal of her now that you're back on the job." He opened the door, looked at Janice, and ordered, "On the double."

Janice rose and advanced without haste. She was a natural ash-blonde with very dark eyes and a redheaded temper, usually restrained. She was also neatly and provocatively put together.

"Yes, sir?"

"Come in. This is Whitney Dennis." Mr. Norton put a solid arm around Janice's shoulders. "And this, Whit, is Janice Cooper, who has the honor of being my godchild."

"Nepotism," remarked young Mr. Dennis. "Can she type?"

"College," said Mr. Norton. "Advanced courses in shorthand, typing, business and commercial law; also tax courses. She was assigned to the office pool on graduation. When Emma retired, I kicked Janice upstairs."

"What does she like?" inquired Dennis. "Geraniums and smoked salmon? I'll take her out to lunch."

"Run along," said Mr. Norton benevolently. "I have a luncheon engagement too."

"Okay," said Dennis. "Get your hat, if any—I hope you're hungry. I like healthy girls with hearty appetites. I trust you aren't on an unnecessary diet."

Janice said, "Thank you very much, Mr. Dennis, but I'm not free for lunch."

"Where do you live? I'll pick you up at eight for dinner."

"I'm not free for dinner either." She looked at her godfather, who was smiling. "If you'll excuse me, sir . . . ?" she said.

Norton nodded. When the door had closed, he remarked, still smiling. "I anticipated that. Janice has quite an effect on males of all ages."

"Seriously, is she your godchild?"

"Certainly. Her father and I were at the university together. He, your father and I roomed together one year. Bill Cooper's practicing law in Cleveland. Last time I saw him he told me he was going to retire in a couple of years and go fishing. Janice is a nice kid, Whit, one of the best."

"Is this a warning?"

"Of course."

Dennis said, as if in shock, "She turned me down."

"She's turned down a good many high-handed males, including Howard Jr., who hasn't recovered."

"Oh, well," said Dennis cheerfully, "we have our fall meeting soon and I daresay she'll be there, as Emma used to be, with notebook in paw. There's lots of time. . . . Why don't you ask what I've been doing the last six months?"

"I know. Europe, mostly on Corporation and Foundation matters. I keep in touch."

"I thought a small, dark man with a stealthy manner shadowed me all the time I was in Athens."

"Probably some Greek girl's boy friend," said Norton laughing. "How about lunch?"

"You said you have an engagement."

"I didn't—and Janice knows it. Where do you want to eat? Incidentally, I'm on a low-carbohydrate diet."

"How distressing, but you can afford to lose twenty-five pounds or so. How about the Club?"

"Which one?"

Dennis told him, and as they went out through Janice's office, Norton said, "You can reach me at the Princeton Club, Janice, if anything comes up."

"I hope it won't be your lunch," said Dennis, regarding Janice, "and that you enjoy it more than I expect to enjoy mine," he added politely.

"Thank you, Mr. Dennis," said Janice. She had a low, pleasant voice, another piece of equipment of which Mr. Dennis approved.

When they'd gone, she asked the switchboard to connect her with Mr. Manly's office. Janice shared an apartment with Audrey Towns, who was Mr. Manly's secretary; there was a third girl involved in the flat sharing, one who brought what Janice called "a little color" into their legal lives; she was Katie Evans, who worked for a dress designer.

"Hi! Free for lunch?"

Audrey reported mournfully that Tom had to fly to Washington and had canceled their date. "So I'm free, worse luck," she said.

"Thanks, dear."

They lunched in the building, and over coffee Janice, admiring Audrey's pretty face, asked, "When are you and Tom getting married?"

"He'll postpone it once too often," said Audrey, "and I'll marry someone in a rock-and-roll band."

"Why?"

"He'd be so different from Tom. It's hell to be engaged to a fanatically ambitious man. Oh, he loves me, I suppose," said Audrey sighing, "and I'm nuts about him. But he won't be a husband, he'll be a career. I'll have to meet him at the door in a hostess gown with a pitcher of martinis when we're alone, which won't be often. I've been his hostess at his apartment so many times I could write a book about it."

Janice was, as always, sympathetic. She said encouragingly, "I'll miss you when you leave us."

"I may never; or I may, and then come back. I don't know why I had to fall in love with a computer. I wish I could just marry for money, give value received, and let it go at that."

Janice said somberly, "We don't seem to have much choice when it comes to falling in love. As my English grandfather used to say, 'It's a mug's game.' "

"Yep," said Audrey. She knew about Dave Peters. . . . Not many people did, but at the time Janice had given up her own apartment—and Dave—and gone in with Audrey and Katie, she'd been in pretty bad shape; Audrey had helped, so she knew, as did Howard Norton, and a few others.

Janice said carelessly, "If you decide to erase Tom and settle for, say, a hundred million, I can introduce you to Whitney Dennis."

Audrey dropped a fork. "Whitney Dennis," she said. "I thought he was a legend like Midas or Howard Hughes."

"Nonsense. I know he's been out of the country, but he must have come to the office since you came to work here."

"Not Mr. Manly's. Where did you meet him?"

"In my office this morning. He asked me to lunch."

"And you're lunching with *me?*"

Janice said, "I fancy he asks practically any girl not cross-eyed, bowlegged or with any of the dire drawbacks you hear about on TV."

"What's he like?"

"Tall, broad-shouldered, good-looking——"

"I don't believe it."

"I don't either. It isn't cricket. By all the rules of fair play and the law of averages he should be short, fat and repulsive."

"Charm?" asked Audrey cautiously.

"Loaded, I daresay, if you're crazy about hurricanes."

"Next time he asks you," Audrey advised, "latch on to him. It could be a soul-stirring experience."

"I don't think I care to have my soul stirred. He scares me. However, I do attend the Dennis Foundation Board Meetings in the line of duty. He wasn't at the late spring one, which was my first, nor at this past summer's."

"Does he really run the Foundation?"

"It so happens," said Janice carelessly, "that after he and Uncle Howard went off to the Princeton Club, I sort of fell over a copy of *Who's Who* which I'd been using as a footstool. Yes, he runs it. He ran the Dennis Corporation, too, despite his age or lack of it. He worked there summers when he was in the university and full time after graduation, learned the ropes and apparently didn't hang himself. Oh, yes, he took time out for the Navy, too. But for the last couple of years the Foundation has been his chief concern. He's Board chairman in the Corporation now; someone else is president."

"Where did all that lovely money come from?"

"Out of the everywhere into the here. It started, I gather, with his great great grandpa, who thoughtfully bought Manhattan real estate which stayed in the family. Just one son to a generation, it seems. Odd, isn't it? All the energy must have gone into real estate. Dennis' great grandfather bought some more, and his grandfather and father launched little sidelines like hotels, airplanes, steamships and whatever. Quite a heady brew, isn't it, well laced with oil. Oh, yes, computers too—maybe Tom was begat in that organization."

"Makes me feel faint," said Audrey. "Let's pay our check and get back upstairs. I'd lie down if I weren't afraid Mr. Manly would totter in looking for a shoulder to cry on. His case isn't going very well."

Janice laughed. The Honorable Manly (who had once been a judge) was long, lean and forbidding. The shoulder hadn't been fashioned that he'd cry on, not even his formidable wife's.

They went back to the office, and on the way up in a heart-stopping express elevator, Janice asked, "Whose turn to cook?"

"Yours, ducky. But I'll be out . . . I'm having dinner with Bernice and her husband. I love to open my wounds, sit and contemplate young married couples with the dew still on the rose. And I think Katie also has a date. So cook yourself a lamb chop, dear, and wash your hair—not that it needs it," said Audrey with some envy. She was a dark, attractive brunette, but sold on the myth that blondes have more fun. Tom, however—himself a fair-haired boy—liked brunettes.

The apartment was in a brownstone walk-up with a good address. Katie and Audrey shared a big bedroom, and Janice had a small one, to herself. The decor was a mixture of the individual tastes of the three tenants, all astonishingly good.

That evening, Janice was sitting at the kitchen table in a bright green shift, reading a magazine and eating her chop and salad, when the telephone rang.

"Hello," said a masculine voice at the other end of the wire, "May I speak to Miss Cooper, please?"

"You are speaking to her."

"This is Whitney Dennis."

"I was afraid of that," said Janice, but her smile came through her voice. "How did you find me?"

"I could have asked your boss," said Dennis, "but I hate resorting to blackmail. Then I thought of hiring a Pinkerton man, but it occurred to me to look in the telephone book. I can spell, you know."

"How clever of you."

"You're at home," deduced Dennis brilliantly. "Are you entertaining?"

"Not very."

"Then—how about dinner? I know it's late but——"

She said, "I'm having my dinner now, thank you," and hung up.

He rang back immediately.

"That was rather rude," he said reprovingly.

"I'm sorry, Mr. Dennis." She stifled an audible but genuine yawn. "I didn't mean to be. I just thought there was no real reason to continue the conversation."

"Lunch tomorrow, in lieu of an apology?"

"Apology from whom?"

"You, Miss Cooper."

"No lunch," said Janice, half angry, half amused.

"Okay. But I'm persistent."

"I'll see you at the next Board meeting," said Janice and added, not too far under her breath, "Unfortunately, it's inevitable."

This time *he* hung up; and she was laughing when she returned to her chop (getting cold) and salad (going limp) and magazine (rather boring).

Before the weekend, Howard Norton said casually, "I understand Whit Dennis has been pursuing you to no avail."

"That's right," she agreed indifferently. "Why, Uncle Howard? Droit-de-Dennis Foundation?"

"You scandalize me, Janice. Whit's a sensible, delightful and extremely clever man. So he likes you. I thought he might provide you with a little amusement. . . . This summer on your vacation, at the Cape, I'd rather hoped——"

She said brusquely, "I know you mean more than well, and I've seen mail marked personal, postmarked Cleveland. Father or Mother, or both, put you up to something . . ."

She was sitting by the desk, her elegant legs crossed, her notebook in her hand. He looked at her—at the shimmering hair, heavy, uncut, coiled at the back of her slender neck—and said gently, "We all love you, my dear."

"I know, and I'm grateful. As for the Cape, it was just Tom coming down to see Audrey, and the quarrels ending in reconciliations; and always the extra man, dragged there by Tom to amuse me, as you say. It's no use."

She raised her eyes. They were large, luminous and almost black under the fair, slightly penciled brows; they were also somber.

"I'm sorry," he said inadequately.

"Me, too," said Janice, and tried to smile. "Don't think I haven't fought it. I've been reckless, I've been stupid, and I'm still stupid." She rose. "I'll get the letters out at once," she said.

"Wait," he told her and as she halted at the door, he said. "I daresay my vocabulary isn't exactly nineteen sixty-eight . . . but Whit's no wolf, Janice. You don't have to be afraid of being afraid."

"Who's afraid of the big bad Dennis?" she inquired. "I'm not afraid of anything, any more, Uncle Howard, not even of myself. Zillionaires with six—or is it eight?—domiciles don't tempt me, not even when they look like a maiden's dream . . . supposing one is a maiden."

She went out and closed the door between them gently. Norton picked up the telephone and said to the invisible switchboard, "Get me . . . No, on second thought, never mind." He thought: I'll call Whit from home.

He did so, over his before-dinner drink.

"I did my best. She'll have no part of you."

"Why not?" asked Dennis irascibly. "I'm young, reasonably attractive and filthy rich."

Norton laughed. He said, "But Janice isn't interested."

"Well, I am," said Dennis, "and I'm not giving up easily."

As Norton returned to his living room, his pretty wife, Edna, asked tolerantly, "What was that all about?"

"Whit's taken a fancy to Janice."

"And?"

"Nothing. She wouldn't give him the time of day if she had two watches, both running."

Edna said, "Well, that will be a new experience for Whit." She looked anxious for a moment, then added, "I'd so hoped Janice was getting over it."

"She isn't. Sometimes I think she's just stubborn. She made an error, she paid for it. But she's determined to go on suffering," her husband said, refilling his glass.

"Maybe she's being wary; once bitten, twice shy, to coin a phrase."

"Don't be absurd, darling, you've known Whit since he was born. When he was seventeen, he began running; he still is——"

"Sometimes he runs toward," said Edna.

"Of course. That's up to him, isn't it? You know he either quits uninvolved or plain bored. If and when he becomes serious, that will be another matter."

"You think he's serious about Janice?"

"How in hell could he be?" asked her husband crossly. Dinner was announced and they went in to sit at a small table by the terrace and look out over the lights in the park. "He's seen her only once."

"But," said Edna, "she's apparently unimpressed. Which, with his record of love 'em and leave 'em, should start him off in hot pursuit."

"Women!" said her husband. "I give up. Where is our son?"

"Out, as usual. Janice really struck him a body-blow," said Edna. "I could hate her for it if I didn't love her. I would have liked to have her in the family."

"Me too. And how," asked Mr. Norton, "is our natural daughter, her monster children, and her husband? I saw a letter on the hall table."

"They're all fine. They'll be coming up from Boston next weekend. You're to take the kids to the Zoo, Jim has a client to see and Gwen and I have some catching up to do."

"Heaven help me," said her husband gloomily.

"Maybe Janice will go along? The kids are crazy about her——"

"The kids are crazy period," said their grandfather.

Janice went. She liked the Norton grandchildren, the Terrible Twins; she liked the Nortons' daughter, Gwen, and her husband. She liked the Central Park Zoo, although cages disturbed her; she knew how the animals felt. There's no future in cages. She was enjoying her lunch, and the laughter, until . . .

"May I join you?" asked Whit Dennis amiably and the Twins rose as one, and cast themselves upon him, screaming, "Uncle Whit!"

Janice looked accusingly at her godfather and Howard said, "I'm sorry, Janice."

Whit sat down. He ordered lavishly. He said, "This is on you, Howard, unless Janice offers, or the Twins' allowance is burning a hole in their pockets."

The girl twin said, "We'll take you to lunch, Uncle Whit," and the boy twin asked, "Whatever for? He's got tons of money."

"Don't blame your boss, Janice. I telephoned and Aunt Edna told me where he was and with whom," Whit said.

Janice arched an eyebrow. "Aunt Edna!" she said. "Then why not Uncle Howard?"

"I feel older than he is. . . . Look, I'm starved. Let's eat and then go look at more animals. I'm harmless, Janice, up to a point."

She looked at him, at the very blue eyes, the thick dark hair and the somewhat crooked eyebrows; at the firm mouth and stubborn chin, and burst out laughing. She really liked him, she decided.

"Good," said young Mr. Dennis. "You like me. Let's take it from there."

They had a fine afternoon, and Mr. Norton and the Twins went back to the apartment exhausted, the Twins happily so. Whit Dennis took Janice home in a cab. "Taxi?" she said. "I thought you had five cars."

"Six or seven . . . I didn't want to throw my weight around."

At her door, he asked, "May I come up?"

"No. I really do have a date tonight."

"Pity. Never mind. Think you could bring yourself to have a date with *me?* Or are you scared?"

"Of what?" she asked indignantly.

"I dunno. Me, or just men, in general."

"I'm not scared," she said, smiling, "merely immune. Yes, to a date if you like."

"I like. Dinner? Theater? Whatever you say. I have to be out of town Monday. How about Tuesday?"

"All right, Mr. Dennis."

"Whit."

She asked, "What time?"

"Let's skip the theater. There's nothing very good on at the moment. I'll pick you up, as I once suggested, at eight. We'll go somewhere to eat, and just talk. You like Spanish food?"

"*Sí.*"

"Good. *Hasta la vista.*" He smiled at her and went off in the waiting taxi which had been ticking away.

Janice went upstairs. He was fun, she decided. The arrogance which had at first annoyed her was probably put on. He wasn't really arrogant. He was vital, genuine and likable. Tuesday would be amusing.

It was. The Spanish place was small, the food was good and the music tolerable. They talked. He said, "Tell me about yourself," and she answered, "But Uncle Howard has told you, I was right there."

"Oh, sure, the résumé. I mean your real self. . . . Love life, for instance."

She looked at him stonily and said, after a moment, "Quite sufficient, thank you."

"Aren't you interested in mine?"

"Not really," said Janice truthfully. "Tell me more about the Foundation. Oh, I know about it, from taking notes at a couple of Board meetings, and also from reading about it. What interests you so much? I would have thought the Dennis Corporation exciting enough for a lifetime."

"It is," said Whitney Dennis, "but the Foundation is something else again—medical research and scholarships—helping to bind up the infected wounds of the world. I wanted to be a doctor," he said soberly, "a surgeon, actually. But from the time I uttered my first—if not last—squawk I was committed to the Corporation and also the Foundation. My father set up the Foundation when he was fairly young. He died three years ago, and after a while I took over. I haven't deserted the Corporation, but it goes along on its own momentum under good direction. As for my family——"

"Your mother?" she asked.

"Mother, married sister, a couple of aunts. They live mostly in California, San Francisco, and the Springs, when they aren't in Europe. Anyway, they think I'm out of my mind. Plenty of people to run the Foundation, they say."

"Are there?"

"Of course, but someone has to steer the ship. Trouble with an organization like this—shoals, reefs, rocks . . . and shallows. Too many have nots, too much greed. You have to chart a course, and keep a lookout. When I was abroad recently, it was partly on Foundation business. We don't just operate here, you know."

When he took her home, he said, "Okay, so I can't come up."

"But you can," she said. "I'd like you to meet the

girls." She'd told him about Audrey and Katie. "I think they'll be home."

So he went up, admired the apartment, charmed the tenants, finally looked at his watch and said, "Tomorrow's another day, probably. Thanks for a good evening, Janice."

She went with him into the little vestibule. They could hear Audrey and Kate talking.

"About you," said Janice. "Want to creep to the door and listen?"

"No. I don't suppose you'd kiss me good night?"

"I'd be delighted," said Janice warmly. She kissed him before he could kiss her—a nice, brief, friendly kiss, and Whit said, "Well, I'll be damned!"

"Good night," said Janice, "and thanks."

When she went back into the living room, Audrey said, "You should have warned us. I'd have fetched Grandma's smelling salts. He's divine."

"I doubt it," Janice said.

Katie, who had chestnut hair made artfully red and a wide mobile mouth, said solemnly, "I thought money couldn't impress me. God knows I see enough of it flitting in and out of Cher Raoul's salon, but for two cents I'd give up the job and camp on Mr. Dennis' doorstep, wherever that is."

"But he has so many doorsteps," said Janice.

She went off presently to her bedroom. Brushing her heavy shining hair she looked in the mirror. She thought: You're an idiot. Even without what Audrey called 'all that lovely money,' this is a very attractive man. Not that he'd ever be serious about me; and not that it would matter if he were.

For a moment, she put her head down on her slender arms, there at the dressing table. Dave, she thought forlornly, *Dave*. . . .

TWO

SOME WEEKS LATER Janice told her employer that she had been seeing a good deal of his client, and added with anxiety, "You don't mind, do you, Uncle Howard?" They had completed a long dictation session, no one was in her office or in Norton's, so she felt unrestricted. She rarely uncled him at work.

Norton shook his head, "Of course not. Whit's good for you. I don't need ESP to tell me that. Shakes you up, doesn't he?"

"In what way?" inquired Janice, raising an eyebrow.

"Oh, hell," said her godfather. "I don't mean whatever you think I mean . . . simply that he gives you something to think about and talk about, generally amuses you, probably antagonizes you often, and I trust feeds you well."

"Oh, yes, all that," she agreed. She looked at him thoughtfully. "But to return to what you thought I thought you meant, which is a simple three-letter word, I also find him physically attractive, which is a fringe benefit —like his being able to afford to feed me well."

Norton looked alarmed; Janice laughed.

"Not to worry," she assured him. "He doesn't attract me to the point of no return . . . or should I say, returns? That won't happen, ever again."

"Do you know how he feels about you?" Norton asked, ignoring her last statement. "I can't ask him, although we're reasonably close. He'd think I was inquiring, or prying, *in loco parentis*, about to produce a shotgun—figuratively anyway—and ask, 'What are your intentions?' although I can't imagine your father doing so."

She said quietly, "That's right, he didn't—until it was too late. Much as he worried, disapproved, and was hurt—as was Mother—he was quite aware that I was over twenty-one and knew—after a while at least—what I was doing. Both Mother and Father talked to me and advised me; otherwise they kept their hands off. Actually I should have been beaten, locked up, sent to Europe or whatever parents used to do. Not that it would have done any good; you recover from beatings, you pick locks, you can stowaway. Now, of course, they're still forced to come into social contact with Dave, which is hard for them. I suppose I have one hurt which is permanent—the knowledge that I hurt them so much. What I did to myself is of less consequence."

Norton cleared his throat and said, "Well, Whit's apparently a candid fella, as revealing as an open sandwich, one layer, you'd think, exposing wholly what in a real sandwich would be the filling. Don't let him fool you. He can be most un-outgoing; the clam is noisy and revealing compared to Whit Dennis. So you don't ask him really personal questions unless you're damned certain he won't mind or unless he deliberately leads you on——"

"Oh, I can tell you how he feels about me," said Janice. "He likes me. It's mutual, as I like him. I didn't at first. I thought he was arrogant and a super-playboy type."

"You've discovered he isn't?"

"That's right. Also, I'm not repulsive to him; although I admit he hasn't made passes." She thought: A kiss now and then. Who thinks of that as a pass any more?

"He won't," Norton predicted.

Janice had a quirky little grin, something more, and also less than a smile. She said, "You're not trying to sell me on the idea that he's a Galahad . . . or something even less normal?"

"Holy mackerel, what's considered normal nowadays? No. As far as I can ascertain Whit's on the receiving end of passes, and very selective. I've never heard of him being what I used to call 'serious.' "

Janice rose. "Okay," she said. "It's fun. I enjoy it, and I'm not serious either. So I'll stop worrying over the possibility that I might lose you a valued client."

As she went back to her office, Norton drew his heavy, still-dark brows together. He'd like to shake her, literally, until her excellent teeth rattled. Women in this era, and many before it, didn't go on dedicating themselves to the lost love, the impossible dream. As a matter of fact few ever had, despite the torch songs. Most of 'em got over it, like a bad case of flu. Oh, sure, some remained nostalgic and persuaded themselves that if things had been otherwise, they would have been romantically happy for the rest of their lives. However, they usually settled for second-best, which frequently added up to first-rate. Sometimes in the magazines Edna read and which he glanced at occasionally, there were stories of grown-up boy meeting grown-up girl twenty years later; but for one or the other, or both, the lovely illusion had perished, what with overweight, receding hairline, dentures and domesticity; also sprightly conversation about their legal spouses and the dear little kiddies. Which reminded Mr. Norton of the Terrible Twins, although by no stretch of the imagination could they be called dear little kiddies. Mobile monsters was a better term. He smiled fondly and returned to matters of more immediate, if perhaps lesser, importance.

Autumn ran its unpredictable course, bringing a Board Meeting and a special Executive Meeting, at which Janice observed Whit with considerate admiration, even some awe. This was not the man who took her to dinner, sometimes kissed her good night, and sometimes didn't (which took her a little by surprise); who demanded as much of her weekends as she'd give him when he himself was free; and who took her to art shows, museums and for long brisk walks, or drove her into the country in one of his fast, savage cars. Nor was this the man with whom frequently she agreed—books, theater, art, politics—and as frequently disagreed, on the same subjects.

Audrey and Katie were spellbound. Audrey said, one night when none of them had a date, but contented themselves with hair setting, scratch suppers, manicuring and lingerie washing: "Cautious, multimillionaire—flowers, candy, books!"

"Some of the flowers make you sneeze," said Katie, "and now and then you throw a book across the room at night—I hear you—and you hate candy."

"Oh," said Janice, imperturbable, "but expensive flowers, books and candy. You were expecting, maybe, a sable coat?"

"Of course," said Audrey and Katie in unison.

"He's well brought up," Janice explained kindly, "and so am I. Flowers, books and candy are traditional."

Audrey shook her head. "Gosh," she said, "I'm glad Tom wasn't born to tradition. He breaks down now and again. I've tons of hope-chest goodies laid to rest that I haven't looked at lately, but I imagine they're rotting quietly." She glanced at her good medium-sized engagement ring. "Diamonds last," she consoled herself aloud.

Katie yawned and said, "I could go for Whit, Jan, except I wouldn't have a chance; besides I'm having too much fun to attempt allurement."

Christmas neared with lighted trees, carols, Santa Clauses, fascinating store windows and, for the record, a little snow on and off, gilt on the gingerbread.

"What would you like for Christmas?" Whit asked one night as he and Janice were returning from dinner in Connecticut.

"My parents—and they're coming."

"Do you think they'll like me?"

"Probably not, at first."

"Why?"

"You're too attractive and you have too much money; they'll think you have baleful designs on me."

"How quaint!" Whit remarked. "With all my money and charm you'd think they'd be the first to hurl you into my arms."

Janice chuckled. "They'll like you, given time," she said.

"To return to my question, what do you want?"

"Flowers, books, candy. . . ." She laughed. "That will impress them favorably. Of course their era wasn't Victorian, on the contrary, but to their ancestors such stately offerings spelled courting. You might even break down and send me perfume."

"What kind?"

"Well, none, actually. I don't use it."

"So I've noticed."

"Still," she mused, "it would be a daring gesture. I know you can get it wholesale—your forefathers took a diversified view of investments—and I can always give it away. Which reminds me that Audrey and Katie think you're a mite penurious. They figured you for a sable coat—which of course, I'd have to return."

"How about something modest in mutation mink?"

"No, thanks. I don't like furs much either. I keep thinking of those poor defenseless animals."

"Is there anything you do like?"

"Oh, food, light wines, drives in the country, un-pop art, quiet music, good plays, not too avant garde—and of course, you."

"In that order?"

"More or less."

He took his hand off the wheel and touched her cheek. He said contentedly, "You're a good kid, Janice."

"Nicest thing anyone has ever said to me," she said lightly. But her heart tightened. Dave had said that once, which wasn't like him; he usually employed more ornate descriptive phrases.

The Coopers came in from the Midwest, laden with packages, and signed themselves into a small suite in a good hotel, which they had booked weeks before. They were special people: young enough to be fun, old enough to be wise; attractive enough to charm everyone from bellhops to maître d's and Whitney Dennis. He turned up at the Nortons for Christmas dinner, also loaded with packages. For Janice, books, flowers, candy and a large bottle of something smelling expensive. For the Nortons, a case of champagne, chauffeur carried; and for the Coopers, an I'm-glad-to-meet-you smile.

Janice, in the Norton living room, replete, after dinner, opened the Dennis offerings and cried, "Oh, no!"

"What's the matter?" asked her pretty mother, "I think Mr. Dennis had excellent taste."

"But you saw the apartment last night," said Janice. "It looks like a well-bred funeral parlor, an elegant lending library, the perfume counter at Bergdorf's and the section of imported sweets from the gourmet shop.

"You sent all that too?" asked Mrs. Cooper, turning astonished eyes upon young Mr. Dennis.

He murmured, seemingly abashed, "One gets in a rut."

Everyone laughed and Whit, looking thoughtfully at Mrs. Cooper, said, "I might transfer my attentions if Mr. Cooper doesn't mind."

The day after Christmas books, candy and flowers flowed into the Cooper hotel suite like the Amazon in flood.

On their last evening, alone with their daughter, the Coopers took stock. Mrs. Cooper said, "I like your new follower."

"Who doesn't?" asked Janice.

"I like him too," said her father and scowled, "but all this sedate, if costly, gift business—is it a put-on or what?"

"I guess it's a what," said Janice. "As I told Audrey and Katie, he's been very well brought up—like me."

Her mother asked anxiously, "You're not serious about each other, are you?"

"Lord, no," said Janice. "Can you imagine me presiding over half a dozen far-flung houses, a pied-à-terre in Paris, one in London and probably—although he hasn't told me so—a castle in Spain—to say nothing of the seagoing yacht and all the rest?"

"Sure," said her father, "you're a capable girl and probably he has housekeepers and slaves *ad nauseam*."

"He has," said Janice, "a paragon named Mr. Meeker, who acts as major domo cum traveling companion, and who hires and fires; each house has a resident housekeeper; she engages her staff. It's hard for Whit to remember all the housekeepers' names, so he calls them collectively Mrs. Smith."

"I don't believe it," said Betty Cooper.

"It's true," said Janice straight-faced. "He has a captain for the yacht, who hires the crew; and also a couple of pilots for the plane."

"I thought he *worked!*" said Mr. Cooper.

"He does, very hard. But occasionally he has to have a place to lay his head, or the old salt fever overcomes him, or the wild blue yonder calls. His personal secretary is a middle-aged gentleman named Mr. Foster. I've talked to him a time or so, after I've spoken to his secretary; she's a Mrs. Lowell."

"Well, good God!" said Mr. Cooper, not at all profanely.

On the way home, Mrs. Cooper asked, "Do you think she's in love with him, Bill?"

"No, worse luck."

"Why worse luck?"

"Because I think he'd be right for her, even with all the money—or without it."

"Do you think he's in love with her?"

"Damned if I know. I had a little talk with Howard. He doesn't know either, but he doesn't think so."

"Heavens," said Mrs. Cooper, who watched TV, read books and had Heard Things, even about the sons of some of her friends. "Do you think he's a little . . ." She hesitated and her husband said, "No, I don't. . . . Here's a crossword-puzzle book he sent to amuse you on the flight and keep your mind off bad landings, fog and traffic. Try figuring one of those out instead."

"You're not worried about Janice?"

"No."

But he was; not that he believed she'd make the same mistake twice. But he didn't want her hurt again, not in any way; and from what Howard had said, young Mr.

Dennis, pursued by almost every woman he met under eighty—over, too for all Howard knew—was an habitual refugee from matrimony. Why, only Mr. Dennis knew.

During March, when Mr. Norton would be away, Janice took a vacation and told Whit beforehand, "I'm going away in mid-March for a couple of weeks."

"Where?"

"Jamaica."

"Girls going too?"

"No. Tom's finally decided he and Audrey can afford to get married in June. And Katie's not due for a holiday. I'm not either, but I'll work this summer."

"Alone, then?"

"I like it that way: sun, beach, sleep, palm trees, the whole bit, dancing, new people——"

"Where in Jamaica?"

She told him, adding, "I can't run to the elegant hotels, but Uncle Howard knew about this guest house. It's on a beach; they take very few people. He went there once from Montego Bay to see friends. Good food, air-conditioned, a little bar, patio, and all informal."

"I'll miss you," said Whit.

"I'll miss you too. Please don't send flowers, books or candy. Flowers grow for free, I don't intend to read anything but paperback mysteries, and candy, if it doesn't melt, wouldn't look well in a bathing suit."

She went off to Jamaica and three days later, when she was beginning to tire of an improbable moon and calypsos, Whit, accompanied only by a couple of stewards and pilots, flew into Montego Bay and went to the suite reserved for him and his pilots, who were respectively Fred and Harry, and his good friends.

He found Janice on the beach next morning, contemplating idle little waves and listening to the rattling of palms. She was wearing a comparatively modest bikini, its aquamarine shade becoming to her beginning tan.

"Hi," said Whit, sitting down. He wore shorts and had a towel slung around his shoulder. He also had a permanent tan, as during the year he was to be found on various beaches for varying lengths of time. He also had a beach bag, which he unpacked, producing a single orchid in a small box, a candy bar and *The Owl and the Pussy Cat* in French.

Janice burst out laughing. She said, with affection, "You're an idiot. How's the Foundation making out without you—and the Corporation?"

"They can manage for a spell; maybe I won't be away that long. It depends on you."

"Me?"

"Sure. How'd you like to marry me?"

"Not very much," Janice said. Then she sat up straight, glistening with oil and water, and more or less besprinkled with sand. "For heaven's sake, Whitney Dennis," she exclaimed, "you're *serious!*"

"Never more so."

She contemplated him for a moment and then asked quite sincerely, "Don't you feel well?"

"Never better. . . . How about it? I won't rush you. I won't say, 'Pack up and fly with me to Tahiti.' You might not like Tahiti. Also you're a conscientious critter; you'd want to give Howard sufficient notice, and break in the best available girl. And your mother has to have time to prepare the wedding feast, send out the invitations and everything, according to protocol."

"You're crazy," said Janice, her eyes enormous. She was half in shock.

"Thanks. No, I'm not. Having seen you with great

frequency over the last six months or more, I've made up my mind."

"You've made up *your* mind!" She began to come to a slow boil.

"Of course. So I came to see if you'd make up yours."

She said angrily, "It's made up."

"Yes or no for starters?"

"No."

"Why not? Do you find me physically repellent?"

"Of course not."

"Does all that stuff in the banks and elsewhere scare you?"

"Not at all."

"Then why not? Cool it, Janice. Stop cooking in the shell and give me one good reason."

She cooled it. She said, "I like you very much, Whit. I'm very fond of you, actually; and you are attractive to me. But I'm not in love with you."

"Of course you aren't," he said triumphantly. "That's the beauty of it."

She said, "Don't give me that old 'You'll learn to——' "

She stopped. "*What* did you say?" she asked incredulously.

"I said, 'That's the beauty of it.' I don't *want* you to be in love with me. If I'd thought you were or were going to be, I'd have folded my tent weeks ago."

Janice stared at him. He said kindly, "You look like a fish; close your mouth."

"You mean to say you don't want a wife who loves you?"

"Of course I want a wife who loves me," he told her easily, "or, as you put it, is fond of me; but I don't want a wife who's *in love* with me."

"You're impossible . . . and also I'd better tell you something."

"I'll spare you the trouble. You're still in love with a guy named Davidson Peters . . . Oh, sure you hate him, but you're in love with him."

Janice was crimson. She said furiously, "If Uncle Howard——"

"Howard hasn't said a word. I have other sources."

"Why—you——!"

He said gently, "Simmer down. It wasn't too difficult to assemble the dossier and no one was embarrassed. You and he grew up together. He was a year ahead of you in high school. You were a smart little girl, worked hard, made straight A's. He was a football hero and all that. So, the innocent romance; well, almost innocent. Then you were both in the university. You were going to be married after you graduated, which would give him time to get going on a career. But instead he married a friend of yours, the local banker's daughter."

"Whit . . ."

He went on inexorably. "That gave him a head start in a small, solid industry, backed by the bank. His wife's father owned stock. Peters had to come East often. . . . You lived alone then. . . But before I met you, it broke up——"

She said furiously, "I broke it up!"

"Yes. Why?"

After a moment she answered quietly, "There was no future in it. But I don't see why, knowing all this, you asked me to marry you."

"I thought perhaps you'd burned yourself out, romantically speaking. And you're everything I want in a wife, Janice," he told her.

She said slowly, "I was in love with Dave, and I hurt people—some who didn't know about it—his wife—I've never known if she knew. And they have two very small children. . . . But I don't understand what you want in or expect from a wife!" she ended, suddenly curious, if still incredulous.

"Affection; I've told you that; warm, responsive sex. The ability and willingness to bear children. More than one, I hope. I don't much like the Dennis record. Compatability. A sense of humor. Honesty."

She said, "She'd have to be a good hostess too, wouldn't she?" She looked at him thoughtfully. "And should speak six languages?"

"Why? I don't. When I get stuck, there are trustworthy interpreters."

"What else?"

"Complete fidelity."

After a stunned moment, she remarked, "How very reactionary!"

"Isn't it? It goes back to the primitive. When I have a son, it has to be for sure. I'm very fond of you, Janice. You aren't beautiful. You're merely bewitching. I like that. Beautiful women can be tiresome. They look over your shoulder into a mirror. Also you are healthy. Small, but healthy. That's a must. And we're friends, which doesn't often happen in romantic marriages. People violently in love are natural enemies. You have a lot to offer; so have I."

"Such as?"

"Affection, as I've said. Companionship, sharing in a life we'd both build; and, of course, money. Do you like money?"

"Naturally, I like it——"

"Well it's there and no strings attached."

"Fidelity?"

He frowned. "I don't know. I think so now, but I could be wrong. I have normal instincts—just in case you think I haven't. They're brief. I don't really like women *per se* much," he added.

"But——"

"Oh," he said, "basically they're possessive, devouring and jealous. I've had all that. You know a little about my family, mother, sister, aunts . . . possessive types; and the girls I fell in love with from college on, till I learned better. Scenes, demands, tears. I've too much else on my mind to have to cope with that. . . . What are you thinking about?"

"Dave."

"I see. Well, I suppose you would at this point."

Dave had been possessive, demanding, jealous—without—once he was married to Madge—any right.

Whit said, "Remember Eliot's prediction—'the world ends not with a bang'—I'm not trying to be funny—'but a whimper'?"

She said miserably, "I've tried not to go on being in love with him."

"You'll make it someday. Meantime, you'll have me. For always, I'm afraid. If you get tired of me, no divorce."

"Why ever not?" asked Janice, astonished.

"I don't approve of it. If I take a pledge, I mean it and I keep it."

"Fidelity's in the usual vows," she reminded him.

"Oh, I know. But if I were stupid enough to consider a small flutter, I'd be very discreet about it; and it wouldn't mean anything. Besides, you aren't in love with me. You'd be angry or annoyed, but not jealous. When I say no divorce, that goes for me too. Consider the Victorian husbands. Their wives—no matter how they felt, lying around on sofas crying into handkerchiefs soaked with eau de cologne or in the smallest toddler's golden curls—had the upper hand. Papa always came home to roost."

He got up and pulled her to her feet. He kissed her. "How was that?" he inquired solicitously.

"Just fine."

"Good. Go get some clothes on. I'll go back to my hotel and pick you up around seven. Meantime I'll send some cables: to Howard, to my family—I'll have to call New York and ask Joe Meeker where each one is—and to your parents. We'll have dinner, we'll dance, celebrate. And I'll introduce you to Fred and Harry."

"Who are they?"

"My pilots. Want to fly back with us?"

She answered after a moment, as they walked toward the guest house, leaving the flower, book and candy bar on the beach, "I don't think so. I'd like to stay here another week and think about it."

"What's to think?"

"Oh, sort things out. I haven't said yes, Whit."

"You have actually. But I'll give you until after dinner; we'll postpone the cables till morning."

He left her at the door of her room which opened onto the beach, said, "Be seeing you," smiled and walked off, the towel about his shoulders.

She thought: Gosh, the beach bag. And when she heard the car start, she went back to find the bag. It was there, with the book and the orchid. But a couple of kids scampering down the pink-pearl beach had evidently found the candy bar and Janice thought: This isn't happening to me.

But it was. She thought further: How do I feel?

Excited? No. Calm, if astonished. Happy? No. Just interested and content.

"And what else?" she asked herself.

The answer was—*safe.*

THREE

STRICTLY SPEAKING the Cooper-Dennis wedding was not a Happening if the term refers to a sort of spontaneous combustion. It took time, Janice discovered, to marry money; also to find the available and intelligent girl for her employer, who was torn between fury at losing his secretary and delight that his godchild, to whom he was devoted, and a young man whom he admired and of whom he was fond, were presumably to live happily ever after. Presumably was the key word. He took Janice to dinner and refused to include Whit. "You'll have time for a great many dinners," said Mr. Norton.

"Now," he said, installed in a private corner at one of his hushed, expensive clubs. . . . "Of course you know Whit is making a very large settlement on you, Janice."

She nodded, flushing a little, and admitted, "It seems —well—fantastic."

"An overworked word. What I want to know is, are you happy?"

She looked at him, her dark eyes brooding, brushed a recalcitrant lock of hair from her forehead, and answered hesitating, "Yes—no—that is, I haven't had time to consider how I feel."

Norton sighed. He asked bluntly, "Are you marrying him on the rebound, Janice, or—and this is what a lot of people will ask—for the money?"

"Neither." She added after a moment, "I can't imagine Whit *without* the money; it's part of his background, and personality; without it, he'd probably be a different man."

"Then you're in love with him?"

She took a long time to reply to that, and when she did, she spoke slowly and quietly. "No one has attracted me as he does; not in a long time," she said.

"You haven't answered my question."

"All right. No, I'm not in love with him—which is exactly what he wants."

Norton regarded her in a stunned silence. Then he said, "But that's absurd."

"Yes, isn't it? And you're the only person I could say this to. I couldn't to anyone else, not my mother nor my father nor my best friend, if I had one other than yourself."

"But how do you know this?" he asked uneasily.

"He told me so in Jamaica. . . . I—well—I told him about Dave, or started to. I didn't have to finish. He knew all about it."

"Well, I'll be damned!" said Mr. Norton inadequately.

"So," she went on cheerfully, "it's even steven. We like each other, we're compatible in most respects. I'll make him a good wife, he'll make me a good husband." She had at the right-hand corner of her mouth an evanescent sort of dimple which now briefly exhibited itself. "We can make a good life together, although there are moments when the sort of life I'm expected to share seems difficult. Scares me to think of it." She looked at her left hand, and remarked idly, "Sometimes, when I have the strength to raise my hand, I fancy people must think I'm gnawing on cracked ice. I'd have settled for something very much less spectacular and I told Whit so. He merely remarked that it was expected of him. Did you know he's giving me pearls for my wedding gift, as well as matched luggage and a few other trifles, cars and——?"

"No. How about a half a dozen fur coats?"

"He knows I don't like furs," she said. "But I like cars." She added, "Do you know how he feels about divorce?"

"Yes."

"Well, that's it," she said. "Wish us luck."

"I wish you more than that." He put his hand on what he could find of hers weighted down by the diamond. "And you know you can talk to me always. I feel no disloyalty. Whit knows he can talk to me too. Although," he added gravely, "I doubt that he would about personal matters."

Whit reported by cable and telephone to his family. "They are, as one woman, shocked to the core but bearing up nicely," he told Janice, "and somewhere along the line I'll have to present you for inspection."

"Will it be grim?"

"Certainly. My mother is a brisk, pretty person, who looks as if she were my older sister. She keeps herself in terrific trim, fights away all suitors like Penelope, although her Ulysses will never return. My older sister—married to an amiable man whose interests lie in their two girls, first editions of obscure poets and very good paintings—is a carbon copy of my mother; my father's sisters, Heloise and Hilda are widows, and have no children. They're all loaded, as the saying goes, and are equally upset by my venture into matrimony."

"Why?"

He shrugged. "There's been a cold war ever since I was born."

"But your sister has children!"

"Girls."

Janice shook her head. "I give up," she murmured.

"Last thing you must do. Fight back. I've been waiting a long time for someone to rescue me and now that the cavalry has arrived, heaven forbid it should about-face and gallop back to the post."

She said, "All right, but I don't understand."

"You will," he assured her.

They were dining at the airport, as he was seeing her off to Cleveland.

"Don't wait till the plane goes, Whit——"

"Why not?"

"I don't like it," she said uneasily, remembering when she'd waited to watch Dave through the gate.

"All right."

When the time came, he kissed her and said, "Don't get all worn out with fittings, arrangements, reporters——"

"Reporters?"

"Sure."

"But I thought I'd finished with them in New York."

"You'll never be finished with them. But you handle them very well, darling."

Now and again he called her that—carelessly (everyone calls everyone else "darling" in this era). She wished he wouldn't. But she could hardly say, "Anything but that." He'd know why.

Back to Cleveland, and Quaker Heights and the family, just her parents; later the clan would assemble from Canada, California and heaven knows where. Her parents were mildly astonished that Whitney's family would not be present at the wedding. Mrs. Dennis was taking the waters somewhere in Germany, Whit's sister Lily and her husband were in Greece—Mr. Turner was also interested in archeology—and their daughters were in Swiss boarding schools. As for Whit's aunts . . . Heloise was in London and Hilda in Cannes.

"Seems as if they could fly back," said Mrs. Cooper.

Janice said evenly, "They don't approve."

"Of you?" asked her parents in unison and anger.

"Not me, exactly; I gather they're just unhappy that Whit's getting married."

"Silliest thing I ever heard," said Mrs. Cooper. "Does it worry you, dear?"

"No."

She reflected: That's curious. If I were even mildly in love with Whit, it would; now it's unimportant.

Fittings, photographs, the minister who'd officiate; arrangements for rehearsal, for Audrey and Katie to come on—they'd stay at the Coopers', as would the Nortons—and of course for the reception at the house.

"Although how we'll manage I don't know," said Mrs. Cooper.

"Not to worry," advised Janice. "Only family and close friends. Remember?"

"But they're so many of them and the people I haven't asked will be livid. Whit's list isn't terribly overpowering, however."

But everyone had to be represented, including the Foundation and the Corporation and half a dozen university cronies and their wives.

The wedding gifts streamed in and Janice could visualize the frantic donors hunting through the various great stores, demanding something for someone who has everything, short of a sacred white elephant, Thailand pagodas, a launching pad or a seat on the Stock Exchange. What was left?

Reporters came, from the society pages. Janice had talked to some in New York. She could, as Whit had said, handle them—with ease and amiability. She'd been spared the columnists' gossip and speculations. The fact that Whitney Dennis was marrying someone of whom these ladies and gentlemen had never heard was news, and had to be mentioned of course, but only that. Young Mr. Dennis rarely crept into the columns. His lawyers and the various PR people who were employed by him personally or by the Foundation and Corporation saw to that.

A few days before the wedding Janice and her parents went to their small cottage by the lake. It was cool, being the end of April, and it was quiet. There Mrs. Cooper put Janice to bed for part of each day and there she cooked their simple meals. They went for walks. They sat about the fireplace evenings and talked. They wanted to know if Janice was happy and she said, "Yes," and was, for the moment, just being there with them. But sometimes she woke at night and wished herself back in the apartment, going to the office in the morning. Sometimes she was knotted inside with a kind of nagging fear; sometimes memories gnawed at her mind like rodents.

But Whit telephoned twice a day, morning and night. Once he said, "Scared, aren't you?" And she admitted, "A little." And he said, "Me, too, in a way," and laughed until she did.

Before returning to the city:

"You knew Dave and Madge aren't coming," said her mother hesitantly and her father murmured, "Quite properly." And Mrs. Cooper went on, "Madge wrote that Dave had to be in San Francisco."

Janice said, "I saw their present." She had. An antique silver box and the correct Mr. and Mrs. card. Madge had selected it, she assumed.

Whit and his friends, their wives and people from his offices turned up. Ushers were plentiful; and he'd taken over a good-sized motel. Howard Norton was to be his best man. Janice had, as matron of honor, an old school friend with whom she'd kept in touch. She'd asked Whit if his sister would consent to that position and that's when he'd said, "None of them will attend; don't fret about it, Janice." As bridesmaids, two girls with whom she had grown up, and Katie and Audrey. The parties and the rehearsal went well and Whit gave the supper afterward.

The wedding day was cool and sunny and everything as smooth as the icing on the cake. Sunlight . . . people . . . photographers . . . alleged society reporters from the local paper, from New York and elsewhere . . . a big church and an organ playing.

Janice's mother helped her to dress, while Katie, Audrey, the matron of honor and others hovered. They all said, "You're beautiful."

Well, close to it anyway, in the simple lovely dress of ivory satin. Janice had thought when they'd selected the dress: The bride wore white—well, off white. The lace veil that had been her grandmother's, Whit's flowers.

She remembered very little of that day, in detail; it blurred, it dizzied her, as psychedelic pictures do on a screen. Last-minute wedding presents, cables, telegrams; Whit assuring Janice's mother that she need not worry about the gifts. "It will all be attended to and shipped; all we'll want is the list. I'll lash my bride to a chair and make her write 'Thank you so much . . .' "

Walking up the aisle and down again, she had the this-isn't-happening-to-me feeling. But it had happened and it was irrevocable.

Everyone yearned to know where they were going on their honeymoon. "Horrible word," said Janice to Whit before she left for Cleveland, "like lollipops and mush."

Few were informed. Janice, of course first. Whit had said, "We're going to Vancouver for a couple of weeks, which is all the time I can spare at the moment."

"Vancouver?"

"Yes. You'll like it. And no one knows us there. My

friends there are now in Malay and have lent us the house."

"Lent us their house?" She'd burst out laughing.

"Sure. No Mrs. Smith, no local curiosity, no reporters ——"

"What about the yacht?" asked Janice, enjoying herself.

"Not enough time. Besides, how do I know you're a good sailor?"

"I'm not so sure either. But I thought there was a modest houseboat in Florida."

"There is. But Florida's full of people."

"And the North Carolina lodge?"

"Mrs. Smith."

"The East Hampton house?"

"Let's just say, Mrs. Smith."

"Okay," said Janice. "How do we get to Vancouver? Fred and Harry?"

"I'm giving them time off. We go by commercial plane to Seattle, and then on."

He'd taken her hand, looking at it as if he'd never seen it before. "Pretty," he said contentedly, "and capable. Vancouver's fine the end of April and early May; flowers, beaches, sun—we hope. Spring begins there in January. We'll do some touristy things, also walk on a beach, sit in the Richards' garden, look at the view."

"You didn't consult me."

He gave her an astonished look and said, "I rarely consult anyone, except of course your godfather and Joe." He scowled at her thoughtfully. "If I had, where would you have suggested?"

Janice said, "I haven't the remotest idea. Actually," she added, "it's rather nice to have someone making decisions for me—not that I'll always agree with them."

"Par for the course," he commented cheerfully and kissed her, satisfactorily.

Dave had also made the decisions, including the one not to marry her. . . . Later his decisions had been the careful ones which, by their very nature, she hated—hole-in-the-corner places, dark restaurants, out-of-the-way motels. Discreet decisions, very.

After the wedding, the crowded reception, the farewells, laughter and tears, and Janice's father saying to Whit, "Very cliché, but see that you take care of her." Whit gave him his straight, startlingly blue regard and said, "I shall." Janice's mother cried a little and Whit kissed her. He said, "Not to be outdone in the cliché department, always remember you're not losing a daughter but, for better or worse, gaining a son," which made her laugh.

The private executive jet was waiting in what Whit called the backyard of the big textile company owned by the Corporation. The backyard had an airstrip because the company executives used a company plane. Fred and Harry, who had been at the wedding, along with Joseph Meeker and Mr. Foster and others of Whit's friends and staff, were waiting each with a large smile and a bottle of champagne, saying in chorus, "If you don't mind, sir?" (normally they called him Whit) and promptly kissed the bride once on each cheek, to which she responded warmly. She'd flown with them before, back in Montego Bay, a short hop over clear, bright blue water and therefore knew them and the steward Scotty.

The plane had the usual equipment, including engines and wings; also a large lounge for working or loafing, as well as bedrooms. On the short flight to New York—and no one, at Whit's request, saw them off—Scotty brought them sandwiches and champagne. He was, of course, a

Scot, redheaded, stocky, with a nautical roll and a slight engaging burr.

"Gosh," said Janice, discovering she was hungry; she had eaten very little at the reception. "No gorgeous hostesses?"

"On call."

"Well . . . really!"

"You are an indelicate old woman. Now and then I fly the directors—and sometimes their wives—around. I particularly recall one rather curious jaunt to Expo—and then, we provide a hostess."

"Where do you get them? Do they moonlight?"

"Oh," he said, "I borrow them."

She'd forgotten that the Corporation owned an airline.

"Did I remember to give you the cables?"

Janice nodded. The cables were from her recently acquired mother-in-law, sister-in-law and aunts. They were cordial, if restrained. His mother's added that their wedding gifts would be presented in person, in New York.

"I thought it was a little odd," Janice said, "that they hadn't sent some of the family silver."

"My dear, I already have the family silver. . . . No, from word received through the underground, I think we're going to own a few more paintings, which we don't need—probably selected by Ned Turner—and of course you'll get the diamond dog collar and what goes with it, such as a small, but imposing tiara."

"You're putting me on."

"No. These are valuable, hideous and involuntary bestowals."

"What do you mean 'involuntary'?"

"They're entailed. Originally my grandfather bought them for his bride. It is understood in the family—and is I believe legally binding—that they are always to be given to the bride of the oldest son. You're it. I'm it. And don't ponder on having the stones—which are very good—reset. That's *verboten.*"

Janice reflected in silence and Whit asked, "By the way, did I tell you you were, and are, a very charming bride?"

"Other people said 'beautiful,' " she told him austerely.

"Oh, well, in the eyes of the beholder. . . . I like that suit."

"You should; you dictated the trousseau colors."

Scotty appeared, earnestly inquiring if they lacked anything and then took the trays away.

"Tired?" Whit asked her.

"A little."

"Panicking?"

She considered that and then admitted, "Somewhat."

"Splendid, and so traditional." He flipped a thumb and forefinger against her cheek. "In case you're interested, our plane doesn't leave until noon."

She said sleepily, "I hope I packed the right things for Vancouver."

"If you're taking what I suggested, you have."

They landed at the Westchester field where the plane lived when not in use and one of Whit's more sedate cars met them, with Mortimer driving. Janice knew Mortimer too. After a while, she reflected she'd learn to know the various Mrs. Smiths.

Mortimer congratulated them, standing at attention. He all but piped them aboard. The doorman at the mammoth apartment house was congratulatory too. The luggage was wafted to the penthouse and, by way of a private elevator, Janice and Whit.

She'd been in the penthouse before of course, on a number of occasions: for dinner with Whit and the Nortons; with her parents, during their Christmas visit; with Audrey and Katie; and, alone. She knew—if not intimately—the butler, whose name actually was Smith and the cook, his wife, who really was Mrs. Smith. There were, she assumed, parlor maids and such; she hadn't encountered them.

Whit produced a key and handed Janice a duplicate; except that hers was gold. He opened the door, and halted. Janice asked, "What are you waiting for?" And he said, "The luggage, my idiotic wife; after which, the ceremony."

The luggage came; the caravan departed. Whit picked her up and whooshed her over the doorsill. He said, putting her down, "It's lucky you don't weigh much. I seem to be out of condition."

No one was there to meet them.

"And where," inquired Janice, sitting down on the nearest chair in the big square hall, "are all the slaves?"

"In bed, I hope. They won't be back tonight, nor," he added, "until after we leave. You're sure you can cook?"

"Must I?"

"Certainly. Coffee, bacon, eggs, three minutes, toast, juice. A child can do it."

"I grew up," said Janice.

She cast her little hat aside, looped her fingers through the pearl choker—"Sports jewelry," he'd said, giving it to her, and with the longer string, "This for showing off." "I'll never make the stairs," she murmured.

"I'm not carrying you," he said firmly.

She did not pause to look at the big and beautiful rooms she'd already seen, nor did she go out on the terrace to look from an incredible height across the park. She went doggedly upstairs, stumbling once, and thought in alarm: Either I'm having a heart attack or behaving like——

"Like what?" she asked herself angrily. "An unwilling bride, or a virginal bride?"

Whit opened the door of a bedroom she recalled from her first inspection of the penthouse. "All yours," he said. "I'm next door."

Janice looked about the room; it was not exactly as she remembered it. She said, "It's different." And he answered, "Perhaps a little less masculine."

She sat down on the bed, a big one and he stood in front of her smiling. He said, "As you see I can compromise between today and yesterday; for today, separate rooms . . . for yesterday a double bed in each."

He sat down beside her and took her in his arms. He said, "No maid. Think you can unpack, or shall I? Incidentally, we'll have to get you a maid."

"I learned to tie my shoes when I was two. I don't want a maid."

"Madame," he said, "must learn that her status requires it, for packing and unpacking, for the laying out of dinner frocks, for the necessary comforts and consolations. . . ."

"And who looks after you?" she inquired.

"Oh everyone, in a manner of speaking." He rocked her a little and presently said, "Get to bed. . . . I'll wake you up tomorrow. I have a new alarm clock."

She'd given it to him, a gold traveling clock. What do you give the man who has everything for his personal wedding present?

"If anything disturbs you," he said politely, "like waking in a strange bed and place, call me. . . . Good night, Mrs. Dennis."

He went through the door which Janice knew led to his dressing room, bath and bedroom and closed it quietly.

Janice went into her own dressing room, showered, came back with a towel cinched about her narrow waist and took her night things from the overnight case. She went back to brush her teeth and returned to put on a nightgown her mother had selected for her. She sat on the edge of the bed again, stroking the chiffon folds lightly, and her eyes brimmed over. She got into bed and switched off the lights. She thought: I can't sleep. I should have asked Mother for a sleeping pill. No . . . she would have thought that very odd indeed. . . . And slept.

She woke before dawn. The room was dark, the curtains moving in the wind from open windows; the shadows of the furniture were dim, the bed was strange. She sat up confused and unhappy. She had never felt so alone.

"Whit," she called. "Whit."

He came in at once. He apparently hadn't been asleep. He sat down, and drew her close. "It's all right," he said in a quiet matter-of-fact voice.

Suddenly she was crying. She said, "Don't leave me; please don't leave me."

"I won't," said Whitney Dennis.

FOUR

JANICE WAS AWAKENED by a bell, not harsh or loud, but ringing with a dogged silvery persistence. She rolled over, said crossly, "But I turned off my alarm. That's Audrey's."

The bell went on functioning and she sat up, in a vast room with light filtering through the long curtains. Her pillow had been punched into shape; the other, dented.

She reached out and picked up the telephone. It was, she realized hazily, having had it explained to her the night before, a house phone.

"Hello," she said faintly and her husband ordered crisply: "Hit the silk!"

"Whit . . . where are you?"

"In the kitchen, idiot. Wash your face, brush your teeth, slip on something, a towel, wash cloth or the bedspread, and get down here on the double. It's not every day that I cook breakfast."

She was laughing. "Where is the kitchen?" she asked.

"Follow your nose," he advised, and disconnected.

Going downstairs, she was smiling. Her last thought before she slept returned to her now. She'd thought: Calling him like that . . . how stupid can you be? And how embarrassed you are going to be!

She was not in the least embarrassed; she felt fine and today they were going to Vancouver.

She followed her nose. Coffee, bacon . . . she shuddered, finding her way through the dining room—which wasn't too big but big enough, and which she well remembered—to a gleaming, antiseptic, electrified and electrifying kitchen. Whit, fully dressed except for tie and jacket, and wearing a butcher's apron was at the range. He said, without turning, "Good morning, Madame."

"Good morning. Is that bacon?"

"It is. How do you like your eggs?"

"Not at all, nor bacon either; coffee, lots of it, black; juice, whatever's handy; a piece of toast, no butter."

"Is that your usual breakfast or just the morning after?"

"My usual."

He turned, smiling, put his arms around her, hugged her hard, and kissed the curve of her cheek. He said, and his eyes were serious, "How do things look to you this morning?"

"Splendid."

"Good." He waved her to the kitchen table, which was laid for two. "Coffee's ready." He poured her a cup, and added, "I'll go on with my catering if you don't mind. I'll have to teach you to behave like a normal, healthy human being. It's all right to skip lunch if you must, but breakfast, never. Will you watch the toast?"

When he joined her, she looked at the eggs and bacon with mild horror. "I suppose I'll get used to seeing the animal being fed mornings," she told him.

"You will." He raised his cup. "*Salud,*" he said. "Happy days."

Janice burned her mouth, but responded, "To your very good health."

"You look pretty, mornings," he told her. "Now don't

dawdle. We have a little repacking to do, and a plane to catch."

She said idly, "I didn't hear you leave."

"You were sleeping the sleep of the innocent, figuratively speaking, so I silently departed. I thought, just today I'd let you off the domestic bit."

"You'd better. I can't fry bacon and as for eggs——"

"You'll learn. . . . You didn't tell me you snored."

"I don't," she said, startled.

"You mean no one's ever told you," he said calmly, "and you don't snore enough to tell yourself." He relented, adding, "Not a snore really, just a rather engaging wuffling sound."

After their second cup, he went off somewhere and returned with the morning papers. He said, "We'll just read the headlines," and they did so in a companionable silence, broken only by occasional profanity from Whit.

"The society page——" she began.

"Oh, sure. I've already seen it. Creditable job. I like the picture. . . . Going to keep a scrapbook?"

"I never keep scrapbooks."

She had once, long ago.

He said, "I do, or rather the slaves clip and paste for me. This one will be preserved for posterity."

At an appointed hour Mortimer brought the car around. "To the airport," Whit ordered grandly, and Mortimer permitting himself a slight grin, answered, "Yes, sir."

Janice looked at her watch, a wedding present from her parents. She'd looked at it and any other handy time piece frequently in the last more than half hour; she was accustomed to arriving at airports at least an hour prior to flight time.

"Stop fidgeting," said her husband.

"But you pointed out to me that we'd a plane to catch and I mustn't dawdle. But you did. Now, we'll be late."

"We are never late," Whit said royally. "So why don't you ask me if I have the tickets?"

"Have you?"

"No, dear; Joe has."

"Joe?"

"Joseph G. Meeker," said Whit patiently. "You've met him, and you saw him at the wedding."

Of course. The paragon! A moderately tall, thin man with almost frighteningly intelligent eyes and the kind of imperturbable face you expect to encounter in the FBI, the CIA or any similar organization.

"He wasn't with us after the wedding——"

"Certainly not."

"Then how did he get here, wherever he is?"

"Commercial wings, and he's at the airport as of now."

Meeker was, indeed. He was curbside, and had commandeered a porter and after the greetings he said, "Meet you in the usual place, Whit."

"Follow me," said Whit to his bride.

"Is it permitted to walk beside you, Sahib?" she inquired, with timidity.

"If you wish," he answered benignly.

She put her hand on his arm. "Is it also allowed to ask, *Quo vadis?*"

"Well there's a room which public relations makes available for heads of state, royalty and such, and even motion picture stars."

"I thought you were traveling incognito."

He said, taking her down a corridor and opening a door, "I don't travel incognito with my wife. But I have so traveled," he admitted warily. "Sit down, have a cigarette, compose yourself."

"On what occasions?"

"Secret missions," he said carelessly, "plus a touch of dalliance now and then."

She was trying not to laugh. She asked gravely, "What names have you used under such circumstances?"

"John Doe, John Smith, Lefty Jones, and sometimes 007."

"Come again, you're not trying."

"Would you believe Till Eulenspiegel?"

"With you, I would." Now she was laughing. Then she asked, "Do all your employees call you by your given name?"

"The various Mrs. Smiths wouldn't presume, except for the one on the Island; she knew me when I was a charming child. Foster doesn't. Freddy and Harry do, also Mortimer, when we're alone, and of course, Joe."

"Why?"

"Navy," said Whit, "all of us."

"And the captain of your yacht?"

"Navy also. The crew, however, and the household help remain on formal terms."

"I understand everyone's job so far, except Joe Meeker's" she said thoughtfully.

"Meaning?"

"Frankly, from the little I've seen of him, he seems wasted running errands for you, smoothing your way. And don't tell me he's well paid for it. I'm sure he is."

"Oh," said Whit, "he has other things to do, much more important. Shall we say the courier-cum-major domo job is a cover. . . . Here he is now."

Joe Meeker knocked and came in. He had the tickets, the seat selections and the luggage checks. And the information that they'd board in about ten minutes; maybe they'd better start for the gate.

At the gate he shook hands with them both and said, "Have a good trip." And Janice had an uneasy feeling that he was looking at her with more than routine and unsmiling attention.

"Watch dog too?" she suggested as she walked with Whit through the modern covered wagon to the plane.

"Who?. . . Oh, Joe? You might say so."

The plane began to move exactly at noon, then sat on the runway. The pilot was soothing. It would be a while before they were cleared for takeoff, he told the passengers. No smoking; seat belts fastened.

Music played.

Janice could see the patient planes ahead of them, and in back. She asked idly, "Couldn't we have come in your plane?"

"I daresay."

"Then why not?"

"Same regulations obtain," he said, smiling. "Oh, you didn't mean that? Well I thought a nice public plane would give you time for reflection, and your own thoughts. A private plane, no. . . . By the way, ours has never had a name. How about 'Mrs. Dennis'?. . . No, that's no good."

"Why?"

"My mother's also Mrs. Dennis," he explained. "But to go on with what I was saying, we'd have been alone except for Fred and Harry in the cockpit—and Scotty. You'd have to make small talk. In fact, you think you have to make it now. You don't. And in the midst of a great many strangers you can't unfasten your seat belt and scream 'Stop the plane. I want to get off.' "

"It would never occur to me," she said.

He pinched her ear and opened the magazine a stewardess had brought him. "Think away," he said, "at least till lunchtime."

She had taken off her absurd small hat. Now she leaned back and closed her eyes. She thought: This is one situation in which, if you have an ounce of decency, you don't make comparisons. She hadn't last night, or this morning. All she had permitted herself to think was: *Different* . . . a sort of unassuming expertise and gentleness.

The delay was for almost an hour. At intervals the captain reported their position. Eventually he said in some triumph, "Now we are number two," and Whit murmured, "Trying harder?" and nudged Janice. "Wake up, dear," he said.

He'd put his magazine aside some time ago and studied her vulnerable sleeping face, serene, yet somehow a little lost, and watched her quiet breathing, the pallor of her skin and the shadows beneath the closed eyes which, open, were so astonishing. He brushed back a lock of her hair and said again, "Wake up."

She did, fully, looking startled. "And don't ask, 'Where am I?' " he admonished her. "We're about to take off."

After the takeoff and the smooth, seemingly effortless, lift upward, the equally smooth drinks and luncheon, Janice said happily, "This is good. I was hungry," and added, "Won't we be late?"

"There you go again. You remind me of the White Rabbit. Yes, we'll be late, but it's not important. We had a couple of hours at the Seattle airport anyway. How was your nap?"

"I didn't know I was asleep." She smiled at him, and added, "You're remarkably patient with me."

"As with a new employee?"

"Something like that; like someone who knows it will take time to adjust to my surroundings."

"And duties?" he inquired.

"I don't think so," she said, frowning a little, "except perhaps the social bit."

"That will be easy. All you have to do is look beautiful."

"You said I wasn't——"

"Oh, but there are other opinions. Be charming. Listen. Don't talk too much. Ignore the infuriated girls who once baited hooks for the goldfish. Ignore secretly, but not outwardly, my mother, sister and aunts."

"Honestly, Whit!"

"You'll see!"

"I must also adjust to the—I believe it used to be called 'the trappings of great wealth.' "

"It's now called 'crass materialism.' That won't be hard. Remember the old Spanish proverb—at least I think it's Spanish—'Take what you want, God said, and pay for it.' "

She considered that a moment. Then decided, "That's scary."

"Isn't it? But on the surface level again, you can afford to. . . ."

Their luggage had been checked through. A pleasant man met them at the gate and said, "I hope you had a good flight," and introduced himself. They shook hands and he took a key from his pocket, saying, "If you'll come this way . . ."

Another room, empty and very comfortable. Their guide indicated a desk telephone: "In case you wish to use it," he offered. He asked for the tickets, said he would return them.

"Joe Meeker again," decided Janice, lying back on a great couch with her small feet up.

"Joe, yes. Also courtesy of PR and a special representative of customer service."

The telephone rang and Whit picked it up. She heard him say, "Yes, everything according to plan, Joe. . . . Oh, the delay, of course, but it doesn't matter. No, I'm not intending to show Janice Seattle. We're very comfortable as we are. . . . Let me hear from you in Vancouver."

He hung up, smiling. "Joe's a dedicated sightseer; you'd never expect it of him, but I remember——" He broke off and shook his head. "Suffice it to say, when he takes a vacation he goes poking around strange islands, or curious cities with practically a knapsack on his back and a stout stick in his hand. He thought we might have time to hire a car and scoot around Seattle."

"Do you mean to say he'd permit you to hire one on your own?"

"Oh, occasionally he lets me off the leash."

Their sponsor in Seattle returned with the tickets. All was well. He went with them to the gate and wished them a happy landing.

On the plane for the short flight, there were two enchanting Oriental girls and a family which looked Indian or perhaps, Janice thought, Alaskan.

Customs immigration. When that was over, and they went out of the airport, a car was waiting and a young Japanese was waiting with it.

Whit said, "Hi, Hiroshi," and added, to Janice, "my good friend Sato Hiroshi— this is Mrs. Dennis, Hiroshi. . . . How'd you manage a parking space?"

Hiroshi said, "It's a parlor trick," saw that the porter disposed of the luggage and opened the door for his passengers.

Janice made inquiring eyebrows.

Whit said, "The Richards from whom I borrowed the house also left me a car and Hiroshi. . . . He's studying at the university, incidentally."

"Hardly incidentally," remarked Mr. Sato from the front seat. "I'm practically knocking my brains out. I don't know how I was ever persuaded to attempt to take my Master's."

"My wife's never been in Vancouver before."

"I wish I could drive you all around," said Hiroshi.

"Don't you trust me? I've been here before; besides I can always ask directions."

"I don't know, Mr. Dennis," said Hiroshi. "Will you be able to remember a thirty-mile speed limit?"

"I'll try," said Whit gloomily. To Janice, he said, "Relax. This is a relaxing place. Also, in case you haven't noticed it, it's spring . . . more spring then we left behind us."

She had noticed—the trees and leaves, the buds and flowers; also, even in traffic, the clear air.

"I feel as if I hadn't been breathing before," she said.

It was not a long drive to the Richards' house and when Hiroshi stopped the car, he said, "I'll put it away unless you plan to use it, Mr. Dennis."

"Not tonight. Here, give me some of that luggage."

They carried it down an incline, and Janice had a glimpse of gardens. Then she was in the house and Hiroshi asked, "If Mrs. Dennis wishes to go upstairs . . . ?"

She did and she did not. She had seen the great windows overlooking the water . . . and the curving mountain range beyond.

But she went obediently up the stairs to a big, cool, quiet room and Whit said, "Suppose we leave you for a while? I'll be up presently and help you unpack."

She heard them go downstairs laughing and talking, Hiroshi saying earnestly, ". . . but she must see the university. . . ."

Presently she opened a suitcase and took out a thin wool dinner dress and then stood dreaming in front of the windows, looking at the clarity of the sky.

She had just finished showering and dressing when Whit knocked. He came in, said briskly, "Early dinner, therefore early drinks. Hiroshi is coping. Run along down and look . . . it's beautiful any time of day, although sometimes I like night best."

So she went down alone in a strange house, which was nevertheless as welcoming as familiar arms about her. The living room—and the two studies—each with the view. She looked down on land sloping steeply, on the Richards' front lawn which was in little terraces, on a small pool and on the flowering dogwoods and azaleas and rhododendron. She looked down to a beach, and could see people walking by the water's edge.

Hiroshi appeared and said, "You like it?"

"I love it," said Janice. "Were you born here, Hiroshi?"

"Oh, yes." He wore a white jacket now. He said, "When Mr. Dennis comes down, perhaps you would like your drinks in here? I have already laid the dining table."

"May I see the kitchen too?"

He took her in, smiling a little. Women always wanted to see the kitchen. But all she did was shake her head. "It's lovely," she said, "and utilitarian. Do you think you could teach me to cook?"

The dining room was small and charming. "On this floor," said Hiroshi, "there's also a guest room and bath, and another in the basement . . . which isn't really a basement, just on another level. When the Richards' nephews come to visit, they bunk downstairs. There are two bedrooms and a shower."

She was standing by the living-room windows when Whit came down. He said, "I like your dress. I haven't seen it before."

It was turquoise, ankle length, full, soft and simple. With it she wore turquoise, a loop around her wrist, and a ring.

"Nor those," he said, indicating them.

"My grandmother's. . . . Look, someone's running on the beach."

"Yes. Come out in the garden in the back for a moment. You can hear them—the children, I mean."

So they went to look at the jonquils and tulips and flowering fruit trees.

"And there's still snow on the mountains," said Whit.

"Tell me about the Richards."

"Old friends. He's a senior professor, off now with his wife in France, doing some research. . . . They're very comfortably off—in their fifties, and childless. Kate writes children's books, very good ones. . . . Look, it gets cold suddenly this time of year; we'd better go in. Hiroshi makes a marvelous martini, and is a superb cook."

"What's he taking his Master's in?"

"English. He plans to teach."

He took her hand and they went back to the house in an easy silence. The azaleas flamed around them and the house waited, knowing they were there.

FIVE

THE TWO WEEKS IN Vancouver were as delightful as a pleasant dream and if, occasionally, Janice nudged herself awake, just as unreal. Flowers bloomed riotously. The weather was exactly right, except for a spell or two of rain: warm, by day—but still too cold to swim, although youngsters ran on the beaches in shorts, and skippers in bathing suits sailed their dancing little boats. At night, it was cool.

Hiroshi cooked as if inspired, and on his evenings off they went out to excellent restaurants, particularly one Japanese place owned by an uncle of Hiroshi's, where there were indoor gardens, sliding panels to insure privacy and, under the inches-low tables, concealed places into which a diner could inconspicuously lower his legs—a blessing in Whit's case. They were served by pretty girls, kneeling.

"I wonder if one of the Mrs. Smiths could train our various waitresses or even butlers to kneel," Whit reflected. "Have some more sake."

They went walking down the steep street to Spanish Beach, and once took an hour's hike to the university beach and climbed the steep path through the greening woods to the university itself. Whit had a guest card, thanks to the Richards, and they lunched there that day.

Hiroshi was available only evenings and some afternoons if they wished to give a cocktail party. They didn't.

So Janice—outwardly sighing but inwardly entertained, depending on Hiroshi for the lavish contents of the refrigerator—made salads and sandwiches, and sometimes Whit produced a superior omelette. Janice steadfastly refused to cook breakfast; she could not face eggs at such an hour she said, so they developed a routine: Whit brought her a tray of toast, coffee and juice, sat with her for a few minutes and went whistling off to the kitchen where he fixed himself a proper meal; sometimes chops, or a small steak, or a little fish, and in between the inevitable eggs.

Often, early mornings she would quietly leave him asleep, slide her narrow feet into slippers, huddle a warm robe around her and go downstairs to look from the great living-room windows at the dawn-blue water, at the mountains and, to the left, emerging like something Utopian, the soaring buildings of the university. At night the view was, as Whit had promised, spectacular with myriad dancing lights.

They did a little sight-seeing with Whit driving; they went to West Vancouver and sat looking at the water in a park, where people were sunning themselves, most of the men with their shirts off.

It was a Sunday. "But not like park Sundays at home," Janice commented.

"Why?"

"Oh, I don't know; none of the hurry and fever to unpack, to picnic eat, repack. Everyone's relaxed; even the kids don't make as much noise as at home."

They went down from the top of the hill to a bench and Whit wandered off to return with coffee and hot dogs.

"Well," said Janice, biting into hers, "the universal language."

"What language?"

"Hot dogs . . . hamburgers too, I suppose."

At the Richards' house the garden was sunny with the last of the daffodils and the early tulips; an ornamental cherry was in full pink blossom and wherever one looked there was color, pink and blue, yellow and white.

They talked a great deal.

"No one comes calling," said Janice, once.

"No. . . . Would you like it if they did?"

"Of course not. But I wondered. The Richards must have many friends, and friends always drop in on your house guests."

"They have hundreds of friends," said Whit. "I've met a few—painters, writers, university people, lumber people; you name it—but when we talked this over . . . oh, sure I flew up to see them."

"When?"

"Before Jamaica."

"Why, you—you were that sure of me?"

"Let's say, I hoped I could be sure. When I saw them, I suggested no callers, however talented, hospitable or curious. I left it to them to figure out why we must be in seclusion. Leprosy, perhaps. Or one of us convalescent from a terrible accident or both of us writing books; or even an Arabian prince and his newest wives."

Janice laughed. She said, "But Hiroshi——"

"Hiroshi is a gentleman," said her husband, "and gentlemen do not gossip."

They talked about themselves. He said once, "I like to hear about you when you were a kid. Meeting and marrying you was like opening an exciting book about a quarter of the way through." He added after a moment, "But there are, of course, chapters which remain unread."

"Only one. Do you mind?"

"No."

In his turn he talked about his family. He gave her

graphic pictures of his mother; his sister and her scholarly, pleasant husband; of their children—"nice kids. They've been dragged up all over the earth"—of his aunts. One was insane about dogs and fancied herself a poet; that was Heloise. The other was a do-gooder, who wrote mediocre verse but was a fabulous organizer of charitable balls, luncheons, dinners or what have you.

"You don't even like any of them?" she asked incredulously.

"On the contrary, I'm devoted to my mother. She irritates the hell out of me, but she amuses me too. I'm fond of my sister, although I haven't the remotest idea why; if we weren't siblings and I met her somewhere she'd madden me. And I like the aunts. Each is, in her own fussy, absurd way, a darling. But all these *women!*" he said. "I was smothered by women; they doted on me, they spoiled me, and each, individually, consumed me, or tried to."

"Why?" asked Janice. They were in the big living room, the soft lights on, the paintings glowing from the quiet walls, Whit flat on a couch and Janice in a deep chair beside him.

"Oh, only boy I suppose. Each was jealous of the others; all proffered bribes. But you'll get to know them, Janice, and you can form your own opinion. Don't be influenced by me. I'm merely the only son, only brother, only nephew."

"I suppose they'll hate me," she said rather unhappily.

"Oh, I don't think so," he said indifferently. "None has much emotion—except of course possessive jealousy. They'll be jealous, of course, and therefore a little suspicious."

"King Cophetua?"

"Probably—although anything less like a beggar maid than you, Mrs. Dennis, I cannot imagine—but they'll thaw out; the ice is mainly surface, except perhaps in my mother's case. And once you've had a baby, they'll coddle you; if it's a boy, they'll fall down and worship, and of course endeavor to consume him too."

Janice said firmly, "I'll see to it that they don't. That's a no-no." She looked at him warily, "You're not suggesting that I get on with it, are you? I'd like a little time."

"I'm not suggesting anything. I've never even mentioned the inhibiting pill."

Janice was silent a moment, then she said, "I saw my doctor at home, you know. I thought—for a little while—until we became accustomed to each other . . . ?"

Whit shrugged, which isn't easy to do while lying almost flat. He said, "A year, two years if you like; just not so long that I'll be old and gray. I'd hate to have my son regard me as a grandfather."

"You'll make a lovely grandfather," said Janice, "not at all doddering; probably rather like Uncle Howard with the twins."

"Not at all like your Uncle Howard. Come here, darling."

Janice rose and went to the couch. She said, sitting down, "Over there I felt rather like an analyst."

He sat up halfway and pulled her down beside him. He asked, "Any twins dangling from your family tree?"

Janice considered this thoughtfully. She said, "No. . . . Wait, I think . . . yes, on the English side—that is to say, my mother's. Her father came to the States as a young man. I knew him; he died when I was about eleven. . . . my grandmother's given name was Vanessa, but I don't remember her."

"Get back to the twins."

She said vaguely, "Cousins or something a long way back."

"Vanessa? I like that. We'll call a girl that, maybe."

"Don't rush me. Besides, I assumed I was elected to be the mother of several splendid sons."

"Certainly. But girls are rather nice. . . . Tell me, do you like me as well—no—are you as fond of me as when we were married?"

"Yes."

"Fonder?"

She considered that also. After a time she said, "I don't think so, Whit."

He sat up straight and she nearly fell off the couch. "Well, I like that!" he said indignantly.

Janice pushed him back, and sat up, her chin propped in her hands. She said, "Once you told me that you desired honesty in a wife."

"I did. I do. Here, lean back. You don't need to prop up the great brow in the little hands."

She said, "I couldn't, I think, be fonder of you than I was almost two weeks ago."

"A fortnight," Whit corrected.

"It's different, however," she told him. "Naturally, I know you—perhaps even understand you—a little better."

"God forbid!"

"But," she went on serenely, "it's simply because we're married and have——"

"Tell it like it is!"

"Oh, well . . . the fact that we're sleeping together," said Janice obediently, "hasn't changed anything except that it's a closer relationship. You're a very nice man, Whit"—she paused, and added—"as you said of Hiroshi, a gentleman. What's the matter? Were you afraid you weren't adequate?"

"No. What an idea!"

"Or are you afraid I've fallen in love with you?"

"Have you?"

"No, dear." She rose. She said, "I like things the way they are."

"So do I. . . . Where are you going?"

"Upstairs to change. It's time for Hiroshi. I hope there'll be bonfires tonight."

"What do you mean? Oh, the booms. The spring cleaning on the beaches."

Janice loved the simple, mathematical patterns of the booms and the blazing fires consuming the broken, discarded logs. She said, "I can't decide which is lovelier, night or day; by night the fires, the stars and a new moon waxing; by day the flower drifts—I especially love the azaleas, particularly the Richards' big white one—and the far mountains laced with snow, and the nearer ones, and sky and water, and students studying on the lawns, and all the colors. Let's come back every spring."

"Of course, when we're free to . . . but we can't always have this house. That's something I can't buy you. The Richards treasure it. You'd have to settle for a rental of sorts, or a hotel."

"No, just this house."

On the stairs she turned and looked back. "I'm glad there's something you can't buy," she said.

Whit lay down again, smiling.

It was working out beautifully. He had had misgivings now and again before their marriage. But this was no usual marriage, all romantic dreams, hopes and sex; nor was it a marriage for money, position, security. This was a rational, soberly considered commitment, upon which they had entered, having weighed the pros and cons. It was like buying stock for growth—solid unspectacular growth, yet one which also paid dividends, not recklessly or grudgingly either, but carefully, looking toward the future. He'd never been interested in speculation in the market or anywhere else, but of course the sensible man occasionally took a calculated risk.

Perhaps Janice in her own fashion felt this way too. So far he'd not encountered any of the surprises—some of them shattering—which he had often heard discussed on planes, in bars, in clubs and among his friends. Janice had not changed—nor had he—because they'd stood before an altar. She was as he had known from the first day: honest, amusing, very intelligent and appreciative of most of the things he liked. She had humor and compassion. She liked people, she liked being alive. Also she had heat lightning flashes of temper, soon over, and a deep, quiet fund of reserve, which he respected. Physically, they were beautifully compatible and he had not been astonished by her generous warmth and response.

As for the life she would now lead with him, there would be adjustments on both sides; which is as it should be.

He liked her parents and her friends; as for what she'd think of his family, he was not worried. She might like them, she might not. She'd take her time, making up her mind, and however she made it up, it would not disturb their personal relationship.

He was very fortunate; he had looked for a long time for that which he had now found.

The night before they left, Janice crept downstairs and stood looking from the windows at the lights of the city and the white buildings, at the dark mountains and the water. Tears stung her eyes briefly. Peace and tranquility—but a dream world. And no one outside of a mental institution lives long in a dream world. She had been happy here in the Richards' hillside house; not crazily, violently, destroyingly happy, but gently—as she had hoped she would be. Lunacy, rapture—that was in the past and had brought with it despair, depression, regret. It was something she would not know again. That period of her life had been like a stormy voyage, uncharted and headed for nowhere; the journey on which she had recently embarked was a course that was fixed. Oh, she thought, squalls and disturbances, but they'll pass.

When she went upstairs, Whit asked, "Where were you?"

"Downstairs, saying good-bye."

"I thought as much. You're shivering. Here, come to bed."

"If you thought so, why didn't you do something about it?"

"Such as what?"

"Come and say good-bye too."

"Goody-byes are private." He put his arm around her. "Go to sleep Mrs. Dennis," he said. "Tomorrow we return to a semblance of reality. God knows what's happened since we've been away, but nothing world-shaking or Joe would have zeroed in on us."

Hiroshi took them to the airport. The farewells were said and, on the plane to Seattle, Janice asked, "Which is his last name?"

"Sato is his family name. It's always backwards in Japan. I'm surprised at your ignorance."

"You'll get used to it," Janice said serenely.

The return to New York was uneventful, the pleasant attention in Seattle during their wait, the smooth flight to New York; and Joe there to see to the porters and luggage and take them to the car. He said, "Hello, Mrs. Dennis," and smiled at Whit.

"Janice," said Mrs. Dennis. "Now I'm one of the family."

Joe looked at her, frowning a little; then he said, "Thank you—but it may take a while."

"Take as long as you like," said Janice.

She was sleepy. Too much dinner, two drinks, and the time change caught up with her. She was aware of Mortimer driving through the night, and of Joe and Whit talking. Now and then she caught a word or a phrase and none of it made much sense.

"Wake up," said Whit and shook her.

"Are we there?" She had dozed off and had been dreaming. She could not remember the dream, but it left her curiously sorrowful as if something she'd found had slipped from her grasp.

Eventually they were home, in the apartment. The staff was present. Bags were whisked away. Later Whit came in from his adjoining room at her plaintive cry and unzipped her. He said idly, "Joe's found you a personal maid."

"But I don't want——"

"Let's not go through that again. There'll be times when I won't be around to zip and unzip—and I will not have my wife sleeping in her outer garments nor running about the city, unzippered, half naked."

"But——"

"If you're going to suggest the household staff, forget it. Cooks cook; butlers buttle; housemaids housemaid and tweeneys, tweeney. You may not know your place, but they do."

Janice chuckled, yawned and looked around the room. "Pretty soon it may look familiar," she predicted.

"Want to call your parents?"

"Not tonight. How about your family, wherever it is?"

"They're in the process of assembling and will be

properly met at various planes. Joe will see to it. Mother has an apartment around the corner; Heloise and Hilda share one, and Lily and Ned, another, all in the same building. They're often in New York, so there are what they call skeleton staffs in residence. And the day after tomorrow we turn up and dine with them at Mother's."

"Merciful heavens! What shall I wear?"

"A bare neck, in case she gives you a diamond monstrosity."

"I'd rather my pearls," said Janice, with some animation.

"Suit yourself. Have a good night's sleep. You'll need it. You interview your personal potential nanny tomorrow."

"It's disgusting to be rich," said Janice.

"You've found it so already? Pity. Maid's a misnomer. She's a widow, a Mrs. Cecil. First name, Susan; British, about fifty and comes highly recommended by Joe. He says she's personable, accustomed to high wages, and low duchesses—hey, you'll fall off!"

He scooped her up from the dressing table bench and deposited her on the bed. "Brace yourself," he advised, "we're now back in the mainstream; it's sink or swim."

SIX

AT ELEVEN THE next morning Janice interviewed Mrs. Cecil in what was known as the morning room. It was a small pleasant sun-filled room off the library, with a couch, comfortable chairs, an antique but practical desk and a great window beneath which plants lived in a long lined box, complete with pebbles. The first time she'd been shown the room, before her marriage, Whit had said, "This is yours," and she'd asked, "What for?"

"Interviews, consultations with the staff, or girl talk with good friends. Like the library is for me, half office, half social center."

Whit had gone to the Foundation offices; they had breakfasted together, he had announced he'd be home at the cocktail hour and departed. After which Janice went to her bedroom to bathe, dress, write notes and conduct a long conversation with Audrey, who was in a state of shock as her wedding day approached.

Smith knocked. Janice said, "Come in," and he reported that Mrs. Cecil had arrived and was in the morning room.

Descending, passing a rather pretty maid in the hall—which one, Hattie or Vera? They looked enough alike to be twins—she found herself as nervous as though she, and not Mrs. Cecil, were applying for a position.

The woman who sat on a straight chair, facing a small Renoir, maintained a more ladylike attitude than Janice was used to—legs crossed at the ankles, hands folded in her lap. Now she stood up. She was tall, and the word "well-nourished" flashed through Janice's mind. Susan Cecil had a serene face, good skin, dark eyes; her hair was also dark and neatly assembled under a small hat. Her suit and blouse were gray. She wore no make-up.

"Mrs. Cecil?" Janice moved toward her, put out her hand and Mrs. Cecil's large strong hand engulfed it. Was it Janice's fancy or did her rather heavy dark eyebrows lift?

"Good morning, Madam," said Mrs. Cecil.

Janice said, "Please sit down. On the couch," she suggested.

Mrs. Cecil waited until her prospective employer was seated, turning the desk chair to face her, then she said, "Mr. Meeker has my references, but in case you haven't seen them, I have copies." She produced them from a large handbag and Janice waved them away. She said, "That won't be necessary. I'd just like to know something about you personally."

A flicker of astonishment disturbed Mrs. Cecil's placidity as a very small pebble does the surface of a pool.

"Personally?" she repeated. "In what way, Madam?"

"Your life," said Janice. "Not just your positions. I'm sure that Mr. Meeker has all the facts. . . . But I'm interested in knowing how you happened to choose your profession."

Mrs. Cecil contemplated that for a moment; another flicker, this time possibly amusement. She said, "I was born into it so to speak, Madam."

"Would you tell me about it?"

She thought: I simply can't have this woman under foot day in day out and not know something about her as a human being; I'd as soon hire a robot.

Susan Cecil regarded Mrs. Dennis thoughtfully. She

was not one to make up her mind in a hurry. Occasionally she acted on instinct, but never through impulse or emotion. In her half century she had experienced only two overwhelming emotions. The gnat stings of anger, irritation, the dull ache of boredom she could control. As for her employers, some she had mildly disliked and others, rather liked; she had not made them aware of either slight involvement.

"It's an ordinary enough story, Madam," she began.

"I really must do something about this Madam business," Janice told herself crossly.

Susan Cecil, born Susan Lewis, was the daughter of a gardener on the estate that dominated the village of which Susan was a native. In 1917 he had married the ladies' maid who "looked after" the two older daughters in the household. She was from London, but of French extraction. Mrs. Cecil barely remembered her father. He had not been called up, owing to an injury received as a child, but had been killed in an accident. Susan's mother had been moved into quarters in a house with her child, and had continued to work, as she had up until a few months before Susan's birth, in the Cottage Hospital. Susan's grandparents, her father's people, had a small farm, and had wished to take Susan and her mother. Her mother had refused. "She didn't care much for farming," Mrs. Cecil explained.

Her mother had trained her and when Susan was sixteen "just out of school, Madam," her mother had died of pneumonia. But Susan had been kept on, the household staff having dwindled. "I did a little of everything. I was grateful to learn," she told Janice quietly, "whether downstairs or up." When she was twenty, the big house had been closed, there having been deaths, to say nothing of taxes, and eventually with her small savings and a generous present, she went to London, where she entered service, this time with an actress. At twenty-three she had married. When her husband had been called up, she'd gone to live with his parents, who had a small shop. She added, "He was killed. I lost the baby, and when I was well again, I went into war work. When the war ended, there were still people who wanted what I could do, so I went back into service."

Janice said, "But why did you——" and stopped.

Mrs. Cecil was regarding her as if tolerantly. She said, "I suppose I could have done something else, Madam. I'd had some"—she hesitated—"training during the war. But I liked being in domestic service."

"When did you come to the United States?"

She'd come seven years ago. She added that she had a cousin here, and there was no one left, as she put it, at home. She had taken out her papers.

All the rest, of course, Janice knew she could find in the references: for whom she had worked, here as well as England; when she had left and why. Now, Mrs. Cecil said, she had not had a position for two months; there was not a great demand for her type of work. Mr. Meeker had found her through the agency with which she had registered. She was living with the cousin and her family on Long Island. She mentioned a duck farm and her nostrils quivered a little.

Janice said, with the funny little scowl, which to those who knew her indicated merely thoughtfulness and some puzzlement, "I think I'd better tell you, Mrs. Cecil, that I've never had a personal maid."

"Yes, Madam," said Mrs. Cecil, still tolerant.

Janice laughed suddenly. This whole thing was pretty absurd. She added, "I'm afraid you'll have to train me."

Mrs. Cecil's face relaxed. "Then you are willing to try me, Madam?" she asked.

Janice said, "Would you mind very much calling me Mrs. Dennis?"

"No Mad—Mrs. Dennis, not at all," and added, with another flicker of humor, "My ladies have always called me Cecil."

That was that. "Mrs. Cecil" would be unheard of (except, of course, for a head housekeeper) and Susan would be for parlor maids.

Janice said, "It's pretty and rather like a first name when you come to think of it." She rose and Cecil also got to her feet. "When do you wish to come?"

Cecil thought about it. She said, "If Mrs. Dennis would find it convenient, the day after tomorrow?"

Mrs. Dennis did find it convenient. She did not mention hours, or wages, or duties. Certainly Joe had covered all that. She thought: I'll have to play it by ear.

Which reminded her of Smith. She rang, made the necessary explanations, and Cecil was escorted from the morning room.

Janice went back to her room. She was to meet Audrey for lunch. She thought: Well, if Whit's family considers I'm not too well put together tomorrow night, I'll just tell them my maid hasn't as yet arrived.

Presently she went off to meet Audrey at a small restaurant they both liked. She listened to her grasshopper agitation, made some suggestions, including an offer and finally went shopping with her. She returned home in time to rest and reclothe herself and was downstairs talking to Smith when Whit rang the bell and Smith hastened to admit him.

"Hi, Luv," said Whit.

"Hi."

He came over and kissed her, and she asked, "Don't you ever wear a hat?"

"Sometimes, when it snows."

"Or carry a key?"

"Why bother? Someone will answer the door. I lose keys. Joe carries most of mine for me. Why don't you ask me, 'How did things go at the office?' "

"How?" she asked docilely.

"All right. Corporation meeting, the rest of the time at the Foundation. What have you been doing?"

She told him and said eventually, "You know Audrey's position, I think. No parents. An aunt out in California somewhere. Tom's is similar; that is, he has a mother and a stepfather in Arkansas. There's no question of anyone coming on. . . . Audrey and her aunt aren't very friendly, and Tom hates his stepfather. They plan to be married in the church Audrey attends. She was talking about a small reception—just their friends—and I told her we'd give it for her. She wanted to know if it would be all right with you."

"So what was your reply?"

"I just said, it didn't matter, because *I'd* give it." She looked at him and smiled. "After all, I have my own money," she reminded him with dignity.

"So you have. My mistake. I should put your weekly allowance in the cookie jar. Tell Audrey we'll give her a send off."

"The question is—where? . . . You're an awfully nice person," she told him suddenly.

"Here. Where else? Leave it to the Smiths and a caterer and if she hasn't decided on someone else, I'll give her away. I suppose we'll have to do the same for Katie?"

"She's still playing the field."

Smith came in with martinis and canapés, and Whit raised his frosty glass. "Here's to Audrey," he said, "and also to us. . . . What else did you do?"

"I went shopping with her."

"Buy anything for yourself?"

"No."

"Get busy. You need clothes, over and above the trousseau."

She thought: I suppose it is—well—exciting at first, but after a while what? Shopping? Seeing old friends, meeting Whit's, entertaining, being entertained.

"You look thoughtful."

"I am. Whit, isn't there something I can do at the Foundation?"

He looked at her, briefly startled, and asked, "Bored already?"

"No," she said frankly, "but I could become so in time. I'm not accustomed to the idle rich bit."

"I can't put you on the payroll," he said with his engaging grin, "because one, you're family; and two, you're apt to take off with me at any moment."

"I know, but perhaps you could use a volunteer? I'm really a very good secretary. Uncle Howard will testify to that. I've had some experience in handling people, and I can do odd jobs."

"Dusting, filing, sending down for coffee?"

"All of those. What's more important I know a little about the Foundation." She hesitated, "I won't antagonize anyone, Whit, especially Mr. Foster and Mrs. Lowell," she promised.

"You might distract me," he said. "However, we can put you somewhere out of my sight and reach. Okay, you're hired, a dollar-a-year woman." He took out his billfold and gave her a dollar. "Frame it," he suggested, as Smith came in to announce dinner.

Laughing, they went in to sit at the smaller table by the windows and Smith looked at them with approval. Re-entering the kitchen, he said to his wife, "I believe she'll do."

Mrs. Smith inclined her head. She said, "A lady and she doesn't interfere," and added in a less stately manner, "Wonder how she'll get on with his folks?"

Janice wondered also, as she had wondered ever since her engagement. She was annoyed with herself the next evening for being nervous. She thought: Well, I look all right.

A simple dinner dress, one of her prettiest. And no pearls.

"How do I look?" she asked Whit before they went out to the car and he said, "Ravishing, of course. But wait till you see yourself in the dog collar."

"Woof," said Janice with resignation.

The apartment house had not been spawned recently. It was elderly, staid, solid, the lobby furnished in sober excellent taste. Casey, the doorman and elevator attendant, greeted Whit with moderate enthusiasm, for everything about this multiple dwelling was moderate—except the rents. It was not a co-operative.

Janice's small hands were damp in her gloves. In the uncrowded elevator Whit put his arm about her shoulders. He said, low, "Take your foot off the panic button. Casey approves, and present company."

The senior Mrs. Dennis lived on the top floor. Whit rang, the door opened and Whit said, "Hi, Jasper. . . . Janice, this is Jasper who has known me for thirty years."

Jasper was long, lean, and dark brown; his slow smile revealed superb, natural teeth. He executed a courtly little bow to Janice, said he was happy to see her, and could he offer congratulations? Janice shook hands with him and said, yes, he certainly could.

Someone whirled into the entrance hall, a woman who looked younger than she was, not entirely because of stated intervals spent at places called farms or ranches. She was dark, vivacious, slender, and Whit bore no resemblance to her. She said, "For heaven's sake don't just stand there," and whirled on ahead of them.

"My mother," said Whit to his wife. "Her name's Martha."

They went into a quietly furnished living room. This old building had high ceilings and big windows and, as Janice soon discovered, an incomparable situation on the East River. In the room, a gathering of women and one man.

"This is Janice," said Martha Dennis superfluously.

Hand shaking, a kiss on the cheek, all around. And Mrs. Dennis said briskly, "Do sit down; don't hover. We'll all have a drink and relax."

Jasper appeared, orders were given, and then Mrs. Dennis said, "Let me look at you, Janice."

Everyone looked thoughtfully.

Janice was sorting them out. Aunt Hilda, relict of Oscar Dalton, ten pounds overweight, fair, pleasant in an absent-minded fashion. She was the one who wrote, painted, and was a dog lover. Dogs appeared as on cue and made for their mistress, two smartly groomed miniature poodles, apricots. Aunt Heloise, very like her sister, relict of Francis Lemington, the one who wrote verse and guided charitable organizations. Lily Dennis Turner, a couple of years her brother's junior. Excessively thin, with eyes like Whit's and salon-frosted brown hair. Her husband, known as Ned, perhaps eight years her senior, a charming balding gentleman, friendly, but living, Janice judged from Whit's thumbnail sketch, in a world of his own.

"I must say," remarked Martha, taking a small sip of her drink, "this was a surprise to us all."

"An agreeable one," said her son-in-law.

Heloise said sadly, "Whitney rarely writes us."

"It's hard to keep track of any of you," said Whit.

"But if he had written," said Lily, "I doubt he would have mentioned you, Janice."

"Oh?" said Janice. She found herself smiling. This wasn't a sheathed claw; it was probably merely the truth.

"I didn't meet her a couple or three weeks ago," said Whitney. "We've been going steady for some time, and would have been married earlier, if, earlier, I'd thought she'd accept me."

"Ridiculous!" said Aunt Hilda, shocked.

Janice decided it was time to cease and desist from the nods and becks and wreathed smiles. "Yes, wasn't it?" she agreed, "when you consider Whit's charm, looks, and incredible amount of money."

There was a small sigh, almost of astonishment. Jasper wafted in; refills were in order. Janice refused. She said lightly, "Until I get to know people, one's my limit."

Ned Turner looked at her, smiling. He had nice gray eyes under blond brows. He asked, "Did you take a long time to consider?"

"Not really. Jamaica," said Janice, stone-faced, "is a romantic place. And besides," she added blandly, "no one better had offered."

"Do tell us something about yourself," said Mrs. Dennis.

Janice shrugged. "Oh, but I'm sure Whit has, and possibly Uncle Howard. You must have a complete dossier," she said.

Whit grinned. He said, "See, girls—and Ned—she can, if necessary and with her back to the wall, fight back."

Dinner was announced. Ancestors adorned the wall; the service was vermeil, the food excellent, the wines light and fragrant, the conversation general; such as: "Do tell us about . . . Where was it you went . . . ? Vancouver?" Or, "I do hope to meet your parents, Janice, if we happen to be anywhere at the same time."

After dinner, Janice coped with names. Lily, yes. Ned, yes. And of course the aunts. But they announced firmly she must call them Hilda and Heloise.

"And you?" Janice asked Martha. She couldn't imagine calling her Mom; and she'd be damned if she'd call her mother; only one person qualified for that title.

"Belle-mère's affected. Martha will do, since I can't be granny until you have a baby," said Martha, running a bright dark glance at Janice's figure, beautifully revealed in the simple, becoming frock.

"Wait a minute," said Whit. "In fact wait a couple of years."

The concerted whisper of a sigh again, this time disappointment, and Whit said, "Janice is perfectly capable of producing regiments of little Dennises, but I didn't marry her entirely for that reason and she can take her time about it."

"Look," cried Lily in delight. "She's blushing!"

Janice said crossly, "I'm sorry. I do—too often—it's just something in my skin or nature or whatever. Think nothing of it."

They were drinking coffee and for those who wished, liqueurs. Jasper cleared and departed. And Janice said, "What a nice man. Does he travel with you, Mrs. Dennis—Martha?"

"She'll answer to hi or any old cry," said Whit. He went around back of the couch and ruffled his mother's artfully arranged hair. He is fond of her, thought Janice.

Ned was talking about his little girls. He had pictures in his wallet. Vicky, twelve, and Betsey, ten, were currently in school in Switzerland and, he said, his face lighting up, "We'll go over to fetch them in June—haven't decided where we'll go from there."

"How about home?" suggested Whit lazily, and Lily said, "But languages are so important."

"Including English," said her brother.

Lily shrugged her too-slender shoulders. "Well, of course, when they go to college, it will be in the States," she said.

Janice was studying the pictures; Vicky had a remote look of Whit about her; of course, Whit's eyes and Lily's. She was tall for her age and thin; Betsey was very fair, like her father; she was round and laughing. They looked like natural, healthy little girls. She said so to their father, "Charmers," he said putting the pictures away. "I do miss them."

Now Heloise was asking Janice earnestly, "Is your mother involved with charities?"

"She has a very good record as a volunteer at one of our hospitals; when she was younger she was in scouting," Janice said.

"It's most important," said Heloise, "to give your time to worthy causes. . . . I've never been able to interest Hilda or Martha, yet in our position it's practically a mandate."

Martha admitted, lighting a cigarette, "I gave it up when I found it was easier to write checks," and Hilda said indignantly, "You know I take an active interest in the SPCA."

Lily said nothing, so she probably did nothing.

"I hope," said Heloise, "you will identify with a charity which appeals to you, Janice." Well, of course, Janice thought, liking her, Heloise would consider the money a responsibility. She didn't need to "identify" for social purposes, as a woman does coming to a strange city and starting up the ladder, or as a businessman must for business reasons.

"She's decided to go to work for the Foundation—on her days off," Whit told his aunt.

"But that's family!" said Heloise, shocked.

"Nepotism? We're not paying her. She's going to be a sort of floater, where needed, or dogsbody generally"—one of the poodles yapped sharply and Whit said, "No offense, old boy. . . . Also she's conversant with the setup to some extent, having read reports, taken dictation, and been generally useful at Board meetings in her capacity as a legal secretary."

His mother asked, "Did you suggest it, Whitney?" But it was Janice who answered, "I absolve him. I volunteered," she said.

"It will all be very flexible," said Whitney, "because I'll need her at home and abroad."

"Speaking of abroad, why don't you two come to Switzerland with us? You usually have business somewhere, and there's the Paris flat," Ned said.

"I won't be going over for a while," Whitney told him. "I'll be busy, here."

His mother said, "Your aunts and I plan to go down to the Island for a couple of weeks at the end of May, or in early June, before we return to California. You can surely take time off for that, if only weekends. You should use the house more. I'm certain Janice will love it."

"Of course she will and we'll see you there, but the first weekend in June we have a wedding on our hands."

"Anyone we know?"

"No. Friends of Janice's . . . just recuperating from her own, she's staging someone else's."

"Which reminds me . . ." said Martha, and rose. "I'll be back in a minute."

She returned followed by a tall, spare woman in uniform and hard on her heels, Jasper.

The maid carried a large velvet box, Jasper some paintings and a jewel case.

"There," said Martha when the box and case were on the coffee table and the paintings leaning up against the couch. "Take the wraps off, Jasper, please."

A small Picasso, from the Turners, for Janice and Whit; a not very good painting of the Big Sur from the artist, Hilda; and from Heloise a promise. "I'm going to buy you a dog," she said, "since your last one, Whitney, has been gone for some years. The question is, what breed? We can talk it over later."

From the jewel case, gold and enamel cuff links. Janice thought: He has at least twenty pairs, but his face was suddenly like a boy's as his mother gave them to him. "Pop's," he said and turned them over in his hands. "I didn't know you'd kept a pair."

"Just for this occasion," said Martha. She opened the big velvet box. "Whitney's grandfather had this parure designed and made for his bride; it was given to me when I married Whitney's father and it is to go to the bride of the oldest son in every generation."

Janice took the box in her hands and looked down at the faded lining; the dog collar—she hadn't really believed that—a small tiara, a bracelet. The glitter was overpowering; the stones in the outmoded settings not too big or too small, but a multitude of flawless diamonds.

"I expect Whitney has mentioned them," murmured Martha.

"Just recently," said Janice, aghast.

Lily said to her husband, "We did try for a boy." She added in her clear light voice, "But Vicky and Betsey being girls, are spared." Turning to Janice, she explained,

"Anyway we're out of the running. After Betsey was born, no more children."

There wasn't much you could say to that. Janice still looking at Grandmother's wedding gift, said, "They're beautiful, of course."

"Nonsense," said Lily briskly. "They could be. Even the old-fashioned cutting would appear to advantage in modern settings, but Grandfather fixed it in his will; nothing can be redesigned nor reset."

"Let's try it on for size," Whit suggested. He took the dog collar from the case and put it around his wife's neck, standing in back of her, and fastened it. "Grandma had a slender neck," said Whit, "as you have."

Martha spoke to the maid. She said, "Bring a mirror, Mary, please."

"There's one over there, on the wall," Janice said.

But Mary had left the room and returned in a moment with a hand mirror. Janice regarded her small face over the glitter, and gasped; she felt weighted down, choked, and Lily said, "It does even less for her than it must have for you, Mother. By the way, I don't recall your wearing it——"

"Oh, occasionally, when your grandfather was alive. It pleased Father, Whitney. Your grandmother often wore it."

Janice said, with a resignation she didn't feel, "I daresay you have to be dark. It washes me out."

"All diamonds, and no Janice," said Whit cheerfully and released her from bondage. "Now try the tiara."

It was less a tiara than a circlet, the main diamonds rising up from the center. "This I must see," said Janice, walking to the wall mirror. She lifted the tiara from her head. It also did nothing for her, as Lily had said of the dog collar.

"Cheer up," said her husband, "there's always the dog

Hilda is going to buy us, except that I'd rather not have a female."

Mary departed presently to put the parure and its case into a small attaché case. Jasper rewrapped the paintings, and Martha said, "You remember Mary, don't you, Whitney?"

"Of course, she's been with you a dozen years. I remember most all of 'em."

"Very capable woman," said Martha, "and often a great comfort. We must see about finding you a personal maid, Janice."

"Joe's attended to it," Whitney said.

"I honestly won't know what to do with her, but she seems very capable. She's coming tomorrow," Janice told her mother-in-law.

"She'll give the orders up to a point," said Martha, "and I do hope she's satisfactory. There's nothing like a well-staffed house."

SEVEN

❀❀❀

IN THE CAR going home, Mr. and Mrs. Dennis conducted a staid, comfortable conversation. Said Janice, indicating the attaché case, "What are we to do with that?" and Whit replied, "I'll entrust the contents to Joe and the bank; the case will be returned."

"And the paintings?"

"Suitable wall spaces can be found," he assured her.

"How about the potential dog?"

"Don't you like dogs?"

"I love them. One of my major heartbreaks was when, while I was in college, my cocker died. I refused to have another, ever. Mother and Father always have dogs. Didn't you see them flitting in and out of the reception? Dachshunds."

"Had a lion or two emerged, wolfing goodies," said Whit, "I wouldn't have noticed. Frankly, I was terrified—and not of lions."

"You. . . ? Why?"

"I was never married before; somehow it comes as a shock."

When they reached home, Smith was waiting. He took the paintings away and Whit carried the attaché case to his bedroom where, hidden by another painting, there was a wall safe. This he opened, saying, "Remind me to give you the combination in case you want to put any trinkets away."

She said, horrified, "I never thought of it. The pearls and all the rest are in my jewel case."

"That's all right. No burglaries so far. This place is bugged—bells ring, fireworks go off, and the fuzz presumably rush to the rescue."

After a moment she said mournfully, "I'll probably never learn."

"Come," he advised and led her into her own room. "Let's have a companionable drink, in the bedroom, like the lower classes. Smith will be along with them presently."

He cast himself on the bed, and Janice sat sedately on the chaise, asking, "how in the world did your mother find that apartment? It's charming."

"The Corporation owns it."

"Oh." She added wistfully, "I don't imagine it's very large."

"Martha's? No, two bedrooms, hers and a guest room, with baths and what you saw, aside from the quarters for Jasper, his wife, and Martha's handmaiden. Lily's has three bedrooms to accommodate the kids when here; and the one the aunts share, also has three. Why?"

She said, "I wish ours were smaller. Whit, why in the world do you need such a big one?"

"I don't. The Corporation owns it."

"I give up," said Janice, as Smith knocked and came in and Whit said, "Thanks. I won't need you any more tonight. We'll just throw the glasses out the window."

"What about Cecil?"

"Who?"

"My new maid," said Janice, sighing.

"Lemme see—next door to this room is your little sitting room in which, were we less depraved, we should now be drinking our sedative tisane . . . and next to that Cecil's room and bath."

"Owned by the Corporation?"

"Naturally, plus all the houses, the plane, the leases on various flats—London, Paris, the yacht, the works. From time to time, we all use them . . . the houses I mean. Martha takes off on the yacht when the fancy seizes her; so do Lily and Ned. The aunts get seasick. I'm the only one who uses the plane. They prefer to be just folks, first class, on commercial flights. Incidentally, what did you think of your new family? . . . You don't have to answer that," he added. "Except to say vaguely, 'wonderful.' "

"I can't answer it," she said truthfully. "I took a liking to Heloise somehow, she's so—well—earnest. Hilda . . ." She hesitated. "Cloud nine," she said finally. "Lily scares me a little; she has a sort of hard polish. As for your mother—honestly, Whit, I don't know. . . . Which leaves Ned Turner. I liked him at once and I felt——" She stopped, and then said, "This is absurd, after just one evening."

"Tell me what you were going to say."

"I felt sorry for him," she answered flatly.

"Very perceptive of you, Luv."

"In the aggregate," Janice said thoughtfully, "civilized and attractive people. But I can't sort out my impressions of them. I don't *know* them, Whit."

"It will take years, perhaps," said Whit, "unless there's a crisis, at which point they'll all rally." He finished his drink and smiled at her. "I would have suspected you of understandable deception had you run over at the mouth about them. We won't see very much of them, Janice."

She asked, concerned, "Don't you miss them?"

"Frankly, no . . . except my mother occasionally. I suppose that's normal, but never enough to be abnormal. The one member of the family I always missed when we were apart, which was often, and have missed since he died, was, and is my father. . . . Look, get to bed. I'll unzip you. After tonight you can ring for Cecil, except when I'd rather you wouldn't."

"Ring?"

"Oh, sure, there's a bell." He indicated it. "Before I moved in here this apartment housed various occupants, one of whom was an old lady—she had your room—and her companion, who had what is to be Cecil's."

When he unzipped her, he kissed the nape of her neck. "It's better without diamonds," he assured her. "You acquitted yourself nobly tonight."

"I wonder what they said after we left."

"You'll never know. I won't either. I imagine the jury is still in session and that the verdict will be, 'She'll do.' "

"How nice," said Janice stepping out of her dress and going into the bathroom to retrieve her nightgown, robe and slippers. Emerging she said, "There's one thing I don't understand."

"Only one?" he asked, from his dressing room.

"Well, among others," she conceded. "If, as you've told me, your mother, and I assume your aunts, are so obsessed with the idea of your producing a child—preferably a son—how come they didn't approve of your marriage? I'd think they would have aided and abetted."

"You were not their selection, darling."

"Was anyone?"

"Often; various maidens, or so we must assume, were trotted out for my inspection at one time or another; here, in California, on Long Island, in London—you name the place—there was always a marketable maiden."

"Golly," said Janice with wide hypocritical eyes. "What were they like?"

"Good stock. Some had money; others were reasonably poverty-stricken; all appeared to be healthy. Some were quite lovely to look at," he added. "Jealous?"

"Not at all," she said cheerfully.

"Not even of the girls I selected myself?"

"As wives?" she asked. "Provided you thought of a harem."

"Not as wives. Temporary playmates." He had been talking to her through the connecting doors, and presently appeared, saying, "Will you shut up, Mrs. Dennis, and go to bed?"

Janice yawned. She was sleepy; the evening had taken more of her nervous energy than she'd realized. She said, docilely, "To listen is to obey, Master," and went to bed.

"I should hope so," said Whit and flicked a switch which turned off all the lights except the one on the night table near him. He put his arm around her and said contentedly, "Go to sleep, at least for the time being."

But she was already asleep. Smiling, he turned out the bedside lamp and lay wakeful for a time reflecting upon the evening just passed. Cautious amity—which was better than guarded hostility . . . not that it would have mattered seriously, except that he would not have Janice hurt. As for himself, he was his own man and had been since he was three, despite female efforts to shape, enslave and mold him.

Following her first deep sleep Janice woke, muttered unintelligibly, turned over and fell back into the healing darkness; but not for long. She dreamed that she and Whit were giving a formal dinner in some vast house unknown to her and that she stood in an enormous, glittering drawing room, alone. Double doors opened slowly into a dining room, and there at a table stretching into infinity, the guests were standing motionless and silent by their places, all looking at her, at which point she became conscious of the fact that she was wearing the diamond tiara, the dog collar, the bracelet and absolutely nothing else. Her own scream woke her from this technicolored nightmare, and also woke Whit from his own dreamless slumber.

"For heaven's sake," he said, fully alert. She was half laughing, half crying, and he put his arms around her. "What's the matter?"

"Oh how silly!" said Janice. "I had a dream."

She told him about it and he inquired gravely, "Did you recognize any of our guests?"

"A few, just staring; your family, mine. . . ." There had been two others—Dave and Madge. Theirs were the first faces she had seen. She didn't report it.

"Where was I?" asked Whit. "Helping to ice the champagne?"

"I didn't see you. . . . Whit, what about entertaining?"

He looked at his watch on the table beside him. "What about entertaining at two in the morning—not that it couldn't be——"

"But we have to invite people."

"Relax. I'll give it due thought. The family, of course, and one evening just Joe. I'd like you to begin to know him. It takes time. On other occasions Fred and Harry, and now and then some of the office staff . . . and of course the Nortons."

"What about outside of family and associates? You must have friends, Whit."

"Oh dozens, and some turn up unexpectedly from Tibet, Hollywood, White Plains. They phone. Then I call you, and you brief the Smiths. Diamond Lil, I am not a member of the jet set and I rarely have what's known as a social obligation. My friends will come and go; yours too. And in early autumn we can throw a cocktail-buffet bash, when people flee cityward from beaches, mountains, lakes and Europe. You can then be properly presented."

"I thought I'd already met royalty."

"Thanks. But there are hostesses who once had me—without gratifying results—on their eligible unattached men list. We'll ask 'em so they can gnash their capped teeth on canapés and over you. Your role is to look and be charming. Have you wondered why you don't have a social secretary in addition to Cecil?"

"I haven't given it a thought! So, why haven't I?"

"I'm it," he told her. "Mother and the girls have such people on tap when they need them—usually for Heloise, who can't keep her engagements straight. For heaven's sake go back to sleep unless you want to watch the late late show."

The television sets lived in various rooms concealed behind sliding panels.

"No. I'm sorry I woke you," she said apologetically.

About six she woke him again. This time she shook him and he sat bolt upright, crying, "For God's sake, Janice, what is it now? So far, you've been an exemplary and quiet sleeper."

"Cecil!"

"How did she creep in at this hour?" he asked wearily.

"That's just it . . . will she? With morning tea and opening the curtains—Whit, will she do that with you here?"

"Only if you say so—and I'm your husband, remember. Look, you've been reading too many English novels—old style. Smith who looks after me, when necessary, doesn't come barrelling into my room. Cecil won't come into yours unless you ring. Joe's explained her duties to her. Are you trying to throw me out of your bed?"

"No. I just didn't know and I've been in England," she reminded him.

"Sure. Well you aren't now. When I'm away, and you're alone, ring Cecil if you feel ill, have bad dreams, or want breakfast in bed. That's it. Otherwise I'm your personal bodyguard. And it's futile to go back to sleep now," said Whit.

At breakfast he asked, "What's on the agenda?"

"I thought I'd buy a dress for Audrey's wedding and maybe shoes and things. Now that I know we don't have to do a lot of outside entertaining, I won't need much."

"Think over our projected cocktail-buffet. We might give a 'come as someone else' party. It's been the fashion for a long while. I'd suggest coming as the person you most hate."

Janice laughed. She said, "I couldn't. I don't hate anyone."

"Sure?"

"Certain," she said serenely. It was true enough; she didn't really hate Dave or Madge. "Unless——" She paused.

"What?"

"Unless I'd feel compelled to come as myself," she answered.

"Psychologically unsound," Whit said severely. "The first rule is to love and forgive yourself, which enables you to love and forgive others."

"So I've read. Where did you discover it?"

"I read too—the do-it-yourself columns, the syndicated psychologists, the printed pulpit preachments." He smiled and then suggested, "When you go shopping, take Cecil with you."

She looked at him, startled. "Why?"

"Because I'd rather."

She argued with a flash of annoyance. "But that's absurd. Even movie stars don't do that. No one does, except possibly," she amended, "the wives of heads of state or something."

"Take Cecil along, Janice."

"Honestly, Whit, I'd feel absurd."

"I said she'd be your personal Nanny."

"I know, and it's infuriating. I'm perfectly capable of going into a shop and selecting what I wish, unless you think Cecil has better taste than mine from her association with duchesses!"

"I fancy she has excellent taste," he said absently, "and I know you have. But I prefer that you didn't horse around alone."

"I went out with Audrey."

"Yes, I know. And you're permitted to lunch and dine with anyone, as you please. I'd simply rather you didn't go alone into crowds."

"In case I'm bumped off," she said furiously.

"Don't lose your cool. The answer to that is, leave no stone unturned, as someone might pick it up and hurl it. Cecil won't get in your way."

"Audrey will think I'm off my rocker . . . or else ——" She halted abruptly, and her color rose.

"Or else what? You're a genius in the unfinished-sentence department."

"Or else," she said doggedly, "that you're afraid I'd start meeting someone——"

"Mr. Peters? No."

Now she was crimson. "It's having me followed. That's what she'll think!"

"And a written report every night? I told you you read too many novels. You didn't tell me you had a date with Audrey."

"I forgot—anyway it's her wedding."

"So it is. All right, scratch Cecil today. But always take her when you go out alone, daytime or evenings."

He thought: This requires a slight change of program.

He asked idly, "Where and when are you meeting Audrey?" and she told him with open resentment.

He'd see Joe at the office, the matter could be arranged easily. For years there had been the threatening letters from various sources, ninety percent of them crackpots. When he was in school and college, these had been sent to his elders. The police knew. And private precautions were taken. You never knew when what you thought was a psychoceramic turned out not to be.

Heads of State had the secret service; ordinary citizens police protection, when it was warranted. The Dennis family provided its own protection.

Janice asked, "Do your mother and the others go around with entourages?"

"When indicated. . . . Mary, for one; that's Martha's little slave——"

"Has she another name?"

"Of course. But she isn't British, so, she's Mary."

Janice said slowly. "I'm sorry, Whit. I was just being stupid. What you are giving me is protection—although how Cecil could qualify . . . Anyway, you must have good reason."

He said gently, "That's about the size of it, Mrs. D. Heloise talked last night about the responsibility of money, in relation to being of service, in her case, through organizations. Money—if there's a lot of it—presents other problems and responsibilities. I'm not trying to frighten you, and I'm sure you don't easily run scared. Everyone in my situation—or in my mother's and the others'—become targets for kooks and some who perhaps aren't kooks. I should have warned you before we were married that the bird in the gilded cage is exactly that. I'm sorry too."

"Not as sorry as I am. It will be a new experience to know that the eyes of even a friendly Big Brother or Sister are watching. But I suppose I'll learn to take it. When do I go to the Foundation?"

"Suppose I take you with me tomorrow and let Forest and Mrs. Lowell talk with you."

"I hope they won't be upset."

"Why should they be? They're being paid; you aren't. You jeopardize no one. Besides you can be useful, as well as being the boss's wife." He looked at his watch, rose and kissed her. "I've got to get going. Have fun," he said.

"Wait a minute. You didn't tell me why Cecil qualifies for the role of guardian."

"She's had training during the war and always carries," said Whit, straight-faced, "a small atomic bomb in her compact. Self-destructing, of course."

"As well as Cecil-destructing." She was laughing when he went out. A few moments later she went upstairs and, because it was expected of her, rang for Cecil and they gravely discussed wardrobe and bathwater temperature.

Cecil said afterward, "If Mrs. Dennis would permit me, I arrange hair quite well."

"I'm sure you do. But my so-called hairdo is simple enough."

"May I brush it for you, Mrs. Dennis?"

"That would be fine." Janice relaxed at the dressing table and the capable hands moved. It was soothing, and tension-releasing. She was under more tension than she'd realized.

"Madam has beautiful hair."

This time she didn't mind the Madam. "Mrs. Dennis has beautiful hair" would have sounded a little odd, like a language lesson.

When she was dressed for the street, Janice thought of something and it embarrassed her that she had not, before.

"Are you comfortable here, Cecil?"

"Oh, quite, thank you, Mrs. Dennis."

Janice said hesitantly. "Would you mind if I saw your room? I never have, ridiculous as that may sound, and I just want to be sure."

Cecil looked faintly startled. No, she thought, it isn't prying, it's real interest. She said, "Of course, Mrs. Dennis."

They went down the corridor past the small living room Janice had not as yet used. A nice place to write letters, she thought, if you didn't prefer the morning room downstairs. Cecil opened her door. It was a big room, and she said, "It's what we call a bed sitting room, at home."

Studio bed, heaped with cushions; two big chairs; a vanity table, which could double as a desk; straight chairs; a night table and lamp by the studio bed; two windows; sunlight; bright upholstery and curtains; and, opening out of the room, a bath.

The personal touches were few except for the things most women have on a dressing table, a few books on shelves provided for them, magazines on a table—two English, one American periodical. On the night table an enlarged slightly faded snapshot of a young man, laughing, squinting against the light. On the dressing table, other photographs.

Janice said, "Thank you, Cecil. If there's anything you lack, please tell me." She indicated the snapshot. "Your husband?" she asked.

"That's right, Mrs. Dennis," said Cecil and her heart contracted. . . . So long ago, so far away. You just didn't get over things like people said, she thought.

She went downstairs with Janice. She asked, "Am I to go with you, Mrs. Dennis? I can be ready in a moment."

"Not today, thank you," said Janice, making the implied promise that there'd be days when Cecil would go. She said, at the door, "If anyone telephones——"

Cecil said, "I fancy Smith will take the calls, Mrs. Dennis, unless he's not available."

Well, I'm learning, thought Janice, greeting Mortimer and getting into the car. What I need is a chief of protocol. And she asked herself suddenly: I wonder if I'll ever feel really free?

Glancing about Cecil's room, without, as Cecil had concluded, any thought of prying, she'd seen no overt arsenal. She thought, laughing inwardly: A gun, a dagger in the garter—does anyone wear garters?—a police whistle in the handbag? Well, it didn't matter, the gilded cage was after all an outward restriction; within herself she was as free, she thought somberly, as she'd ever been or ever would be.

EIGHT

❀❀❀

JANICE MET AUDREY at a designated shop and bought her frock. She was a fast, no-nonsense shopper; she always had been. She knew what she wanted and if she found it, that was fine; if she didn't, she went elsewhere.

Her selection, a very pale gray green, like very young leaves, met with Audrey's approval and so did the shoes, the little half hat for church, and the handbag. But Audrey said wistfully, "It would all look wonderful under a short sable coat."

Janice gave her charge plate to the saleswoman who, once she'd processed it, looked awed, and spoke to her by name with enthusiasm. Several people looked around, a few gaped.

"For pity's sake!" said Janice under her breath.

They went to lunch and talked wedding, and at an appointed hour Mortimer slid up outside the restaurant and Janice took Audrey home. Katie was there, cursing a spring cold. Janice had not seen her since Cleveland and promptly made a date, for "when you're over the sniffles." They sat around the familiar apartment and talked and Janice felt a curious pang of homesickness, or perhaps nostalgia—something, anyway.

"What are you going to do when Audrey leaves, Katie?"

Katie reported that she was going to share an apartment with two of Raoul's models, which meant having it practically by herself most of the time, she added.

Janice reached home, and went through her present usual routine—rest, look at mail, dress for dinner. She called her mother from her bedroom and found her at home.

"I haven't written, I'm sorry. More fun talking anyway."

Mrs. Cooper wanted to know about Whit's family.

"I met them last night. . . . What? . . . Oh everyone was very cordial," said Janice. "Whit's mother gave me a diamond stomacher."

"What!"

"Well, dog collar, tiara, bracelet—they belonged to his grandmother and are entailed."

"Janice," said Mrs. Cooper, "if I didn't know better, I'd think you'd been drinking."

"Nope, not yet."

"I can't wait to see them."

"They're at the bank and when you come to New York, I'll take you there and we'll just sit, staring."

"Aren't you going to wear them?"

"This is not the season," said Janice aloofly. "When are you two coming East?"

She was smiling when she broke the connection. Her mother was real, and her father. There seemed little reality in her present life, except of course, Whit. He had always seemed real to her. Mad as a hatter, she thought originally, yet real.

After dinner, they went out on the terrace and looked at the lights and the water and the boats going by. The soft spring night was full of sounds: a doorman's whistle, shrill, seeming far away; the remote mute of traffic, the boats. He said, with his arm around her, "You didn't have a very exciting day from what you've told me: Audrey, shopping, the apartment and Katie. . . . I hope you didn't catch her cold."

"I never catch colds and in a way it was exciting. I felt, in the apartment, as if I'd been away a hundred years."

"And regretted it just a little?"

"Perhaps, but not for long. . . . Talking to mother was fun."

"Do it more often, and when I'm around too. Your mother is an enchanting woman. You'll go with me to the Foundation tomorrow; Forest will take you to lunch; Mortimer will pick you up afterward; and I've told Joe we'd like to have him come for dinner—which reminds me, you'd better call him."

She hadn't the remotest idea where Joe lived and said so and Whit said, "Small suite, in a downtown hotel."

"I would have thought he'd live here," said Janice, "at least until you married."

"Never has. Travels with me, of course, but if we're based anywhere for any length of time, he prefers independence."

"How about girls?"

"Plenty, when he has time for them, but no honorable intentions. He's a loner."

"No, not really," said Janice.

"You mean, me? He's fond of me, I think, and almost savagely loyal. Also he quite disapproves of me, usually. But still he's a loner."

"I wonder if Katie——"

"Come off it. She isn't his type."

"Who or what is?"

"Joe likes to relax on his dates . . . he likes them pretty, sweet and rather stupid."

"Really Whit, that went out with *Gentlemen Prefer Blondes*."

"No, Miss Loos was right; there are a good many men

who like to rest their mental and exercise merely their physical capacities. Katie's a clever, ambitious girl; she'd scare the hell out of Joe. You would too, you know, except that you are now in a different category from the unattached female."

"Okay, let's go telephone, though I don't see why, exactly. This is your house, he's your friend."

"Ah, but he's reactionary. The invitation must come, if I know Joseph, from Potiphar's wife herself."

They were laughing when they went indoors and Janice, finding that Mr. Meeker was at home, told him how much she and Whit would enjoy the pleasure of his company.

Joe said he'd be happy to come.

Janice was a little nervous, going into the Foundation Building the next day, walking beside Whit. She hadn't been, going to meetings with Howard Norton. She thought: We must ask the Nortons soon. She had talked to Edna Norton and also her godfather on her return from Vancouver and they'd spoken of getting together. But she reflected, most people still tended to leave the recently married alone.

The Dennis Foundation Building was not imposing as modern buildings go, nor was it in an elegant area. Built during Whit's grandfather's time, and, as an office building, leased to various firms, Whit's father, when the Foundation was set up, had, so to speak, repossessed it and modernized it. Lighting, space, washrooms, carpeting (in a few of the offices and the boardroom). But it had remained an elderly, sober structure. No fountains splashing in the courtyard—there was no courtyard; and no stunning blinding glitter of glass; just windows kept as clean as it's possible to keep Manhattan windows. There was a fair-sized reception room and a fair-sized receptionist. There was no executive dining room (as in the Corporation Building). You went out or had lunch sent in. Whit had installed coffee, soft-drink and cigarette machines. The washroom for women had a small pleasant lounge, with vanity tables. There were no terraces, no bars wheeling out of paneled executive offices. It was a solid and efficient building and worth the ransoms of several existent and previous kings.

The office of the president was also sober, well furnished but without the decorator touch. There were, to be sure, a couple of paintings on the walls which would have paid several annual salaries and as the building was moderately high rise, a view from the windows—but only of city streets.

"Well," said Janice in the president's office, "I didn't know you cared."

There was a picture on the desk, hers, in her wedding dress.

"Oh, I do," he said. "And even if I didn't, this is the required touch."

In addition to a number of extra telephones throughout the offices, he had a splendid intercom system. He pushed a button and said, "Bill."

Bill was Mr. Foster. Janice, of course, knew him. She did not think of him as Bill; she marveled that anyone did. He was a small gray man of indeterminate age, perhaps fifty, perhaps younger. All she knew about him was that he was efficient, dedicated, and had been promoted from a more lowly position at the time Whit came to the Foundation, and that he lived on Long Island with a wife and several more or less grown children.

Mr. Foster came in, and shook hands and Whit said, "This is a family conference; sit down. Where's Emily?"

Emily Lowell was Bill's secretary. His office was a

small one, opening from Whit's, and in it Mrs. Lowell sat, so Janice supposed, in a corner. She was also of uncertain age, perhaps thirty-five. That she had—or at least had had—a husband was to be deduced. She was somewhere between slim and not so slim; her skirt was short, but not too short; her hair was mousy; she had large grave eyes behind bifocals, good hands and wore only the suggestion of lipstick.

Janice had met her also and seen her at the wedding. Whit waved a casual hand as Emily came in. "One big happy family," he said. "Are you willing to accept a peripatetic member?"

They said they were and Emily Lowell regarded Janice with a little smile which was part felicitation and part resigned envy.

"Well, as I see it," said William Foster, clearing his throat—he had an astonishingly deep authoritative voice for a man of his size—"Mrs. Dennis is willing to give us a hand now and then."

"Every working day," said Janice firmly, "provided I'm in town."

"We need help," said Bill earnestly to his employer. "There's a good deal of absenteeism, illness, babies, that sort of thing. And the young ones get married or move on to a more, shall we say, exciting career? And the old ones retire. We can always get people through the agencies, but ——"

Janice said, with her warm generous smile, "I won't be taking anyone's place, Mr. Foster. Still I can do a number of things—type, take dictation, interview people. I'm not much on figures," she said ruefully, "but I can file."

She thought: They know I'm no threat, I wonder if they think I'm to be here as a sort of spy. But, no; they know Whit, they couldn't think that.

Emily Lowell asked suddenly, "Where are we to put her?"

"Not in here," said Whit promptly, "and certainly not in your office, Bill." He looked at Janice severely. "You don't rate an office. If you're a good useful girl, I may suggest to the Board in ten years or so that you be given a seat on it and an imposing title like Representative At Large."

Everyone laughed dutifully except Janice, who regarded him with annoyance. And Foster, a tactful man, asked, "Do you speak any languages, Mrs. Dennis?"

"French, to some extent," she said. "Spanish, a little; and I have enough German to ask my way to the nearest police station."

"Fine," said Foster. "As it happens there's a desk vacant in the overseas office, where," he hastened to add, "the translators work."

Whit said kindly, "We do have overseas business, you know—aid to hospitals, grants to medical students—those who come from Europe and Asia to intern in the United States; those who, after interning here, go to Europe or Asia for postgraduate studies. Also we have medical and research teams in many countries."

"I know," said Janice sweetly, and could have killed him, because he knew she knew.

"Okay," said Whit. "Suppose you show her the ropes, Emily," he suggested. "Bill, I want to talk to you."

Emily pattered off, Janice followed, and presently found herself in the office of the personnel director, a pleasant gentleman, and eventually in the overseas department which went right on with its work. From there she went to the office of the overseas director.

In the big overseas room, there was one vacant desk like an empty log boat in a fleet. And Emily said brightly,

"I know, of course, that you've been here with Mr. Norton, but I'd like to show you around."

Janice followed her doggedly, into elevators and out of them. Her feet began to hurt and she felt exactly as if she were applying for her first job; though she hadn't, really; she'd come straight from college and her extra courses to Howard Norton's law offices; no problem there.

It was after twelve when they finished the tour, and in spite of her feet and her sense of inferiority, Janice was tremendously impressed. This was very big business; not big business in the Corporation sense, but big business in adventure, alleviation, the binding up of wounds, the setting free of young minds, the biggest business of all, which is the business of caring. It cost money to run the Foundation, but if she were any judge, the expenses were kept to a minimum and the profits were incalculable, since they dealt with intangibles; mercy without sentimentality, generosity without fanfare, hope without the usual strings.

She had talked to many people, she'd looked at many maps, she'd read reports, and returning to Whit's office, she said, with humility, "I'll be proud to be even a very small part of this, Mrs. Lowell. I realized vaguely what it was all about when I came to meetings with Mr. Norton, but I've learned a good deal more this morning."

Mrs. Lowell said briskly, "Most of us work hard and believe in what the Foundation is doing. You haven't seen a tenth of it: the work done with the underprivileged in this country; for the children, for the old people, for the clinics and hospitals. It all ties in. Mr. Dennis said I was to show you the works. But that would take a month."

Whit's office was empty when they reached it, and Foster scurried in like a sedate and fearless mouse. He said, "Mr. Dennis has a luncheon engagement at the U.N. I'm honored to take you to lunch, Mrs. Dennis."

She thanked Emily. "I'll see you Monday," she said, as

it had been established that she'd start work then. And so she went out with Mr. Foster to a restaurant in a nearby building which was crowded, noisy and unrelaxed generally. The food was simple and hot, the service good, and evidently Mr. Foster's table was kept for him in a less agitated corner.

She'd come with Whit in a Foundation car, but Mortimer was waiting for her when she emerged from the restaurant. How and where he had been able to park only God and Mortimer knew.

She went home, tired, and also excited. The workings of the vast Corporation machinery would have stunned and amazed her; she would not have been able to grasp even the rudiments; nor would she have been interested. But the Foundation's concerns—dealing in the humanities, education, research and science, relief and rescue—were something she could understand, however dimly. She knew, through her godfather, that an enormous amount of money had created it and that when there was a need, the Corporation filled it, as the well the bucket.

When she reached home, all she wanted to do was take off her shoes, lie down and think, and tonight talk about it. Then she remembered Joe was coming to dinner.

Cecil knocked. Tall and solid in the doorway, she said, "I heard you come in, Mrs. Dennis. Is there anything I can do for you?"

Janice said. "My feet are killing me."

"With your permission," said Cecil. She sat down on the hassock by the chaise longue and took Janice's left foot in her hands. She said, "It's the high heels . . . ," and proceeded to take off Janice's shoes.

"I suppose so," said Janice, comforted by the slow, soothing massage. "I should have remembered my scouting days and worn oxfords or flats or something."

To her astonishment she fell asleep and woke to find

that Cecil had covered her with a cashmere throw and departed. Startled, she looked at the clock and rang. When Cecil appeared she said, "I actually went to sleep in my clothes."

"They can be pressed," said Cecil, "I didn't want to disturb you, Mrs. Dennis."

Cecil the paragon. She had established immediately that the care of Madam's garments was in her hands. She had told Janice so. She had said, "I'll look after your things, Mrs. Dennis, the pressing, and the special laundering. Mr. Smith will arrange it. He says there is ample space in the laundry room."

There was also a grim, gaunt laundress who came daily, functioned and left.

Janice had taken her second tub of the day, and had dressed, with Cecil to zip her up.

"Do I look half dead? I felt it when I came home."

"No, Mrs. Dennis, you looked quite rested. It's all that walking on hard floors; you're not used to it."

Well she felt rested—the nap, the bath, the hair brushing, to say nothing of her comforted feet. She was now able to face Whit, Joe and the world in a soft unadorned Jersey dinner dress—or, hostess gown, as the advertisements read—a deep burgundy in color. She'd worn it in Vancouver, and Whit had liked it. She thought: I'll have to buy more clothes, I suppose.

This dismayed her; the trousseau had been bad enough; she hated fittings.

"This," she told Cecil, "is either a little too long or else I've lost weight."

Cecil said, "I'm an excellent needlewoman, Mrs. Dennis, and I brought a small sewing machine with me."

Oh, thought Janice floating downstairs on her recovered feet, behold the Idle Rich! If it weren't so pleasant—at least, most of the time—I'd run away and live in an attic and guiltily exist on crusts of bread. But she was laughing at herself when she went into the drawing room and asked Smith, who instantly materialized at her elbow, "Did Mr. Dennis say what time he'd be home?"

Shortly before six, she was informed, and dinner about seven.

She hadn't ordered it. All Whit had said at breakfast was "Mr. Meeker will join us for dinner. Mrs. Smith knows what he likes."

Whit came in whistling, asking Smith, "Have I time for a shower?" blew Janice a kiss and vanished. She was half sitting, half lying on the big couch when he reappeared.

"And how did it go at the office, I'll ask you for a change."

"Fine. It nearly killed me."

"Feet? The wall carpet is restricted to the executive offices. How was lunch?"

"Good, I suppose. I was too busy talking to Mr. Foster to notice much."

"He's quite a guy," said Whit. "I'm a lucky feller. I have as many right hands as whatever that Hindu god's name is. . . . Do you honestly want to work there on your days off?"

"Off from what?"

"From me, lovely idiot."

"I do," she said and looked at him, smiling, "I've been saying 'I do' quite a lot lately."

The chimes rang, announcing Joe, who came in and took her offered hand. He said, "Hi, Whit," as if they hadn't seen each other all day. . . . Not that Janice had seen Joe in the office, but she thought: I bet they've talked, if only on the phone.

Mrs. Smith, an excellent taciturn cook, knew what Joe

liked to eat; Smith knew what he liked to drink. He brought martinis, and canapés, for their guest a tall, frosty glass full of a colorless liquid.

"Vodka?" asked Janice.

"Tonic and ice," said Joe. He looked at her with his slight, half-reluctant smile. "I'm an ex-alcoholic, you know."

"I didn't," said Janice blankly. What did one say to that? "I'm sorry"?—Sorry, you're an ex, sorry you can't drink?

Joe laughed. He said, "I thought Whit would tell you."

"Why should I?" asked Whit. "It's your problem."

Janice said, with some indignation, "Neither of you has to tell me anything!"

"I'm dried out," said Joe cheerfully, "and have been for a long time, thanks to Whit."

So that's it, Janice thought. Gratitude as well as affection, but I bet there were times when there was neither. Now Whit thinks he's dependent on Joe; but Joe knows he's dependent on Whit.

She lifted her glass and said soberly, "To you, Joe," and in a little while they went in to dinner.

NINE

DINNER, JANICE DISCOVERED, was what nine out of ten men order in hotels and restaurants: shrimp cocktail; steak, medium rare; baked potatoes; green peas; a tossed salad; apple pie, Joe's à la mode. "An unimaginative so and so, our Joe," Whit remarked.

"He has no weight problem," Janice said, smiling at the tall, thin man sitting across from her at the small family table.

Joe said, "Maybe unimaginative, but safe. I've never had the desire to try new things. Now and then Whit's persuaded me. Escargot," he added with distaste, "like eating rubber bands and garlic."

The conversation was easy and general. Joe asked Janice about Vancouver, "Whit hasn't told me much. That's a place I'd like to go—one of many—with a camera." He was a camera buff, Janice learned.

"Do you ask girls to come look at your photography?" she inquired.

Joe laughed; he didn't often, she realized. He said, "Well, etchings belong to another era. Besides I haven't any and I don't have a hi-fi, being practically tone deaf."

When they went in for coffee (which Joe had also had with dinner in a large cup), Whit settled for a brandy and Janice said, "I don't think I'll have anything further, Smith, thank you."

Joe said, "Not on my account, I hope. Other people drinking doesn't bother me any more. There was a time when I'd backslide." He looked at Whit and shook his head.

Whit's face was momentarily somber, remembering those times.

Janice said, "I really don't want anything. Did you know I spent the morning at the Foundation, Joe?"

He nodded and lit a cigarette. He was a chain smoker, she'd noticed, even during meals.

"I start work Monday."

Joe nodded again and said it was a good idea. The grapevine, thought Janice, was better than jungle drums.

"I hope nobody at the office will object," she said tentatively, and Joe said flatly, "They won't."

If they did, they wouldn't reveal it, she thought. They'd had a briefing—from whom? Whit? Joe? Mr. Foster? Or all three?

She said to Whit, "I forgot to tell you that when I went shopping with Audrey and to lunch, then back to the old apartment, I had a curious sense that I was being followed."

Actually, she hadn't had, until now, in retrospect. She looked from one to the other, for their reactions; there were none. Joe's face was impassive, and Whit's also.

"Doubt it, Janice," Whit said.

Now she was remembering; a small undistinguished man waiting as if for someone at the entrance to the shop; later she'd seen him in the elevators and again hurrying down the street when the car drew up. She couldn't be sure of him in the restaurant, where there were a number of undistinguished men there accompanied or alone; nor had she seen him at the apartment.

Joe looked inquiringly at his host and employer, and

Whit admitted, "I'm afraid she knows that when the occasion arises she's in protective custody."

Joe's deep-set eyes regarded Janice. He said, "Does this bug you?"

"Well, yes," she admitted. "It makes me feel foolish . . . and I'll hate to go through life looking over my shoulder and wondering if the same harmless looking gentleman is patiently on my trail."

Joe smiled. He said, "The less you know, the better, and if it's all right with Whit, I might add that you are followable for other than unprofessional reasons."

Whit said gravely, "That's a compliment, Janice, and he rarely pays 'em."

Janice laughed. "Thanks. That sort of thing I can handle. I've managed all right up to now."

Whit said, "You were once in Italy, weren't you, with your parents? You must have had quite a workout."

"I didn't mind being pinched," Janice assured him, "after the first time."

"It may be a little difficult for you to distinguish between the normal admirer and—well—others," Joe told her. "But we can take care of that. I'm sorry it has to be so."

She said in exasperation, "But it's like fiction. Do you really expect me to be shot, kidnaped or just quietly stabbed?"

"We certainly don't anticipate it," Joe answered promptly, "but we do try for the ounce of prevention."

"It's all that money! Things like that would never happen to a legal secretary," Janice concluded.

"All that money," agreed Whit solemnly. "Bite on the unfired bullet, accept, be resigned."

Joe left early. He had to fly to Dayton in the morning, he told Janice. He'd had a pleasant evening. He spoke to her by name for the first time since his arrival at the apartment. He said, "I hope you and Whit will have dinner with me some evening. I've found, quite recently, an attractive, quiet place. Whit likes French food. Do you, Janice?"

She said she did and asked, "But you can get steak, I hope, while we eat escargots and moules?"

"Moules?" Joe shrugged. "Sounds terrible. Yes, I made sure of steak or roast beef."

"He's learning," Janice said after Joe left.

"What?"

"To call me by my first name; he said it might take a while, remember? It didn't."

"Oh, he approves. He thinks you're good for me."

"You egotistical so and so," said Janice. "Did he tell you?"

"No. But I understand the workings of his devious, if brilliant, mind."

They had just gone upstairs when the telephone rang in Janice's bedroom. Hers was a different number from the other telephones, as was Whit's. All were unlisted.

Whit answered, minus jacket and tie and also his shoes. "It's Joe for you," he said.

"Hi," said Janice. "Down with ptomaine or something?"

"No. I just thought, since I'm going to be in Dayton I might call your parents and say I've just seen you, and that you are blooming—with your permission," he added.

"Thanks, Joe," she said. "I'd like that. I spoke recently to my mother, but she'd believe your report."

He said he remembered her parents with pleasure.

Hanging up, she remarked, "If I didn't know that Cecil was straight British and Joe, mostly American—I gather New England—I'd swear they had a touch of German."

"How come?"

"The Germans always say 'with permission.' "

Ready for bed, she cast herself on the chaise. "It's early. Talk time."

"Bedtime story?"

"In a manner of speaking. Tell me about Joe. I mean, really."

He came to sit on the end of the chaise and remarked thoughtfully, "I've never seen pale hair shine like yours."

"Cecil brushes it. I'm too impatient. Go on about Joe."

"I hadn't started. Background, as you surmised. Good people; his father died when Joe was in high school, his mother about a year ago. College—he worked his way through. Navy in which he enlisted at the time I did. He's older than I . . . and he'd had an excellent job. Also, he was married."

"I don't believe it!"

"It's true. It happened while he was still in college; his wife went on working."

"Did you know her?"

"No. But I heard about her. I daresay you can't imagine Joe Meeker passionately in love, but he was. . . ."

"Did he admit it?"

"No. We trained together and emerged a couple of fascinating young officers, at least, I was fascinating," Whit said modestly.

"I don't doubt it. I'm a little astonished Joe enlisted, since he was married, and older."

"If you knew him, you wouldn't be astonished."

"But . . . the drinking?"

"He drank very little—oh, now and then with the rest of us, but never to excess. When we were discharged, I told him any time he wanted a job . . . you know that sort of thing, but I meant it. He said, sure, if the occasion arose. So he went home and I didn't hear from him, although I wrote him several times. The last two letters were returned, addressee unknown. Then he turned up, here in the apartment, one night, shabby, blind drunk, incoherent. Smith and I put him to bed. I called a doctor. He was suffering from the malnutrition of alcoholics . . . he'd also evidently been in a fight. Smith would have thrown him out on his ear, but I happened to be in the living room. Joe's voice hadn't changed as much as the rest of him."

She said, "Poor Joe. . . . Why?"

"His wife. She took off with what she termed a more exciting man, and one with some inherited money. She divorced Joe in Mexico. He let her. After that he started drinking. He was left where they'd been living, and wouldn't go to his mother's. He had some money; he spent it, and drifted."

"What happened then, after he came to you?"

"Hospital, sanitarium, eventually AA. But, as he said tonight, he backslid a time or two. I gave him work, of course."

"Where did he learn to staff houses?"

"His father owned and ran a good inn, summer and ski-resort stuff. His mother—they married rather late—had been housekeeper before her marriage to people who summered up there in New Hampshire and wintered here in town. Joe had picked up a lot about hiring and firing, by osmosis, I suppose. He also read books."

"And then?"

"When I was as sure of him as I could be, I gave him other things to do—confidential missions, you might say."

"Wasn't it risky?"

"Possibly. But so far, my belief in his capabilities, including his capability to stay away from the sauce, has been justified."

"Tell me," said Janice, "is he employed by the Foundation, the Corporation or both?"

"Both wouldn't be possible. Neither, as a matter of fact. He's employed by me—as all the things, in all the capacities you guessed a while back—watchdog, road builder and smoother."

"Personal FBI and Secret Service?"

"To a degree, but also as roving ambassador and, metaphorically speaking, listener at keyholes and transom snooper."

"I hope you reward him commensurably?"

"If you mean, do I pay him in keeping with what he does for me, that wouldn't be possible. There isn't enough money in the world, let alone in the Dennis Enterprises, to buy loyalty and devotion. But I pay him a hell of a good salary, Janice, most of which he saves."

"What for? There weren't any children, were there? And his mother's dead."

"Yes. He provided for her; not that she didn't have enough to live on from the sale of the inn. And she was a frugal woman. But he supplemented it and carried a big life insurance policy for her. She left what she had to him, incidentally."

"I wonder who he'll leave his to," said Janice idly.

"God knows. I've always hoped he would remarry, but he shows no sign of it. He has, as I once told you, occasional little companions—one at a time—and he's generous to them, I gather. Maybe when he retires, he'll go to a lamasery and lead the contemplative life, in which case, he'd reorganize his surroundings of course. Maybe he'll leave it to me or our offspring."

"Which would be a superfluity."

"Natch. But, I think, to the Foundation. He likes kids and they like him, so he might leave it to the section dealing with children and their needs, probably in this country."

Janice rose. She said, "It's a tragic story, Whit."

"Yes, but not unusual. And Joe's not a tragic figure; he's not even, now, a melancholy man . . . closed-mouthed, yes, and not quick to make friends, but then he was like that when I first knew him."

"Whatever happened to his wife?"

"I don't know. I never asked, and he hasn't volunteered any information."

"I wonder if he still hates her."

"I don't think he ever did," said Whit soberly, "and perhaps he still loves her, which is, of course, the real tragedy."

Later, while he slept, Janice lay wakeful. She thought: "Do I still love Dave? Certainly she didn't hate him, but, as certainly, there were times when she missed him, when she would have thrown this apartment, all the houses and appurtenances she hadn't as yet seen, Cecil, the Smiths, Mortimer; the car she'd not yet driven, but which was her own, waiting patiently garaged for her to take the wheel ("Not in the city, my luv, wait till we get to the country," Whit had said when, on their return from Vancouver, he'd had Mortimer drive it to the apartment house for inspection), plus the diamonds—including the parure—out of any old window just to sit with Dave quietly and talk. This ache, which someone once called "the wound of absence" . . . where had she picked that up? From, she recalled, a poem in a book by Elizabeth Goudge; she'd read it after moving in with Audrey and Katie. She couldn't have told anyone what the novel was about; but she remembered the poem. This ache was far less frequent since her marriage, even since before her marriage. But it was still there, and sometimes when she was alone, she experienced it, with fear and reluctance.

Her voluntary dismissal of Dave Peters had once made her think of a fairy story she'd read as a child, and hated for what she'd considered its cruelty, yet read and reread because she couldn't help herself. The little mermaid, who, given feet, took every step upon knives.

"You're awake," said Whit suddenly.

"I'm awake."

"Want a pill or something?"

"I don't take sleeping pills." Oh, but she had once, every night, intent only upon, and longing for, the almost instant dive into the dark waters, soothing, quieting and stirring no dreams. But that phase had ended long ago. Her doctor had become alarmed. Katie and Audrey had helped, sitting up with her for hours, watching TV, playing muted recordings and talking.

On Sunday—which was the Smiths' day off, as well as alternate Thursday afternoons—the Nortons came to dinner. When, which was rare, Whit entertained without his usual staff, a catering team, man and wife came in and did so well that sometimes Smith looked thoughtful and Mrs. Smith muttered.

It was a good relaxed evening and leaving, Howard Norton said, with his arm around Janice, "I won't worry about her any more, Whit."

"Did you, Howard?"

"Of course I worried."

"I didn't," said his wife. "Naturally I hated you, Whit, despite my affection for you. I wanted her in my family." She beamed at Janice and added, "You'll be happy to know Howard Jr. is recovering from you, dear. He brought a very attractive little girl to dinner the other night."

"Good," said Janice, "but I honestly don't think he ever was on the verge of killing himself, Aunt Edna."

Whit returned to Howard Norton's statement. He

said, "Why did you worry about her? Though I sometimes do, myself."

"She's happy," said Howard Norton. "I never worry when someone's happy."

Going upstairs, Whit asked, "Are you happy, darling?"

He didn't say "darling" often, not as often as the hundreds of strangers she'd met in her life, but he said it lightly, as to a child.

"I'm happy," said Janice serenely.

It was true. . . . You can be happy even when wounded. You can be optimistic; ignore pain, and sometimes it will go away. You are healthy, wounds heal; and you are sensible, you don't encourage brooding. If there were restrictions, problems or frustrations in her marriage, she would, as Whit had suggested, learn to accept them. She was not a child, and she was beginning to understand what Heloise had called responsibility. That there would be many uncertain and tense periods of adjusting to changes of plans, to Whit's friends, his family, and to the considerable extent of what she had once referred to in his hearing as his "Empire." She knew that well enough. And also that there were uncut pages in their own relationship; not that you expected, after you were grown up, always to know what anyone was thinking—which brought her back to Dave; she'd always known with him, or so she believed. She suspected that Whitney Dennis was capable of anger; probably a cold, quiet anger, which could be more frightening than the impassioned outbursts of other men—such as Dave, for instance, who was swift to rage, and quick to repent. She also suspected that in their intimate encounters Whit exercised a certain restraint. . . . Dave had not.

But she promised herself not to make comparisons.

The next morning she went to work with her husband. At breakfast he presented her with an attaché case. "Not mother's," he said hastily. "No parure is contained within. But you'll look more like a career woman."

"I never carried one in my life," she said, noting her initials outside, JCD, and inside her full name.

"It lends status," Whitney explained. "What do you want for your birthday?"

She would have one, mid-June.

"Rubies?"

"For dowagers or brunettes with flashing eyes."

"Sapphires?"

"No."

"Aquamarines?"

"You have 'em. How about emeralds? That's your birthstone. Last degree of Gemini," he reflected, "the Twins. Two sides to every coin; two roads to choose between, unless you can walk on both."

"How come you know so much?"

"Aunt Hilda. She consults an astrologer, a good one from what I hear. She was a little more concerned about you than the rest. She hauled me aside while we were at Mother's for dinner, and asked, 'When is Janice's birthday?' Seems we aren't in the right signs for each other."

"Too bad," said Janice sadly. "Buckets of emeralds?"

"A teacupful, grasping woman. What are you giving me for my birthday?"

She looked at him and said astonished, "But I don't even know when it is!"

"Apparently you didn't read the marriage license."

"And I've never asked," she said ruefully.

"I know. I often wake sobbing in the night while you sleep as if hibernating."

"When is it?"

"September. I'm a Virgo—so-called."

Janice laughed. She said, "I'll look up the date in *Who's Who.*"

Self-consciously she took the attaché case to work. They parted at the elevators. He said, "I told Mortimer to pick you up at four. But if you have other plans, call Smith."

"I haven't. Tomorrow though I'm to lunch with Hilda; we're to go to a kennel in Connecticut and select the dog."

"She'll ask when he was born," said Whit.

Janice put in a full day's work; reports to read, an easy job of translation, filling in as secretary for the personnel man whose name was Landman. She sat in a corner and took notes while he interviewed applicants. Then she went back to what was now her own desk and transcribed the notes. His own secretary was out ill, as were several girls in the typist pool.

Lunchtime, a sandwich and a carton of coffee at the desk.

No one stared, everyone spoke, but when a little before four she took her leave, there were comments.

"Seems just like everyone else," said a girl at a translation desk.

"Except prettier," remarked a young man on his way to the washroom.

"She is basically like everyone else and you'd better believe it," said another young man on his way to ask for a raise. He considered himself a left-wing Liberal. He was loud in his denouncement of The Establishment, but consoled himself by thinking that while the Foundation had been spawned by The Establishment, it was useful to the beat-up, mowed-down underdog. Now and then he marched in protests against almost everything, but he was a nice lad, if still damp behind the ears, and he was good at his work. He'd get the raise.

That evening, when they were alone, Janice had a good deal to report to Whit. She said, "There's so much to learn even in my un-category. I don't feel I'll prove of much value. Whit, I could break the date with Hilda."

"No. Keep it. The understanding was you'd lend us a helping paw when convenient, and wherever needed. Go along with Hilda. You'll have fun, but if you return with a female of the species, I'll murder you."

"You'll get off," said Janice, "before an all-male jury. You'll have a regiment of lawyers and you'd make an interesting widower, and get back on the most eligible list."

It was pleasant driving with Hilda, in the car with Jenkins, the chauffeur who took care of "The Ladies," when they were in New York. Connecticut was green, the dogwoods were clotted cream and wild strawberry jam. The kennels were clean and imposing as was the blue-jeaned, social-registered owner. There were numerous dogs from which to select, but Hilda made the choice. A miniature schnauzer, "bearded like a bard," murmured Hilda affectionately . . . and the owner assured her, a well-trained, well-behaved young lady, a year old. Her AKC name was half a mile long, but she was called Angelica by her friends.

Earlier in the morning Angelica's new belongings had been delivered to Smith; a basket, a leash, a collar, toys, dishes for water and food, a case of the latter, together with certain standby remedies and the card of a good veterinarian.

Mrs. Curtis had provided a carrying case; and a sizable check had changed hands.

Driving home, Janice said, "I've not even thought about where she'll sleep!"

"Near you," said Hilda austerely. "Anything else is out of the question. Your little sitting room would be ideal."

"But who's to walk her?"

"You," said Hilda, "naturally."

"But I can't always . . . I'll be working when I can——"

"Yes, I know. Very commendable of you. We're all delighted."

"And Whit and I will be away, often."

"You have the staff," Hilda reminded her, "and in inclement weather, the terrace."

Janice had a thought or two about that, but refrained, as Angelica woofed despondently from the carrying case.

"You're all right, darling," Hilda told her, "and you'll soon be home. It isn't as though she'd never had a home, Janice. Mrs. Curtis told me she was bought as a puppy for the only child of neighbors. The child died, a month ago; the parents couldn't bear to have this reminder around and returned Angelica to the kennels." She spoke as if this was the greater tragedy of the two. "You talk to her, Janice; after all she's your dog and Whit's."

So Janice spoke to Angelica—"what an absurd name," she said, in parenthesis. "Look, Angel," she said, "control yourself . . . and go to sleep."

Angel obliged.

"Are you coming to the Island?" Hilda asked.

"I think so, after the wedding."

"Bring Angelica. There's nothing she'd like better than a romp on the sands." She added, "Of course dogs are not permitted on public beaches, poor dears."

From which Janice deduced that the beach on which Dunewalk fronted was private.

She had rather dreaded introducing her wedding present to the staff, but they'd been briefed or forewarned and they all liked dogs.

When they reached the apartment house, Hilda issued pronouncements and orders. She would walk home; their was nothing like regular exercise for man or beast, and New York was pleasantest in spring and autumn. Also she had eaten too much at the inn near the kennels where they'd lunched. She added, "I hope they fed you properly, Jenkins," to which he responded, "Yes, thank you very much, Mrs. Dalton."

"We won't need you until theater time," she informed him. "Now if you'll just see Mrs. Dennis safely into her apartment . . . ?" And she departed briskly, waving and crying out to Janice, "Do take care of the baby," which caused several nearby heads to turn.

Jenkins inquired, "Should I take the little dog around the block first, Mrs. Dennis?" and Janice said, "No, I think we'll introduce her upstairs first."

So they went upstairs, Jenkins left, Smith and Janice released Angelica from her unwelcome confinement. "She does carry on," Smith commented, watching her capers. He scratched her rough little head. "Nice dog, Mrs. Dennis."

"We'd better show her where she'll live," said Janice and she and Smith proceeded upstairs, the dog at their heels, Smith carrying her luggage. Mrs. Smith erupted from the kitchen and called Hattie to put the case of dog food into a supply closet. Vera looked around a doorway, Cecil stood on the landing, and everyone came tagging along.

In the little sitting room Angelica's luggage was in

place. "But how did you know where?" asked Janice suspecting Smith, not for the first time, of magic. But he said, "Mrs. Dalton telephoned me before Jasper brought her things."

The bed basket was in readiness, the toys were in it, and now Angelica's collar was fastened—Janice thought of the parure—and the leash affixed. Water was put in the water bowl which rested on a rubber pad; food would come later.

"How about a drink?" asked Janice, but Angelica shook her head, looked up at Smith and said something to the effect that she'd like to leave the room.

Smith smiled. He said, "Suppose I take her for a run, Mrs. Dennis. I have time . . . and when I don't, well, there's enough of us here and the building staff as well."

That evening Angel was presented to her co-owner. He walked in, looked about him, sat down and Angel sprang to his lap.

"A female, after all," he said. "But a good city size. What's her name?"

"Angelica. For short Angel, for shorter I think——"

"I don't. That's ridiculous. I'll call her Herman."

"Which will confuse her and everyone else."

"Okay, Angel," he said to the dog and she promptly removed herself from his knees, sat down on the floor and regarded him with a slight sneer.

"Come here, Herman," said Whit authoritatively and she sprang back, lavishing caresses upon him.

"You see?" he said to Janice. "Now there's a splendid medical interpretation of that, but we won't go into it here. I can see that she's too young. By the way, how has it happened that she kisses me and you do not?"

Janice complied. Herman sulked, a little.

TEN

THE DAY WAS fair and warm; the bride, dark and glorious; the groom, nervous. There were not a great many guests, but the honorable personality boy himself, Audrey's employer—she had decided to work for a while longer, Tom being of a thrifty nature—and his formidable wife were present, as well as the Nortons. There was a scatter of office staffs, Audrey's associates and Tom's. No fanfare, in the church, simply a pleasant clergyman, a good organist, and two attendants for the bride, Janice and Katie. True to his promise Whit gave Audrey away and the bridegroom was so in shock that his best man—Tom's immediate superior in the CPA firm by which they were both employed—kept murmuring in his ear before the ceremony. "Brace up, think of the tax deduction!"

Everyone went to the reception of course, friends and also the strangers who wanted to take the tour of the Dennis apartment and observe the gilt on the gingerbread. One girl from Tom's outfit looked with incredulity at her hand after Whit shook it, as if the Midas touch were no myth, and she expected her little paw to turn to gold.

After leaving the reception, Mr. and Mrs. Thomas Warren were wafted to a midtown hotel by one of Mortimer's colleagues, who would pick them up the next morning and convey them to the Dennis plane, where in the cheerful, discreet company of Harry, Fred and Scotty they would be flown to Bermuda. When their ten-day stay was over, the plane would fly them back to the business of prosaic living in Tom's adequate apartment, or, if it so happened that the plane—as yet unnamed—was suddenly not available, Whit had reserved tickets for them on a commercial flight. These, plus the reception, were his wedding presents. Janice's to Audrey, a bracelet of heavy gold links, and supplementary crystal for the rather monastically furnished flat.

"I can never thank you," Audrey told Whit before she left, after changing in a guest room and tossing her flowers over the banister. They were caught by the girl with the invisible golden hand who couldn't believe her luck.

"No need," said Whit. "I owe you a debt. I think you were always on my side."

When they were alone, except for Herman who had been banished from the party, Janice and Whit sat comfortably together in the morning room. The Smiths and helpers were cleaning up the living room and library and the caterers, restoring the kitchen. Janice, with Cecil's assistance, had changed from her pale green frock to slacks and a bright shirt. "It was a lovely wedding, Mrs. Dennis," said Cecil—she had been in the back of the church, probably in case Audrey fainted or became unzipped—"I do like weddings; they always make me sad."

Before their late, light supper, Janice repeated this to her husband. "Do they make you sad?" she inquired.

"As a rule, no. I've attended them in various capacities for years. They always lifted my spirits . . . being then a free man."

"And our own wedding?"

"Ah, of course, the exception. A melancholy occasion."

"Thanks a lot."

"Don't mention it."

She asked with genuine curiosity, "If you so valued your freedom, why did you voluntarily relinquish it?"

"You know the reasons, or most of them. Don't tell me you've forgotten our discussion in Jamaica? Also, frankly, I was mortally afraid you wouldn't be happy."

"Still afraid?"

"Not as much." An agitated yapping floated downstairs from Herman's quarters and Whit said, "Do me a favor, small, blonde and often exasperated, and let Herman out of her plush prison. I'm bushed. Who'd ever think that at my age I'd be giving brides away?" he added moodily.

They went, with Herman, in Janice's car to East Hampton on the following weekend, but Whit wouldn't let her drive. He said, "The parkways are murder. You can practice on country lanes and such."

"I've driven since I was knee-high to a Rolls Royce," she argued indignantly.

"That was a long time ago," he said. "Cars, drivers, highways, thruways have altered since, and you've never driven in New York, have you?"

"I didn't have a car."

But she'd driven outside of the city, in New Jersey, Pennsylvania and once in Virginia when Dave had been with her and rented a car.

Dunewalk might have been unimaginatively named and was certainly without architectural beauty. It sprawled, weathered by ninety years of sun, sea, and wind, on a rise in the land above a long stretch of beach. The dunes, altering minutely in shape each year after nor'easters, hurricanes and ordinary wear and tear, marched above the beaches. The air was salt and roses, but the house was too big, and augmented by unused stables, a vast garage and workshop and the cottage in which Dunewalk's "Mrs. Smith," whose name was Rhoda Larson, lived year round. This was also big, as it had once accommodated the three Larson children, who had gone the way of most children, schooling (local), work (local in two instances), and marriage (also local in two cases).

Rhoda's husband, Eric, did the ground work and the maintenance, assisted by various people from the town. The living was simple at Dunewalk, the way Whit's grandparents had preferred it—simple food and service, no cluttering up with gardeners, Larson could look after the informal flowers, and there was very little grass. From the time they built Dunewalk, the Dennises had bought their vegetables and eggs and chickens from native farmers. Dunewalk was their escape. The house inside was friendly and casual, with bright chintzes which had faded, old furniture, some of an unfortunate period, and engaging paintings, mainly watercolors executed by artists of the late eighties and early nineteen hundreds, and all reflecting water, surf, beaches, beach plum and laurel, roses and country roads. Only two or three of their creators had achieved what is known as fame (by now these were avidly collected).

Everyone on the eastern end of Long Island knew of, and about, the Dennises, and had for three generations. Few knew them personally. Martha and her sisters had some friends nearby, as her parents and grandparents had. The tradespeople knew them best. But the Dennises were never long in residence, and some years not at all. The house and property were kept immaculate, in case a Dennis dropped in overnight, and the churches and charities of the section profited through annual donations.

In this place, little entertaining was done; in earlier

days, tea on the tremendous veranda; later, tea or drinks as you preferred. If Martha and her sisters occasionally gave (as their mother had before them) what was known as "a real party," for what were known as "the neighbors," outside help came in. Otherwise, family, or a friend or two, so Rhoda cooked and the daughter nearest to her, served.

And no one, whether guests or residents turned up with menservants (other than chauffeurs, for whom there were quarters over the garage) or personal maids, hairdressers, or what have you. If you required professional nursing care, you didn't come to Dunewalk. Whit had explained this to Janice before they left for the Island.

"I needn't take Cecil?"

"No, m'am, I'll cope."

"And your mother's Mary won't be there, or whomever the others have?"

"The aunts share a dessicated, devoted old gal and Lily has quite a charmer. . . . Good thing Ned is more interested in old books and paintings than in trim ankles."

"But *you* noticed! . . . When did you see her by the way?"

"Last time I saw Lily—sounds like a song—come to think of it, she may have, by now, departed. Lily likes change."

"But I don't understand. . . . You make the Island house sound like a tent pitched for a safari."

"Actually it's mother's idea of a *petit* Trianon."

They arrived at Dunewalk after lunch, having stopped on the way to eat and to walk and water Herman, who proved to be a car-worthy companion, although in her despised carrying case. "We'll have to give her her freedom in broken doses and slowly," said Whitney, "which could apply to a lot of people, places and institutions."

"Tomorrow," said Janice firmly, "I'm going to drive my car somewhere. You can come along if you like," she added generously.

"I'll think about it. Sure you have a license?"

"I've always renewed it," she answered, then laughed. "I never quite know when you're putting me on."

"You'll learn."

At Dunewalk they were greeted with temperate pleasure, except for Herman, upon whom Hilda fell (though not literally) with cries of joy, as if they were the oldest of friends and had been separated for twenty years. She picked her up and looked at her closely. "She looks happy," she said, "and her coat is in splendid condition."

"Did you expect her to deteriorate so soon?" Whit asked.

"Of course not. But it's a big adjustment. I'll take her for a little run." She started off, calling back over her shoulder, "I don't expect you brought anything for her."

"Why should we?" asked Whit. "There have always been packs of dogs around here. Haven't the Larsons some now?"

"Two. . . . Well, everything's set up, in your room, anyway."

Whit said, "Wait, don't call her Angelica, she won't come."

"Why ever not? It's her name."

"Her name is now Herman," Whit informed her.

Heloise and Martha were talking, leading the way, and Larson coped with the luggage. There wasn't much, as Whitney was staying only until early Monday morning. "Mind if I drive your car back?" he'd asked Janice, "and leave you at the mercy of Jenkins and the group?" She would be here through the following weekend, when he'd be down again and they'd return together.

"This is my old friend Eric Larson," Whit told Janice and she shook hands with a tall spare man; undecided whether his hair was fair or silver. His face was as brown as sun and wind could make it and his eyes, blue. He said he was glad to meet her.

In the house was a middling tall, middling plump woman with a brown rosy face and heavy brown hair. She wore a housedress, which became her.

"And this," said Whit, "is my even older friend, Mrs. Larson. Rhoda to me."

"The Smith in residence?" asked Janice, smiling.

Rhoda laughed. "He'd better know better than to call me Mrs. Smith," she said, "and it wasn't until he was way grown up that he called me Rhoda. I wouldn't permit it before."

"I had to be twenty-one," said Whit gravely.

Rhoda said, looking Janice up, down, and up again, "I hope you'll be very happy, Mrs. Dennis."

"Her name's Janice," said Whit. "I won't have you favoring her over me. I knew you first."

Rhoda said, "Pay no attention to him, and thanks for your letter."

The Larsons had sent a wedding present, a small piece of carved driftwood, which was when Janice had separated the Larsons from the Smiths.

Janice and Whit followed Eric and Rhoda upstairs to a vast corner room which contained the modicum of furniture, painted white enamel, a dressing table, wicker chairs in faded rosy chintz, wallpaper with a pattern of roses also faded. White blowing curtains, dim rag rugs. There were no pictures on the walls, but a number of photographs.

When Rhoda had left saying, "The bathroom's next door, it doesn't connect," Janice walked around, looking. Family pictures—Dunewalk in its various stages of evolution; framed snapshots of Whitney and his sister, of the others; of some she didn't know . . . one, a photograph of Whit's father.

She said, "You were an engaging child and teen-ager and, I imagine, a hellion. Look at the aunts, so much thinner; and your mother." She looked for a long time at Whit's father. "You're like him," she decided.

"I hope so. This was his and mother's room. She's never set foot in it since his death, and she came back here for the first time for a little while last summer. They were very happy in this old barn of a house; they got away from things, however briefly. Let's beachwalk . . . you brought slacks and sweater?"

"Yes. . . . Where did Mrs. Larson say the bathroom is?"

"In the hall, next to us. We have it to ourselves. Grandfather put in a couple of baths, father, more, but none connects with a bedroom. I don't know why. Don't let the plumbing alarm you. It's asthmatic, wheezes, huffs and coughs, but it serves."

"Now we'll go rescue Herman," he said after she'd changed.

They went out, down wide steps, rooted in sand, each grass waving around. Janice looked back once from the beach. She could see their own windows and the curtains blowing. "It's quite a house," she said.

Walking on the beach against a stiff wind, they encountered Hilda trotting along—but the wind was with her and Herman. "I took her leash off," panted Hilda, "but I just can't keep up with her." She thrust the leash into Janice's hands, said, "I'll see you later," and slogged thankfully toward the steps.

Herman was having a superior time. She raced to the water's edge, barking, wet; she shook her paws, retreated, ran from a curling wave; she investigated strands of seaweed, advanced and fled before a demised horseshoe crab, became entangled in beach grass at the foot of a dune and otherwise happily exhausted herself.

"A dog of character, our Herman," said Whit. He had Janice's hand, and swung it loosely, as they walked. Her hair, having escaped from confinement, hung loose and free "silver gilt" in the sun. "You look about fourteen," he told her, "but a knowledgeable fourteen."

"Aren't they all now?"

Presently they turned back. She said, "I love this place, Whit."

"We all do, except Lily. It bores her."

Janice stood still. The tide was out, they were walking on firm damp sand and Herman was busy trying to root out some glorious distracting smell.

"I forgot all about her," she said blankly. Aren't they coming?"

"Tomorrow morning. Lily had important things to do today, mainly I suspect, shopping and catching up with some of her city girl friends. Ned was going to a couple of auctions. I doubt she'd be here at all, but Mother probably issued an order: 'We must have a reunion at Dunewalk for the bride.' "

"Can we come here alone sometimes," she asked hesitantly. "Just us?"

"And Herman? Of course. We'll manage a weekend now and then, or even longer. But you haven't seen the rest of the dilatory domiciles."

"I know. But I'll never like any of them as I like this . . . or feel as much at home."

"Nor I, actually. Incidentally, Dunewalk doesn't belong to the Corporation. Mother has the use of it whenever she wants, the aunts and Lily also, but the property was left to me. My father knew how I felt about it. He knew pretty much how I felt about everything."

Reaching the steps, he whistled to Herman; she came with the utmost reluctance, creeping, as if beaten, lying down as if utterly spent, and complaining plaintively.

Whit picked her up. "Despite her daring and originality, which are very masculine traits," he said sadly, "she is after all a female, cajoling, self-pitying, and when it suits her, helpless. It is my Karma to be surrounded by women."

"Is that what you think of us?" Janice asked.

"That, and more." He gave her his straight unsmiling regard. "Don't fret," he said soothingly. "You've passed an acid test. Rhoda likes you."

"How do you know that?"

"She told me so in the kitchen. . . . Come on, it's close to tea and/or cocktail time. Rhoda doesn't approve of cocktails, but she's quite resigned by now. However, I do the bartending when I'm here. 'You want a drink, you fix it yourself,' Rhoda told me many years ago."

That evening after dinner, cooked and served by Rhoda in what she called "family style," Janice became, to her horror, a fourth at bridge. She played a good game; Martha Dennis a better, and, as they were partners, the aunts were the losers. Hilda's game was erratic, and Heloise's completely uninspired. Whit went for a walk with Herman and returned to make a nuisance of himself, looking over everyone's shoulder, shaking his head, making deprecatory sounds.

"Shoo," said Janice, yawning, and he said, "You're half asleep."

"It's the air."

"Finish the rubber and come to bed. Shall I bring you a nightcap?"

"No. I'd fall on my face."

She spoke to Herman, who ignored her. "She's your dog," she told Whit. "It couldn't be clearer."

"I'll be up presently," he said. He had something to talk over with his mother, relative to certain of her personal investments.

Janice staggered upstairs and decided against a bath in the great old-fashioned tub. I'd drown, she thought dreamily. I'd be found floating, like the Lady of what's her name. She crawled into the four poster and went fast asleep, but was awakened after a while by Whit and Herman. Whit was expostulating. "But I never permit even friends in my bedroom" he was informing Herman, "much less a woman other than my wife."

Janice asked drowsily, "Where are you putting her?"

"Well, the room next door is vacant. I'll put her basket and the water in there. Go back to sleep."

But when he returned, the French windows which led to a flat, railed sun deck stood open and Janice was outside in a bathrobe and barefoot.

"You'll catch cold."

"How often must I tell you I never catch cold?"

He came out and stood beside her, remarking, "Full moon soon."

"How do you know?"

"I read almanacs secretly; a minor vice. But this moon will do," he added, looking at the silver path on the face of the water.

She shivered suddenly, and he put his arm around her. "I told you so," he said.

"I'm not cold. Moonlight affects me."

"Romantically, I hope?"

"No. Remember Jamaica, when I said I hated the moon?"

"Yes. I thought you were just playing hard to get."

"How absurd! Anyway, it always makes me sad."

He was wondering: Moonlight on a great lake; moonlight and kids on a campus. He said nothing except, "Lots of people are allergic to moonshine . . . hard drinkers, lunatics, dogs——"

"Into which category do I fall?"

"The lunatics of course. Come on inside."

But she was listening to the ocean. She said, "Just the sound of it . . . oh, there are so many good sounds."

"What are your favorites?"

"Sea on sand, a lake whispering on shore, surf against rocks . . . the wind, sometimes, but not always; boat whistles, very little children laughing, sleepy birds at dusk, and the lonely sounds—the way trains used to sound—loons calling, an owl hooting——"

"How about music?"

"Some. I'm not very musical, . . . but I like familiar things, Brahms, Liszt—especially when André Watts plays . . ."

"Wagner?"

"A little——"

"How about going to bed? I'd love to hear my shoes drop."

The weekend was pleasant, the fine June weather held. Janice drove her elegant small car with the top down, Whitney beside her, as guide. They went past tennis courts and country clubs and she asked, "You've never told me, don't you *do* anything?"

"I work harder than Herman," he said indignantly.

"Sports, I mean—golf, tennis, skiing, surfing. . . . I know you swim and sail—how about riding?"

"I've given all a try," he said. "Sterner stuff too, and I used to be good, but there hasn't been much time lately. I also curl a bit," he said modestly.

"Curl?"

"That's a sport, idiot."

"So it is. I've only seen it on television."

Lily and Ned came, and with their arrival, Rhoda's older daughter came in to help. And on Sunday night Janice asked Whit suddenly, "Do you mind if I go back with you tomorrow?"

"No, although I must be away for a couple of days. But why? I thought you liked it here."

"I do. But can't we go up together and get back for the weekend? I'd honestly rather be working this week."

He said, "A little claustrophobia, perhaps."

"I'm sorry," Janice said.

"Too many female Dennises do smother. . . . Okay. I'll tell Mother that I've remembered we have to entertain some out-of-town friends. She's used to that. Not that she won't guess why you're leaving."

"I hope she won't be hurt," said Janice, distressed.

"She won't be. But Herman will suffer, and not in silence."

They returned to town, over courteous expostulation and Whitney went to the office, Janice with him. She was needed, she found in the PR department—not that she knew anything about public relations, she told the head of PR cheerfully.

He was a nice, rather hardened-in-the-mold man, who drew a sharp line between public relations and publicity. The Foundation did not need publicity; not, that was to say, of the sort which could antagonize people. The Foundation was not in the market for money; no one had to implore the public for funds, or pass the hat. There were no drives and no one need leave the Foundation any money, so all that was necessary was an occasional release, relative to its past, present and future activities.

Whit was away from Wednesday morning to Friday. He went by plane, since Fred and Harry had brought the Warrens back from Bermuda. It was lonely without him; but Katie came that first night for dinner, and Joe Meeker took Janice out on Thursday.

"I thought you'd be with Whit," she said, when he telephoned.

"No. I don't always go with him."

He picked her up, in a taxi. "May as well give Mort a night off," he said and took her to the place he'd spoken of the night he'd dined with them. She ordered a drink, because if she hadn't, he might have thought she hadn't believed him that other night. They had quite a dinner and he talked to her about cameras, and out-of-the-way places, and his boyhood dream of becoming an anthropologist which had, of course, come to nothing . . . and of Whit; he talked a lot about Whit.

Once he said soberly, "He isn't easy to know," and it could have been a warning. Janice laughed. "He said the same about you," she told him.

"I suppose it's true of both of us."

When Joe left her at the door which Smith opened, he asked, "Did you know you were going to the theater Friday night?"

"No. Am I?"

"I have the seats. Whit asked me to get them."

"What are we seeing?"

He told her, adding, "It's a light nothing sort of play, but he thought you'd enjoy it."

"Unflattering, but probably true. Do you like the theater, Joe?"

"Not very much nowadays," he said. "Thank you for this evening, Janice."

Whit called her quite late and asked what she'd been

doing, as he had when he'd called on the previous night. She said, "I went out to dinner with Joe. Did you tell him to take me?"

"I did not."

"Did he ask you if he could?"

"No. When I talked with him today he simply said he was going to——"

"I hear we're going to the theater?"

"That's right. To celebrate my return. Tell Mrs. Smith to kill a fatted something or other. I'll be home for dinner. Did you miss me intolerably?"

"Well, no," she said truthfully, "but I missed you."

So he came home, they had dinner and went to the theater. It was, as Joe had said, a little bit of nothing, but good fun, with pretty girls, amusing situations and considerable wit. People came in late across the aisle from them, following an usher's flashlight, and Janice muttered. She hated people who came late. Thank heaven they didn't come in this aisle.

When the lights went up, she looked idly across the aisle and went perfectly rigid; as Whit's arm brushed hers, he felt it. He looked at her. She was crimson, then she was white, then flushed again. He asked, alarmed, "What's the matter? Are you ill?"

"No." She looked at him with naked desperation in her dark eyes. "But I'd like to go home, please. Do you mind very much, Whit?"

"Of course not. I know where to find Mortimer. Come, we'll walk there."

Leaving, he glanced across at a good-looking man and woman. He had never seen them before, but he was certain of their identity: Madge and Davidson Peters, commonly called Dave, out on the town tonight.

ELEVEN

THEY LEFT THE theater where, in the lobby, people were buying tickets for subsequent performances. A few looked at them curiously, the tall man, the small beautifully dressed young woman. One man standing in line at the box office said, "I thought this was a good show," and his wife, waiting nearby, said negligently, "Maybe they had a fight."

On the street, numerous other people—some emerging from restaurants, others walking aimlessly, looking at the marquees, at the lights and each other. At this early hour many had patiently queued up by stage doors, waiting for current idols to emerge. And one woman, clutching an autograph book, nudged her companion and pointing at Janice and Whit cried, "Hey, aren't they somebody?"

"Search me," said her friend, craning her neck.

They walked in silence, so you might have deduced that, as the woman in the lobby had commented, they had quarreled. But Whit had her hand trapped in the bend of his arm. Presently she asked indifferently, "Where are we going?"

"Garage. It's not far." He glanced at her, his face betraying nothing but concern. She was not crying, but she was close to it.

"Steady as she goes," he advised.

Janice shook her head. She said, "I'm—well—sorry, ashamed, but most of all angry at myself."

It was true enough; after the shock of recognition, fury and humiliation had immediately followed.

He said nothing, but held her hand tighter. When they reached the enormous busy garage, a man said, "Well hi, Mr. Dennis. You want the car?"

It was parked on an upstairs floor. Janice stood quietly in the big area at one side; cars came in, some left; there was noise, confusion and bright lights. Her head began to ache.

The man was telephoning; and presently the elevator descended and the car rolled out. Whit opened the door and said, "Mort, we're going home," and Mortimer nodded.

On the way Janice made an effort. There was no window to roll up between themselves and Mortimer; Whit didn't like cars which cut off driver from passengers.

"Do you always park there?" she asked, and couldn't have cared less.

"When in the neighborhood."

"Corporation?"

He nodded. The building was Corporation owned.

He talked about the play, a thistledown structure, but good performances and added, "We'll have to see the rest of it sometime."

Janice thought no.

"Tired?" he asked. "Lean back." Her body was tense and resistant; but he pulled her toward him so that her head was on his shoulder, and said, "I'm sorry about the headache."

She started to say, "What makes you think I have a headache?" but didn't, realizing that some explanation was due Mortimer. She made another effort and said truthfully, "I seldom have them."

"Well, keep quiet. Cecil will fix you up when we get home."

She asked wearily, "When are we leaving for Dunewalk?"

"We aren't going, Janice. I'll telephone while Cecil is getting you to bed. Mother will be sorry, of course."

"But I want to go!" She thought of Dunewalk as one thinks of a remote country, sea and sand, quiet, and somehow safety.

"We'll go, probably by ourselves next weekend. But there's something I must do tomorrow."

"You make sudden decisions," she said, with bitterness.

"That's right. Rest now, we'll soon be home."

"We'll see how the boss feels in the morning," Whit told Mortimer. "I sure hope she'll be all right," Mortimer said, and Janice remarked, "It's Saturday; no office, anyway."

The night doorman, if astonished to see them, made no comment, nor did Smith. They went upstairs and into Janice's bedroom. She said, sitting down on the edge of the bed, "I don't usually make scenes."

"That was hardly a scene," he told her, "and you have a constitutional right to leave the theater anytime you wish —even if you aren't a critic."

"What are you doing?"

"Ringing for Cecil."

"I'd rather be alone."

"There's no future in being up tight," he said calmly.

Cecil came in, expressionless and Whit said, "Mrs. Dennis doesn't feel well, Cecil, get her to bed, will you? I'll be next door if you need me."

He beckoned, Cecil followed and he spoke to her at his door briefly.

He went in his room, reclosed the door and Cecil said, "Let me help you, Mrs. Dennis."

The jewelry, the pretty frock, the lingerie. I never thought someone would undress me, Janice told herself and stopped; it wasn't the first time by any means that she'd been undressed, to an accompaniment of laughter and kissing; in her childhood—and later.

She said, "I feel as if I were in a hospital."

The bed was turned down, her night things laid across it; when she was ready for bed, she went into the bathroom. She looked steadily at herself in the mirror for a long time and told herself that she appeared normal enough except for her pallor and overbright eyes. She spoke to herself. "Stupid," she said aloud.

Cecil knocked. "Are you all right, Mrs. Dennis?" she asked.

"Yes," said Janice and Cecil suggested, "Perhaps, if I brush your hair . . . ? May I come in?"

At the big marble dressing table, Cecil brushed slowly, soothingly; she massaged Janice's scalp and the back of her neck. "All knotted up," Cecil commented.

When Janice got into bed, Cecil vanished for a moment and returned with a glass of water and a tablet in a smaller glass. She said, "If Mrs. Dennis would take this now . . . ?"

Janice said, with some violence, "I don't wish to take sleeping medicine." She thought: Do I have to go through all that again?

Whit appeared in robe and slippers and said, "Give that to me, Cecil, will you? Thank you. You may go. We'll ring if we need you."

Cecil said good night formally, and went back to her room, prepared to put herself to bed, thinking her own thoughts.

Whit said, "Drink this, as the immoral Alice once did."

"But I——"

"It's just a sedative; it will relax you, so you can sleep. I'll be next door. . . ."

She was grateful for that and for a moment an expression of concern crossed her face, as it had his, earlier. "Poor Whit," she said.

"I'll bear up," he told her, smiling.

Of course he'd bear up, she thought dully. And asked, "Did you call Martha?"

She had heard the murmur of his voice from the next room and he answered, "Yes. As I said, she's sorry. She or someone will call you."

"What excuse did you make?"

"I don't make excuses. I simply said we couldn't make it. They'll be up during the week; we'll see them. Lily and Ned . . . . I made a tentative date for Wednesday night here."

"Why tentative?"

"Oh, you never know what will turn up."

And that's a fact, she thought.

"Take your medicine."

She obeyed, thinking: Affection, concern, these endured, unswayed by the violent, hurting emotions. How about pride in possession?

He said, "Breakfast in bed tomorrow, Mrs. Dennis. That's an order. I've briefed Cecil. I have to go out even if it's Saturday. Joe and I have a sort of conference scheduled. I'll come in and say good morning."

Leaving he added, "Perhaps you'd rather I closed the door?"

"Yes . . . I'm sorry, Whit," she told him inadequately.

"It's okay. . . . I'm a light sleeper; holler if you want anything or ring for Cecil. Shall I switch off the lights?"

"Please."

Now the room was in darkness except for the light from Whit's room. He padded quietly across the floor and said, "Try to sleep, Mrs. D."

Reminder? Warning? She had been Mrs. D. since April. She would be Mrs. D. for many Aprils; that was the bargain.

Now she could cry, but didn't. She put her face in her pillow, she stretched out between the cool sheets. She thought for an utterly idiotic moment about air-conditioning. The house was air-conditioned, but it was not yet warm enough to have it on. She heard ships hooting at one another on the river; she felt a cool and quiet breeze.

Why had that happened? She felt an illogical savage rage against Davidson and Madge Peters, for daring to come to New York and for being under the same roof, however briefly. She wondered if they had seen her and felt the slow surge of blood to her face. Probably not. That would have been an added, intolerable humiliation if they'd watched her leave the theater, running scared.

She'd never for a moment deluded herself that she'd forgotten Dave, but often was convinced, almost, that it was over, far away and long ago. Now she was Mrs. D. and had moved on. She had, she thought, left Dave far behind.

Her eyes stung with tears, but before she could shed them, she slept.

The morning was bright with sun when she woke; in that first split second before full consciousness returned, she wondered sleepily where Whit was.

Then she remembered.

She sat up in bed and shook her heavy brush-burnished hair, as Whit walked in, fully dressed.

He sat down beside her and kissed her cheek. "Sleep?" he asked.

"Yes. What was in that pill?"

"As I told you, a sedative."

"I don't have a hangover," she said.

"No, you wouldn't. Hop out, get washed up, I'll ring for Cecil and your breakfast."

"I don't want any breakfast."

"I'm not suggesting a banquet; just coffee, juice and toast."

He rang, and when Janice came back from the bathroom he said, "Crawl back in. We have plans to make."

"Such as?"

To her amazement and horror he asked her, "Do you know where the Peters stay when they're in town?"

She found herself stammering; no, she didn't know where the Peters stayed in New York. She thought: How could I? Madge was never with him.

"It won't be hard to find out. The offices are closed, but I'll get Joe onto it, so you can call Mrs. Peters."

"Please——" She wanted to say "Please don't." Finally, with an effort she said it. "Please don't. . . ."

Leave it as it is, she thought. I've made a spectacle of myself; leave it that way.

She added with attempted normality, "If Madge wanted to look me up, she could call."

"She doesn't have the number."

"She could have asked Mother or called the Foundation."

"I doubt she'd ask your mother; and the Foundation doesn't give numbers. Stop hedging. You've had a sudden shock; you were not in the least prepared for it. Now you do what's been advised for generations . . . the horse throws you, get back on it; the nettle stings, grasp it."

She said with anger, "Just because I made a fool of myself."

"Forget it. You're grown up, or will be someday. I'll phone you when I find out where they're staying. Ask Mrs. Peters how long they'll be here. If for a few more days, settle on a night for dinner with us. If they're leaving tomorrow, see if they can come tonight, and tell Smith. If they're going today—or gone—your problem's solved."

"I suppose this is an order too?" she said, her voice rising.

"In a manner of speaking." His voice was quiet. He touched her hair, but drew back his hand when she shook her head. He said, "Face it, and the sooner, the better. If it makes matters worse, you'll have to work that out; if better, that's your good luck."

"Are you punishing me, Whit?"

"You're punishing yourself."

She started to say, "You are punishing me, admit it. And at this point you should say, 'this hurts me more than it does you,' but it doesn't hurt you . . . or if so, only your pride." But she didn't say it.

He rose, and Cecil knocked. "Call you later," he told Janice, "and see you at dinner."

She went out before lunch, with Herman, who was distracted by everything—hydrants, people, other dogs. It was a cool bright day; the early summer humidity had not set in. Returning, to Herman's open dismay, she went upstairs and had her lunch at the smaller table. Smith reported, "No, Mr. Dennis had not called, but Mrs. Dalton had, and would call again, from the Island."

Hilda called. She asked how Angelica was—she refused to say Herman. She added that they were all so disappointed when Whitney had canceled their plans. "Lily and Ned came last night," she said, "desolate not to see you. But we shall next week. How can you bear Sunday in town? Whatever got into Whitney?"

Janice replied evenly that they too were disappointed, but Whit had an unexpected conference today and it would be too late to drive down afterward. She looked forward to seeing them all toward the end of the week.

Whit telephoned about two o'clock. He said that Joe had run the Peters to earth. He told her the hotel, the telephone and room numbers. He said "Good luck" and rang off, and for a moment she contemplated that, wondering how he'd meant it. I won't do it, she told herself. I won't. I'll tell Whit they've left, or they're going, or they haven't a free evening.

Childish, shabby, and besides she'd made a bargain.

She telephoned the hotel at which the Peters were registered. She used a downstairs instrument. People could come into or walk by the library. Smith, his wife, Vera, Cecil or Hattie. If they came by the open door with no intention of listening, they were still deterrents, so your voice wouldn't shake.

She waited for the switchboard operator to connect her, praying, also childishly, "Let them be out . . ." and when she'd dialed, she'd prayed that they had checked out . . . up—up—and away.

A voice answered her; it was Madge's, and just as she recalled it, sweet, cool, ice-creamy.

"Yes?"

"Madge," she swallowed and Madge asked, "Who is this?"

"Janice . . . Janice Cooper," she added firmly, "Janice Dennis." (Remember you're Mrs. D., she thought.)

"Why, Janice!" cried Madge, the ice cream melting. "How wonderful to hear from you, darling. Dave and I were devastated that we couldn't be at the wedding."

I bet you were, thought Janice before she said, "We were sorry too."

Pleasant lies.

Madge added, "But of course we heard all about it."

I bet you did, thought Janice.

"How on earth did you find us? I was going to call your mother and get your phone number. I bet it's unlisted," she said archly, "but we came east so suddenly and I was simply rushed off my feet . . . oh, and how did you ever know we were here?" she added as an afterthought.

You couldn't bypass that.

"We saw you at the theater, last night, as we were leaving."

Madge said blankly, "But we didn't see you. Why didn't you send up smoke signals or something?"

Janice said, "We had to leave before it was over. Whit had to meet someone."

"Oh, what a shame," said Madge, her voice edged with —was it speculation or curiosity? "It was such a delightful play."

"Yes, we were sorry we had to go. Madge, I called to see if you and Dave could dine with us . . . of course I don't know how long you'll be here."

"We're leaving Monday," said Madge. "How sweet of you to want us."

"Will you be busy all day tomorrow?"

"Why no. Just a lunch date, that sort of thing. I'll pack in the evening, not that we brought much——"

"Dinner?" asked Janice. "Is seven too early?"

Seven was perfectly fine. Dave would be so pleased

when she told him. She added, unnecessarily, that he was out now and that she was meeting him and some friends for drinks later.

Janice hung up, observing with distaste that her hands shook and that her hairline was damp with sweat. It had been a long time since she'd heard Madge's voice. They had been good, if never close, friends in high school. Madge was a little older and had left to take her last two years in a boarding school in the east. She had remained in the east for college, returning only on vacations, during which she and Janice had seen each other at parties and picnics in which Davidson Peters was always included. Janice remembered now with startling clarity one evening at the Cooper cottage on the lake when Madge had said in her light voice, "You and Dave have been an item for years . . . but with half the men we know crazy about you, I'd think you'd want a little fun and freedom before you settle down."

They were sitting on Janice's bed and Madge had made a comical little face. "Life's so short," said Madge. She then added how fond her parents were of Dave.

Janice had not attended the wedding; that was the summer she'd gone abroad with her parents.

She looked around at the still and beautiful library. She thought: Why aren't we at Dunewalk? Why did we have to go to the theater last night?

She went upstairs, showered, as if to wash off something unpleasant and was lying on the chaise trying to read, when Cecil knocked.

"I heard you. . . . Are you all right, Mrs. Dennis?" she asked as she had that morning.

"I'm fine, Cecil," said Janice, smiling at the older woman, suddenly realizing how much she liked her—quiet, solid and capable; more than valuable; she was like a rock.

"Is there anything I can do?" Cecil hesitated, "Perhaps it's the wrong time, but there's nothing like a cup of strong, sweet tea."

Janice said gratefully, "I'd like that."

So she had a cup, two cups in fact, read, and then dozed a little and when she woke, it was time to dress.

Sitting with Whit in the living room, she asked Smith if she could have some dry sherry and Whit remarked, "You've come all over British. Cecil's influence?"

"In a way. She brought me some tea, quite early."

He inquired casually, "Did you get in touch with the Peters?"

"I talked to Madge. They're leaving Monday, so I asked them to come tomorrow night." She stopped in consternation. "I forgot it's the Smiths' day off."

"Have you also forgotten the excellent caterers? And is there anything anyone especially fancies?" he asked.

For some inexplicable reason that flicked her like a whip. Of course she knew what Dave liked, or at least used to like. She said steadily, "I'm not at all sure about Madge's tastes and I forgot to ask her allergies, but Dave is a glutton for caviar."

Not, she thought, that we ever had it much, except at other people's houses once and, toward the end, in restaurants.

"Fresh Beluga," Whit said thoughtfully.

When Smith came to announce dinner, Whit said, "Some old friends of Mrs. Dennis are in town and dining with us tomorrow night. Will you telephone the Carter Service, perhaps they will have someone on tap whom we've had before."

Smith said he was sure that could be arranged and added that he would leave the usual written instructions.

Janice going into dinner wondered where the Smiths

went on their days off, and then remembered that they had a son in New Jersey with a young wife and a child or two.

Lucky Smiths, she thought, going on a Sunday off to be with people they want to be with.

TWELVE

ON SUNDAY MORNING as they were having breakfast, Janice was admiring the flower arrangements in the dining room as she had in the drawing room, living room, library, hall and upstairs. "They're lovely as usual," she told Smith, "but I've never asked who arranges them?"

"Hattie does, Mrs. Dennis; she has quite a gift."

"I don't know where they come from either," Janice said, and Smith mentioned the name of an outstanding florist.

When he'd left the room, she inquired, "Corporation?" and Whit said, "oh, it just owns the building."

They had not left the table when the doorbell chimed and Smith answered. At his heels, as he returned, were Lily and Ned Turner, and Lily cried, "We didn't wait to telephone . . . we're leaving for Switzerland, practically this minute."

"But why?" Whit and Janice asked. "Is one of the girls ill?"

"No. After school was out, they were going on a sort of special trip with two of the teachers. One of the teachers became ill, so they all returned to school. They'd be all right there; pupils often stay over for varying lengths of time, but Ned of course blew his stack, so we're off to pick them up. We're so sorry not to be at the birthday dinner, Janice."

"What birthday?" Janice asked.

Lily said, "You're not old enough to forget birthdays."

Whit said, "I advanced the date by a couple of days so the family could be with us; incidentally the Smiths are changing their day off; they wouldn't miss this historic occasion."

Janice had forgotten, since yesterday. Before that she had been reminded by packages arriving from home, and had had Cecil stow them away, mindful that she'd been brought up never to open gifts before the proper date.

"Well," said Ned, "we must quite literally fly. Do catch up with us somewhere, you two."

Fleeting embraces, cries of "Have a good flight" and the Turners were gone, Lily leaving a wake of her favorite perfume which was, of course, that of the lily.

"For heaven's sake!" said Janice blankly.

"They're all like that, here one minute, away the next. I hope you don't mind about dinner? I thought we'd celebrate together quietly on the actual day. Anyway," he added ruefully, "I meant it to be a surprise. They'll come, Martha and the aunts bearing tributes. I've also asked Audrey and Tom, Katie and the Nortons, pledging them all to secrecy. I called your parents; they couldn't get away, but they'll talk to you."

She was annoyed by his autocratic decisions and touched by his thoughtfulness, and said so.

Whit said resignedly as Herman came creeping in, "Retire, Herman, you're not permitted in the dining room."

Well, second best, said Herman to her masterful god and, as Smith opened the pantry door, she whisked like a shadow into the kitchen.

"Any plans until dinner?" Whit asked.

"No." She thought: No plans whatever, except wishing it were tomorrow.

"How about having Mort take us to where we can walk in the park, as we can't drive through it? Then perhaps lunch at the Carlyle?"

It would be a time killer; and it was a beautiful day.

They walked, they sat on benches, they looked at kids and adults on bicycles; saw the little boats sailing on a lake, and lovers, their arms looped about each other, walking on the paths, sprawling on the grass. There seemed to be something of a Happening not far away and they looked at that too, and at old people, generally alone sitting in the sun.

Not for the first time, Janice said, "I can't tell the boys from the girls."

"They can," said Whit. "Always observe the south end, especially if they're wearing tight jeans; the north isn't as accurate under flowing shirts, but the view of their south is usually convincing. Flowers aren't, either in the hair or between the teeth. Of course," he added thoughtfully, "shifts are—and the legs beneath them."

"I can't get used to it."

"Oh, you will. It's a phase, and not for the first time in history."

He tried to amuse her by talking of things he'd heard and experienced. She listened, hearing but often not comprehending. June was beginning to turn on, a little late; the temperature, humidity, birds and barefoot young people digging their toes in the grass.

He said something about their air-conditioning; it seemed it too had a mind of its own and turned itself on.

"That's nice," said Janice absently.

"You must take up knitting, Mrs. D."

She looked at him startled. "A non sequitur if I ever heard one," she commented.

"Not exactly, but you should do something with all that wool you've been gathering."

"I'm sorry," she said, a stubborn line about her mouth.

"You needn't be. Let's walk to where Mort will pick us up."

Lunch was excellent. She forced herself to eat and Whit watched her. "The Foundation tomorrow?" he asked.

"Of course."

"Good. I think, at the end of the month we'll take a little cruise. I can manage some time off, and also see people along the way."

"Where to?" she asked. "You mean on the yacht? What's she called by the way?"

" 'Mrs. Calabash.' Jimmy Durante didn't mind; my father asked permission."

She laughed, for the first time that morning. Then she asked, "Where are we going?"

"Oh, the Cape via the Canal, Martha's Vineyard, Nantucket and along the Maine coast. Ever been to Maine?"

"No, nor to the Cape and other places either."

He said, "You'll need company. The car will meet Joe and me at different places, and we'll join you at others. Perhaps in addition to Cecil, you'll want another woman along. Do you think Katie would join us?"

"She'd love it," said Janice instantly, "but I don't know if Raoul will let her. She's had a holiday."

"Tell her to promise him you'll come to his fall showing. That'll do it. Call her when we get home, and if she's in, ask. We can settle the whole thing Thursday night."

She said with a trace of resentment, "You settle things so easily, Whit."

"Not always; don't be deluded. But in most instances, business or social, it's not hard; all it takes is experience, a good staff, know-how and a hell of a lot of money!"

They went home, and Whit disappeared into the library where he used the dictaphone. Janice went upstairs. There was no way in which she could occupy herself usefully between now and dressing for dinner. The Carter service was efficient; the Smiths had left instructions, dinner was ordered, the flowers arranged, the table would be set. She thought: I can't even dust!

Cecil came into the little living room in which Janice was sitting writing to her parents. A book lay face down on the couch and Herman slumbered in her basket with one eye open. She had not been taken to the park and this had offended her, although trotting along with Vera on duty had not been without charm. Herman had met quite a few potential friends.

Cecil wanted to know if Mrs. Dennis wished to shower or bathe and Janice thought: I'm in and out of that tub or shower so much I may grow fins.

She decided on the shower.

Cecil asked, "Would it relax you if. . . . ?"

"I don't need a sedative," said Janice shortly, and wondered how on earth this quiet woman knew that her neck was knotted again and her nerves screaming silently.

"I was going to suggest a massage, Mrs. Dennis."

So she'd been trained for that too, thought Janice.

Massage, nap and shower. She came out of all this looking rested and refreshed. Whit knocked and was admitted as Cecil was zipping the rose-pink frock. It was one he'd liked when she'd worn it in Vancouver—young, flattering, short but not too short.

He watched while Cecil clasped the pearls, the longer strand, and said, "You'll do," approvingly.

Janice thought so too. Dave hated pink. It reminded him, he said of strawberry sodas and bassinettes.

Leaving, "Did you tell our friends not to dress?"

She thought wildly: Should I have? Should I have said

come as you are—naked if you wish? She said carefully, "I forgot, but they're going for drinks somewhere, so I daresay they'll turn up dressed for that."

"Nehru jacket?" asked Whit.

She was downstairs a few minutes before he joined her, having gone to speak to the Carters—they had names but always seemed to be known as the Carters (rather like Whit's Mrs. Smiths). She was walking about, fingering the flowers, adjusting one in this arrangement and another in that one.

Whit advised, "Just take three deep breaths, Janice."

The doorbell spoke and the male Carter, very correct, hastened to admit their guests.

Janice and Whit went to meet them. An embrace from Madge for Janice, a handclasp from Dave, greetings all around, as Carter disposed of Madge's little jacket.

She was a pretty woman, taller than Janice, with dark hair through which ran a spectacular white streak, unfamiliar to Janice, who found herself thinking, hysterically: Has she turned white over night? Only her hairdresser knows for sure. . . .

"Wonderful to see you, Jan," Davidson Peters was saying; the firm, warm hand clasp was familiar; and the fine speaking voice. She looked at him directly and said she was so glad they could come.

They went into the drawing room, which Janice always thought of as the living room, and she saw Madge's hazel eyes darting around, looking at furniture and Chinese porcelains, at colors and materials—an appraisal.

Dave had altered. He was a little heavier, Janice thought, and there were lines in his face which she had not seen before.

Whit was asking about their trip. Dave saying just business, but we managed a little pleasure with it; friends here in town and theater. "Madge said you saw us there, Friday."

Janice was very still. If Whit said, "Yes, but we left because Janice didn't feel well . . ." She'd forgotten to tell him what she'd told Madge. "Pity we didn't get together after," said Dave.

Madge to the rescue. "But Mr. Dennis had an appointment, and they had to leave. Remember?"

"Whit," he corrected her, "as you're old friends of Janice's."

Madge was looking at him with eyes made larger by skillful make-up and he thought, indifferently: With her face washed, she'd be rather plain. Her make-up was well applied, yet a little too much. Her dress was for the cocktail hour, short, black, and beaded. Her hair was not quite all her own, aside from the white streak. But she was pretty.

Diamonds on one wrist, a watch, concealed in a starry case; diamonds at her ears; and an engagement ring.

Now she was admiring Janice's pearls. "So lovely," she said enviously.

Carter was taking orders. Mrs. Peters preferred vodka —"But once home, I'm going on a diet," she said, aware that she was slender.

"You always say that," remarked her husband, ordering bourbon and water, "and easy on the water."

Caviar, smoked sturgeon, elegant small canapés and general conversation; it would have been heavy going except for Whit; he acted as a lever.

"It's just beyond me to think of Janice married," said Madge, with her second drink.

"Why?" asked Whit lazily. "She looks eminently marriageable to me—even now."

"All those followers," said Madge. "You've no idea!"

"Oh, but I have," Whit assured her.

"See, Dave," said Madge in triumph, "she's blushing, just the way she used to—and she turned them all down."

"Fortunately for me. After all, thinking back, she turned me down too. Oh, just momentarily. Perhaps instant refusal had become habit forming."

"I don't believe it," said Madge shocked, having by now evaluated the house, its visible contents, the pearls and Janice's engagement ring. She turned hers somewhat fretfully, on her rather short stubby finger, and added, "Did she ever tell you that she and Dave were—well—half engaged, once?"

"Of course," said Whit. "I never marry anyone unless she signs a full confession."

It was Dave who flushed now. His skin was fair, and his brown hair had glints of red. He said evenly, "We were very young, Whit."

"Youth," said Whitney sighing. "I recall when in college I fell madly in love with what was known as a town girl. She was gorgeous, was Elvira. I wanted to marry her. She must have left a great impression on me because I never wanted to marry anyone else until quite recently. But I didn't tell Janice. I thought now, surrounded by friends, would be the logical time."

"How old were you, Whit?" asked Janice, laughing.

"Sixteen."

"And in college!" cried Madge, making admiring eyes.

Dave, finishing his second drink, said nothing; he looked at Janice as seldom as possible. He loathed and envied Whitney Dennis. He could have strangled his wife, who was becoming a little shrill. Well she hadn't had tomato juice (unless fortified by vodka) in the cocktail lounge; nor had he.

Carter asked if they were ready to be served? They

were and Whit gave Madge his arm, thinking that, as her heels were high and so was she, she might need support.

Janice went in with Dave. She did not take his arm. And he spoke of the weather, the house, the flower arrangements.

Dinner was perfection. The Carters, whoever they were, were as good as the Smiths.

Janice talked, to Dave, on her right, to Madge on Whit's; she talked about the wedding and about Vancouver and the Island. She even talked about Herman. She had barely touched her second martini, but she found herself obsessed by words. She could think privately, while she was talking. She asked Madge about the children and received a full résumé: Debby so like her daddy; young Dave, "so like me, poor kid."

While she was talking, Janice thought forlornly: What has happened to him? What have they done to you, my poor Dave? And didn't know whom she meant by they . . . Madge? The years? Both?. . . But it wasn't as though ten years had passed since he had flung himself out of her apartment and, she'd thought, dying of it, her life.

Later she talked about the work at the Foundation and Madge said, "You really work?" Her tone added: How quaint.

After dinner, they had coffee and liqueurs and Madge asked if they had plans for the summer. Whit answered that they were taking a short cruise presently, as far as Maine and thereabouts and Madge said sighing, "Dave and I never get anywhere but the Lake. . . . Oh a camping trip once, but I'm not a camping buff and after Dave Jr. was born, I wasn't very well. I went to Palm Springs—it was divine—my father had friends who have a house there. Dave couldn't get away more than a week, but I stayed three."

She added that, of course, they had a nurse for Debby and young Dave.

"Perhaps you'd be interested in seeing what the Springs used to look like?" Whit suggested. "I've a painting in the library. My parents went there, before I was born."

He rose and Madge followed him; they were gone quite a while; there was a good deal to see in the library. They could hear Madge's exclamations, which were in italics.

"Damn Whit," said Janice to herself.

She was sitting across from Dave. He leaned over and said quietly, "I have to see you."

"No."

"Will you meet me for lunch tomorrow?"

"No," said Janice, "I will not."

"Just for an hour?"

She said, "You're going back home, Dave."

"Not until late afternoon. I'll call you tomorrow morning."

She said, "I'll be working at the Foundation."

He looked at her; she was familiar with the look. She said, "But there's no use—there's no sense——"

"I'm not trying to——" He broke off and listened. They could still hear Madge's voice, and Whit's deeper tone.

He said, "You must go somewhere for lunch."

"Nearby, with people from the Foundation, or it's sent in."

"Please, Jan, just let me talk to you—the Special Spot—that's not too far, is it? I'll get there at noon and wait."

She felt herself shrinking. They'd gone there together several times, a dim dark place. She'd forgotten if the food was good or bad; at the time it couldn't have mattered less.

"There are things I must explain."

"You've explained before."

He said, "I'll be there. I'll wait for an hour."

Madge and Whit came back into the room and Madge said, "Darling, you must see that fabulous library," and tugged at Dave's arm until he rose and Whit said to Janice, "I bet you've never even noticed the Palm Springs painting; come and see it."

She asked, "Aunt Hilda's?"

"Heaven forbid!"

A little later they were back in the drawing room and Dave was saying he had a luncheon engagement and Madge was saying she had one too; fortunately theirs would be a dinner flight. "I must pack," she said, distracted. "It's been such a wonderful evening and so marvelous to see Janice again and meet you, Whit, and to see her just glowing with happiness, and small wonder. All this," said Madge, with a sweep of her stubby hand, "and Whit too!"

"Package deal," said Whitney soberly.

When the door had closed, he asked, "How about going up and comforting Herman?. . . Better still, I'll take him for a walk and join you later, after Cecil has gone her appointed round.

The round was brief. Mrs. Dennis didn't need anything but to be unzipped. No, not even her hair brushed; nothing. Cecil was dismissed and Janice went in a robe and slippers to the sitting room, sat down at the couch and looked at Herman's basket.

Its owner appeared after a time, skittering in, bestowing an affectionate kiss on a bare ankle and then making for her basket-bed.

"That's right. Settle down," said Whit. He pulled a

chair closer to the couch. "Why haven't you?" he asked.

She said directly. "I wanted to tell you something. . . . Dave asked me to lunch tomorrow."

"From her plans, I take it, without his wife. Incidentally, I do not find her attractive. . . . Are you going?"

"No."

"Why did you tell me?"

She said drearily, "Wasn't this part of the bargain?"

"You're permitted a few secrets, Janice."

"And if I went, you'd know."

"Oh, yes. Go anyway. I promise you, no eavesdropping."

She sat up straight on the couch and danger signals flared. She said incredulously, "You mean, I should go?"

"Of course. If you don't, you'll always regret it and you'll always wonder. If you do, you may also regret it, but you won't wonder."

"Sometimes," she said, "I think you're not quite human."

"Oh, I'm human enough and you know that very well. I simply believe it would do you good to go. It will be as therapeutic as a good cry," said Whit, "and an act of courage as well. I think I know what he'll say. I'm not sure what you'll reply. But no one will listen in, and you needn't report any of the conversation to me at any time."

She said. "He told me he'd wait for an hour."

"Good. Have you called Katie?"

"I forgot."

He passed her, touched her shoulder. He said, "Call her tonight; it's not too late. I'll be in presently unless you'd rather be alone."

"If you don't mind, Whit."

"I mind, but not seriously. You need a little time in which to decide whether to lunch or not to lunch," said

Whit, yawning. He added, "Forgive me, but it was a fairly dull evening."

In the Foundation car, next morning she said, "I've decided to have lunch with Dave."

"I thought you had. You look a little frayed around the edges; it was, I surmise, a difficult decision?"

It had been. Why had she wavered? Why had she weakened? She'd asked herself that, when daylight was like twilight in the room. . . . Because she wanted to talk to Dave, to make it clear that this was for the last time? Or because Whit had goaded her into it? Or both?

She'd know at noon.

Parting, Whit said, "Mort will pick you up at the usual time. I'll be a little late for dinner. You might tell Smith when you get home. I have to talk to a man who knows all about cargo planes. And there's also a Corporation Board meeting. Have a good day and try to remember to call Katie."

She'd forgotten again. She said, "I'll call from the office; she gets up late. I'm sorry, Whit."

"Never be sorry," he said.

THIRTEEN

❀❀❀

JANICE WALKED TO The Special Spot. She thought: How did he know it was within walking distance of the office? It wasn't hard to deduce; he'd looked up the Foundation in the telephone book before last night. How had he known that she spent some time there? He hadn't, until she had told him and Madge at dinner. But perhaps he had considered calling the Foundation to obtain the unlisted number even before she'd called Madge.

It didn't matter. She had learned, during her maniacally happy, supremely miserable association with him in this city that he was devious, and a planner . . . so much had been evaded, and elusive, yet everything carefully planned.

It wasn't, she told herself walking along the crowded streets, crossing with caution—a part of her mind functioned normally at any rate—it wasn't that Dave was particularly clever. He got by in school and college; an average student, but he had a slow, persistent charm which, sooner or later, affected all who came into contact with him; and a direct, seeming sincerity. . . . Her father had once said of Dave, when they were kids picnicking at the Lake, "No one can be as honest as Dave Peters looks."

She wondered who was following her, and at what range. She didn't turn to look, nor stop suddenly in front a shop and determine who else stopped nearby. She didn't care. She knew, and those who watched her knew she knew; she sometimes waved, spotting whoever it was, some patient unnoticeable carbon-copy man and if she were correct, he waved back; on occasions she hadn't been correct and some innocent gentleman, intent on getting somewhere on his own urgent business, had halted, stunned; perhaps delighted; perhaps outraged.

There was, of course, no point in being openly escorted, as to the opera, the matinee, or just casually walking with a friend or acquaintance, making light conversation.

The thought crossed her mind that Dave would be disconcerted, to put it mildly, if he knew that wherever Mrs. Whitney Dennis went, someone was on guard. She almost laughed aloud.

She went into The Special Spot at ten past twelve, and old dog Tray would come in after her, order a sandwich and eat it within, as it were, shooting distance.

It took a moment for her eyes to adjust to the lack of light. In the front room, the bar, small tables; men talking, drinking, laughing, with a color television set where they could see it, turned on high. She went on through to the back room where, when they'd come here, she and Dave had sat. He was there, in the corner with a glass before him and he rose as she made her way between the tables. The back room was not crowded. She saw a slender man come in and sit down, alone, not within hearing distance. He'd had his orders.

"You came," said Dave superfluously.

He pulled out a chair for her and asked, "What will you have to drink?"

"Just coffee, thanks."

"That's right; you don't drink at noon when you're working."

A harried waiter came and Janice asked for a salad and coffee. . . . "Hot," she said, "not iced," and looked at Dave. He hesitated, decided against a second old-fashioned. "Steak sandwich, rare, and coffee," he said.

"Why did you come?" he asked her.

This was the pattern—when not devious, direct.

"Partly, I think, curiosity."

"And if Whit finds out?"

"What's there to find out?" asked Janice lightly. "I told him I was meeting you. There's nothing very spectacular about having a quick lunch with an old friend. Did you tell Madge?"

"Of course not. I said I had a business date; as a matter of fact I had. I broke it this morning. I'm to see the man briefly before I return to the hotel."

"Would Madge have minded?"

"Don't be absurd. You are hardly naïve. Of course."

She asked evenly, "Does she know about us, then?" And he said, "I don't know. We were—careful, but——"

"You were careful," said Janice. "Looking back at the person I once was, I marvel how little she cared about discretion."

"I don't know about Madge," he said sullenly. "There were times when I thought she suspected something; how much I don't know. Perhaps it was just the normal wifely attitude. 'What did you do in New York?. . . Whom did you see?. . . I called the hotel; you were out.' Or 'You forgot to leave the number where you'd be when you went out of the city.' Occasionally she spoke of you. She'd say 'Why don't you look up Janice?' When it all began—when I did look you up that first time, she knew; she'd suggested it."

"We've been all over that a thousand times," said Janice wearily. "Sorry I brought it up."

The waiter came back with their lunch. And Janice said, "It's cool in here."

"I didn't ask you to meet me to discuss past history or the climate," he told her.

"Why did you ask me, then?"

After a moment he said, as if reluctantly, "I miss you so much, Jan; you've no idea."

"I've an excellent idea. I missed you too."

"But you don't, now?"

"Yes, occasionally, to my humiliation."

She pursued a piece of lettuce around her plate and drank some coffee. He wasn't eating. He cut into the steak and looked at it as if it was something alien he had encountered on a journey.

"If you had been patient, if you had listened to reason, we could have worked something out."

"We've been over that too. Once it was, 'When I get my divorce.' Remember? And then, 'We'll work something out.' Madge would never divorce you—you finally admitted that—except for infidelity. And that I assume would have meant me. I had no intention of letting that happen. I care about my parents. As a matter of fact," she remarked thoughtfully, "I suspect that since that time you've given Madge additional cause for divorce."

He said angrily, "Well suppose I have. I never argue with anyone who meant anything to me."

She reflected briefly on the years she had known him: a big boy; later, a big man, with big appetites for exercise, for amusement, for food, for love. He'd told her from the beginning of their crazy, beautiful, futile intimacy that Madge was not interested in him as a lover. He'd said, "What she wants is a husband, a father for her children, an escort, and someone who will eventually provide for her as well as Daddy provided."

Now Janice said, "You once told me what you believed Madge wanted in a husband. I think these requirements still hold. And now she has children to consider."

"Her children, everything's hers."

Janice looked at her watch. She said, "I have to get back to work."

Dave laughed. His eyes slanted at the corners when he laughed. She'd noticed that last night; it had hurt, remembering; it did now.

"Madge was right for once," he said. "How ridiculous—Whitney Dennis' wife going to an office."

"The Foundation is a private charitable institution."

"I'm sorry, Jan. Don't go. Let me ask you this—are you happy?"

She said gravely, "Yes."

"I don't believe you—not in the way we were——"

"That was insanity, and I suppose insane people think they're happy," she said.

"Why did you marry him, or is it obvious?"

"Perhaps it seems obvious to you. . . . No, Dave, I didn't marry him for money. Money's never meant anything to me except ordinary comforts, ordinary pleasure; I didn't marry him for position. My parents gave me that when I was born; a good background, one which is respected."

"Then why? Not that he isn't attractive, I suppose. Madge went into a tizzy about him. I daresay he's very attractive to women."

"Yes, very; with or without the money," said Janice. "Good-bye, Dave," she said, rising.

He said to the hovering waiter, "I'll be right back." He took Janice's hand and held it, hard, saying, "I'll see you again; I must," and walked to the door with her.

"I think not." She detached her hand and went out

into the June sunlight. A slender man came out after her, not hurrying, and fell into step behind her, and Dave Peters went back to his corner table, poked at the cold steak, ordered another old-fashioned. He was fed up with everything; with Madge, with the business which hadn't been going well. His father-in-law had sold his stock in it, but while the old man had influence at the bank, money was tight; and Madge was complaining. She had complained last night at the hotel. "Some people have all the luck," she'd said; "some fall on their feet."

Janice thought on her way back to the office: That's that. Don't think of him. Think of Katie, when I remembered to call her this morning, how excited she was once she was convinced that Raoul, the neurotic slave driver, would let her come with us. Think of how much fun it will be with her again, almost like the old days.

Her mind dismissed Katie as unimportant. Why do you go on caring for people when you know their faults, and shortcomings, their cruelties and deceptions? The mind reasons; the body remembers. It is an illogical instrument, the body. She had resented and disliked Dave, sitting at the corner table in The Special Spot; she had regarded him coldly, with the clarity of vision which had come to her over the long time of their separation and never more sharply than last night.

But resentment and dislike do not always add up to indifference.

His eyes, slanting when he laughed; his hands; the line of his mouth, grave or angry or as, when he asked her not to go, tender and compelling; his touch, however brief—to these she was not indifferent, nor, she told herself in despair, could she ever be.

Alone with her that evening, Whit asked, "How did your day go?"

"All right."

"Did you call Katie?"

"Yes, early. I woke her up. She was cross, but she soon recovered and was as excited as a child when I finally convinced her that Raoul would let her come with us."

"Visions of sugar plums would dance through his head," said Whit. "Sometimes it pays to pull rank."

"I know. I was horrified at myself. I said, tell him I'll come to the fall showing . . . I even said that she and I could talk clothes—after all she does know what I like—on the cruise. And just before I left the office, she called back."

"And?"

"Raoul is *enchanté*," Janice reported with a straight face. "She said he kept her for ten minutes asking about my coloring, what sort of clothes I wore and who had dressed me. But she fielded that one; she could offer him no great name in the changing world of fashion. He probably thinks I was born Mrs. Dennis."

"Just born to be, which reminds me you'll need clothes perhaps for the cruise—shorts, slacks, more sweaters. You needn't give Katie's boss a heart attack. I doubt he provides those. Take Cecil and just go shopping."

She said, "I've promised Mr. Parsons in PR to look over a new brochure with him. He thinks I have a flair. But I could go, latish, before the shops close."

"Cecil can come with Mort to pick you up."

After dinner, she said, "You haven't asked me about lunch."

"I take it you didn't eat much. You did justice to our Mrs. Smith tonight, however. Why? Is there something you want to tell me."

"Actually, no. I dreaded it," she said truthfully. "I could have murdered you for pushing me into it—which is exactly what you did."

"I've always said you're perceptive."

"God knows why you did it," she told him, "but I expect you do. Anyway I've usually taken dares, since childhood. That was what it was, a dare."

"Anyone ever throw you overboard to teach you to swim?"

"No. My father didn't approve of the method."

Whit laughed, regarding her with that curiously veiled look which often puzzled and in a way distressed her. She said suddenly, "Uncle Howard once told me you seemed as open as a Scandinavian sandwich—or words to that effect—but weren't. I think clams also got mixed into the metaphors somehow."

"Smart lad, Howard. But don't believe all he says—he's a lawyer."

"Well if you must know——"

"It's not essential."

"It was distasteful," she said, "it was—oh, I don't know—don't make me try to analyze it."

Whit lifted an eyebrow. He asked, "Who's making you do anything?"

"I nearly stopped and flagged my guard," Janice said. "A nice chat on the way to work would have been in order."

"Next time I'll have him sling a keg of brandy around his neck," said Whit. "So you figured who was who?"

"I think so. Short, slender, going gray. He didn't even have a hat pulled down over his eyes like the men who trail people on TV. No hat, at all, in fact."

"That was Abernathy," said Whit, "I think. He would have been humiliated had you hailed him."

" 'Me and my shadow'?" said Janice, and laughed.

That night, he asked from the connecting door, "Want to be alone, or would you like company?"

She said, "I'd like company. Is anyone available?"

She felt cold and uncomforted. Whit would warm her and console her, alleviate her anger at herself, quiet her curious dull despair, take her into temporary forgetfulness.

Later he reached for the light switch, and a cigarette and smoked, in silence . . . Janice was half asleep when he put out the cigarette and turned off the rosy radiance of his bedside lamp. He put his hand behind his head and said, "You didn't owe me anything, Janice."

She answered after a moment, "I know. It wasn't that —believe me, Whit, it wasn't."

"All right, Luv," he said. "Go to sleep."

Cecil and Janice went shopping the next afternoon. It was warm, cloudy, and threatened to rain. Automobiles were driven by madmen who were bucking traffic in these first, close, humid days. Shoppers were beginning to thin out and anxious people stood at the curbs vainly hailing taxis. Everyone was going somewhere and wanted to get there before it rained. It was thundering a little and the sky was dark when Janice and Cecil emerged from the big store. Mortimer would drive up any moment, as Cecil reminded Janice, to park near the side entrance.

As they turned the corner, Cecil with her large handbag and neatly furled umbrella, there seemed to be a lot of people walking both ways. Janice felt a jostle and a tug and there was a slight scramble as Cecil moved in. No one seemed to notice; people in New York are disciplined not to notice too much. There was a sharp yelp of pain, something clattered to the pavement and Cecil said firmly, "Hurry, Mrs. Dennis."

There was Mortimer, past the side doors, at the curb.

Janice got in the car, Cecil followed. Cecil looked gray but unruffled. "Whatever happened?" asked Janice blankly. "Someone shoved me—and pulled . . . then I heard him or her shout something——"

"I think, a purse snatcher," said Cecil. "He had a knife. You're wearing a shoulder bag. The knife was to cut the strap."

"But shouldn't we have called the police?" Janice asked anxiously.

"I think not, Mrs. Dennis." Cecil cleared her throat. "There was someone near us; he'll do what's needed."

Abernathy or another shadow? Cecil had moved very quickly. Good eyes, and probably a good karate chop to the predatory wrist.

No police; the Dennis family avoided publicity.

Janice told Whit about it that night, and he nodded. He already knew, he said.

"For heaven's sake, explain Cecil to me. How much of all that reference business was true?"

"Alas, no duchesses," said Whitney, laughing. "I just threw that in to amuse you."

"I know she's had training other than as a personal maid," Janice said. "In massage, for instance, and"—she looked at him speculatively—"probably judo, karate or whatever . . . and I'll bet you a quarter, first aid."

"I never bet on a sure thing." He smiled and added, "As you should know."

Janice flushed a little. "She—Cecil that is—told me she'd had training during the war. . . . Police?"

"Loosely speaking."

"And the agency from which Joe got her?"

"Doesn't exist."

"References?"

"They were beautiful," said Whit sadly, "and you didn't even look at them."

"What about the maid bit? She's wonderful, you know."

"Oh, she had to train for that," said Whit, "and for Nanny work too. Her life since the war has been occupied with riding shotgun for the very young, the very old, and in betweens, who might be, occasionally, in precarious situations."

"And where she was born, and her husband killed in the war—is that fiction?"

"No. Relax. Someone meant to annex your handbag. He didn't succeed. But Cecil doesn't want your handbag snatched, not because you carry much money or any jewelry in it, but you do have identification."

She said meekly, "Very well, Master. I'm beginning to think she's really using her Nanny training, as well as the rest of it, with me. What about the relative on Long Island?"

"That's a fact, and so is the duck farm. That's why she came here, highly recommended."

"By Scotland Yard."

"Of course."

"I never know whether to believe you or not," said Janice indignantly.

"It's half my charm. Shall we go in to dinner? You'll regain your balance."

"I didn't really lose it," said Janice.

Thursday was the night of the almost birthday party. Everyone came, including Janice's parents. She had to have one surprise, Whit said when they walked in.

"You said they couldn't make it!"

"But they did," said Whit, "moving heaven and earth."

It was a lovely party. Audrey was glittering with excitement, and even Tom rose to the occasion; Katie was her natural self; the aunts delighted to see and meet everyone; Martha Dennis friendly and relaxed, and the Nortons, charming as always.

The Smiths had supplementary help, the Carters of

course, a different pair this time. Everything was gay and happy and the presents were heaped on a couch in the living room.

Janice said, "I've never had a better time."

It was true; there had been times which were more wonderful, but none better.

She asked her mother, "Where are you staying?"

"Here," said Betty Cooper. "Where else?"

"Why pay a hotel bill?" inquired her father, "when your daughter's humble roof is available."

"But the luggage."

Her mother said, "We came in last night to the hotel, and Whit had most of the luggage smuggled in during the morning, when you weren't here. We kept enough with us to dress for dinner, and checked out. As you know, we're going to the Poconos to visit the Andrews . . . that is, after your real birthday."

"What happened to the bags with the evening clothes?" asked Janice, who always liked things explained.

Whit said, "At the hotel. Mort will pick them up."

Everyone got along very well; Hilda and Bill Cooper talked dogs; Heloise and Betty discussed charity drives; Tom, more animated than Janice had ever seen him, and more outgoing, talked business with Martha; Katie and Audrey gossiped.

"We're short a couple of men," said Whit, and Hilda cried, "Your Aunt Heloise, your mother and I are used to that."

He said, "Well, I thought I'd keep it in the family. As a matter of fact, I tried to get Joe but he was otherwise engaged."

After dinner, the presents: fripperies and frivolities for the most part, including an enormous bottle of perfume from the Turners, worth its weight in gold with a note from Lily saying, "I don't know your taste in scents, but I thought this might suit you."

Whit looked over Janice's shoulder as she opened it; the others came to look at and exclaim over everything. She put the bottle aside with a little shrug; she said, "I wonder if she'd mind awfully . . . ?"

"She won't know about it." He looked at the other women. "Katie, I think, when we go on the cruise."

Janice opened his present last. It was beautifully wrapped. The box containing it had a name written across it in gold in reproduced handwriting. It said "Felicity."

She shook the box before she took the cover off. "It doesn't rattle," she complained.

"No."

"Why should it," asked Hilda, "unless something's broken?"

"Whit promised me a cupful of emeralds," said Janice mournfully, "and they should rattle."

"It's a cup, anyway," Whit said.

A small cup, an egg cup, in gold and enamel; solid enamel rimming it and a band of translucent enamel with small birds running round it; and a monogram—not Janice's—in emeralds.

Everyone exclaimed. Janice revolved it in her hands. "An egg cup!" she said incredulously.

"For a child," said Whit.

"Probably made by Fabergé," said Martha, taking it from Janice. "It's quite lovely . . . and for someone in the Russian royal family." To Whit, she said, "Your father gave me a pair of those fabulous Easter eggs once——"

She gave the cup to Heloise, who inquired, "But what on earth is it for?" And Whit said, "To eat eggs from. Now we'll have to find Janice a spoon."

"So useless!" said Heloise.

"Not to someone who eats eggs. I'm going to teach Janice one of these days that a fresh egg at breakfast is one of life's minor delights."

Martha, wandering across the room, stopping to take a cigarette from a tortoise-shell box, asked, "How's Felicity doing by the way?"

"Very well. In addition to the trinkets she hunts down at auctions and bargains for, she's designing——"

"She always was."

"Jewelry," finished Whit calmly.

"Do you still see her?"

He looked at his mother amused. He said, "Obviously, if I went to her shop and bought the egg cup."

Now Betty Cooper had the egg cup saying, "It's the prettiest thing of its kind I ever saw."

It was fairly late when everyone went home except the Coopers, who were to be in the big guest suite. Cecil had unpacked for them. There was a flurry of good-byes, at least as far as Martha and the aunts went, and they were going as far as California on Saturday.

Martha put her arm around Janice. She said, "Make Whitney bring you out to us."

"I'll try, but I can't make him do anything," Janice said and Whit, kissing his mother, remarked, "It's so hard for me to know where any of you girls are at a given time. But we'll see you."

"Are you going to Dunewalk?"

"After we get back from the cruise."

Katie enraptured by the thought of a cruise had told Janice she didn't have anything to wear and Janice said, "Slacks, shorts, shirts, bathing suit . . . you'll manage . . . some cotton for dinner and the villages . . . Cecil will look after your things."

It struck her as mildly entertaining that she had begun

to think of Cecil as if she'd always had her, and also that you become accustomed to being rich faster than to being poor (if you have been rich).

They sat talking with her parents for a while longer and when Betty rose she told Whit, "It was the most lovely party. . . . Janice, what on earth are you going to do with the egg cup?"

"Keep it upstairs and look at it a dozen times a day," said Janice. "Of all the crazy beautiful presents."

"It isn't your real birthday present," said Whit. "You get that on Sunday morning."

When they went upstairs, she rang for Cecil and suggested, "Perhaps you'd look in on my mother, Cecil, and see if she needs help?" And when the door had closed behind her, told Whit. "Mother will have a fit; father will vanish cursing into the bathroom."

"Then why did you do it?"

"It's time they learned how the other one and a half percent lives," she answered. She kissed him. "Thank you for the party," she said, "the fabulous egg cup, and especially for mother and father."

Later, ready for bed, with her egg cup gleaming on her night table, she said, "Tovarich?"

"*Da*—and that's as far as I can go except *Niet*—what?"

"Who's Felicity?"

"A very good-looking girl, with considerable talent. Christened Sadie, I believe."

"Your mother seemed to know about her."

"My mother has known about every—well almost every—young woman with whom I've occasionally appeared in public."

"Shall I meet her?"

"Felicity? Of course, whenever you wish. The shop

address is on the box—or did you throw it away?"

"I tossed it."

Presently in the darkness she said, "I wish she liked me better."

"Felicity?"

"Your mother."

"She likes you," said Whit. "In time she'll probably be fond of you. She'll even think of you as Janice and not my son's wife."

"You mean I'll have my own identity?"

He muttered something, possibly assent.

"What are you giving me on my real birthday?"

But he was asleep.

FOURTEEN

WHEN JANICE WOKE ON Sunday morning, the sun was making an attempt to penetrate the curtains. Whit was nowhere to be seen, but there was a small unwrapped box on his pillow. She took it in her hand and swung her feet to the floor, went across the room and pulled back the long curtains. Standing there, blinking in the light, her hair tossed forward over her shoulder and the box in her hand she thought first: I must have overslept; second: I didn't hear Whit leave the room, and third: It's going to be a hot day.

When Whit came in, he was dressed—shirt, slacks, no tie. "Happy birthday, old girl," he said, smiling. "Aren't you going to open your present?"

He came over, put his arm around her, and kissed her soundly.

"I overslept," she said, guilty as a child. "Where's everyone?"

"Having breakfast. I hadn't the heart to wake you so I silently folded my tent and so on . . . I've had coffee with your parents. Your mother thinks she's worn you out during the last couple of days."

"We did sort of barrel around." She went back to the bed, sat on the side, and looked at the box. "Not Felicity?" she inquired.

"Nope."

She opened, and took from it a pendant on a thin gold chain. The pendant was a bird cage, fashioned in gold and a tiny jeweled bird sat forever fastened to a small gold perch which swung as Janice moved her hand.

"Just so you'll remember," he said.

"Did you have it made?" she asked, swinging the little cage, fascinated. "It's charming."

"There wasn't time to have anything made, but there's a shop over on Madison which specializes in the more or less unusual and sometimes one of a kind, like this. Do you like it?"

"I love it," she said.

"One drawback," Whit said, going over to stand by the big windows, "the bird doesn't sing." And went on before she could answer. "My father had one . . . in a gold box; you tapped the lid, a bird popped up and sang. It came from the same collection as mother's Easter eggs . . . I haven't seen the bird nor eggs for a long time, they're all in a museum. We'll go and admire them someday."

She said, crossing the room and putting her arms round his neck, "You're very good to me, Whit."

"Little birds take a lot of care," he said gravely, "delicate, restless . . . I'm sorry I've had to clip your wings a little." He kissed her cheek and went out, saying, "Get Cecil, fling on some garments. See you downstairs."

But she did not immediately ring. She went back to the bed and picked up the pendant. The cage swung on the chain, the perch swung, and the bird with it, but the bird had no freedom of its own; it was locked in the cage and moved only when the cage and perch moved.

"Just so you'll remember," he'd said.

For a very brief moment she had a compulsion to

smash it into glittering fragments. But the bird wouldn't escape; even if she could open the door. It could not fly.

She told herself: And it doesn't really want to; or, not often.

After the Coopers left on Monday, there were a few crowded days. Janice went to the office during most of them and was gratified to be told that she'd been missed. Every hour on the hour Katie telephoned. "Honey," pleaded Janice, "please don't call me here. Wait until I get home."

Cecil was busy with a few minor alterations and the packing. Smith produced luggage and packed for Whit. The *Mrs. Calabash* meantime had been steadily heading north from her berth at the Palm Bay Club in Miami, to her destination on Long Island Sound, where, in due time, they boarded her—Janice and Katie, Joe and Whit, and Cecil.

That evening the yacht's launch took them to where she lay at anchor, and they dined and slept aboard.

Mrs. Calabash was not the largest private yacht afloat. The Dennis family did not do a great deal of entertaining aboard. There was room for them all, should they ever decide to reunite on the water—something Whit said he couldn't remember the family doing; there was room for guests; and very comfortable quarters for the Captain whose name was Chris Adams (Boston born, ex-Navy), the steward, his assistant, the chef, and all hands, of which many, and stalwart. It would take Janice most of the cruise to sort them out.

The owner's quarters were Whit's, or whatever Dennis was aboard. *Mrs. Calabash* was a superb example of the ship builder's art—every convenience naturally, and also unostentatious luxury. You would expect excellent service and food, and even music at the turn of a knob; you would be certain of ship-to-shore telephone, but there was also a wireless operator.

"Holy cow," said Katie inadequately, on the afterdeck following dinner. There were other boats, sailing boats and cruisers, small and large, near them. Riding lights were reflected in the water, light streamed from the yacht club and the sky was crowded with stars.

She was lying in a long chair muttering to herself that home was never like this. She didn't think she could stand it.

"Seasick prone?" asked Whit.

"Well once going to Bermuda . . . but most of my sailing has been done on ferries."

"Lots of remedies in the medicine cabinet, everything from dramamine to shark-bite medication. And Richey knows his way around sick bay; so does Cecil."

Richey was the steward, a solid, capable middle-aged man.

"Maybe Cecil gets seasick," Katie said, and Joe remarked amiably that Cecil never lost her cool and probably wouldn't lose her lunch.

That night in the owner's stateroom Janice said, "This is like a dream to Katie. Me, too, really."

"I can take you aboard bigger ships," said her husband, "and noncommercial at that."

"*Mrs. Calabash* is big enough," she told him, "and a beautiful, shapely air-conditioned lady."

"Life aboard," Whit told her, "is informal. No elegance. You can eat on the afterdeck or anywhere you please in your bathing suit and with your feet bare. I hope you'll apprise Katie. She said at dinner that she hadn't brought evening clothes!"

Janice asked, as he stood by her dressing table, smoking a final cigarette, "Are you often aboard?"

"The owner's flag seldom flies for me. I haven't time. I haven't been aboard in a year. I lent her to some friends, which is why she was in Florida, so they could romp around various islands."

"Jet set?" asked Janice, testing her bed which was superb.

"No. Friends, and their son and his wife—you'll meet them, sometime . . . names's Tredwell; the son's boy was killed in Vietnam. His mother and grandmother were close to a breakdown, so we gave the older Tredwell a leave of absence, and also his son. They both work for the Corporation; the older man heads a department, the younger is an accountant. They're very good people, and very unhappy."

"Has island hopping in *Mrs. Calabash* helped?"

"I think so, as far as physical health is concerned."

She thought about that; and about young men whom she'd known, their youth and gaiety destroyed in the second World War, in Korea. After a while she asked, "When are we sailing?"

"Early tomorrow. Breakfast in bed for you girls. We're going to Boston first. Mort meets me and Joe there; we'll see you on the Cape."

His bed was near hers, a night table between. He came over to kiss her. He said, "Pleasant dreams, Mrs. D."

She was wakeful for a time, listening to the water whispering against the boat, hearing faint sounds from shore, and people on other boats talking to one another across the water.

Whit was gone before she woke and they were moving. There were bells from ships' clocks, and also one she could ring beside the bed. It sounded in Cecil's stateroom and Cecil came in smiling. She said, "It's a lovely day, Mrs. Dennis."

"Where's Miss Evans?"

"I took her tray to her half an hour ago when I heard her stirring about. I'll get yours now."

"Please ask Miss Evans when she finishes if she'd like to come calling."

When Cecil brought Janice's tray, she reported that Miss Evans was dressing and would be right along and when Katie came bouncing in Janice was drinking coffee. "You look like something on a magazine cover," Janice said.

Katie wore yellow shorts, a paler yellow shirt, socks and sneakers, and had tossed a sweater about her shoulders.

"I feel like it. I feel like one of our own models. But someone wake me up any minute. This is heaven."

"Did you sleep?"

"I thought I wouldn't, but I did. I hate to miss a moment of this. Do get up." She sat down on Whit's bed and asked, "Aren't you at all impressed?"

"Any red-blooded man, woman or child must be impressed with water and wind and motion."

"You can get that on a ferryboat," said Katie. "I didn't meant that and you know it."

"Well, how about comfort?" said Janice, looking around the stateroom. "Also beauty—*Mrs. Calabash* is beautiful—anyone, even, without blood, would be favorably impressed——"

"I didn't mean that either. I could throw something at you."

"Well," said Janice, "the word isn't impressed. It's more like startled, I think. I don't happen to have yachts in my background. Oh, we had boats; after all, with a cottage on the lake you must have boats—little boats, or bigger ones, but all toys, of course, if you're making comparisons. I've been on yachts, not as big as this, which belonged to friends."

"So you're not impressed?"

Janice said slowly, "I'm just trying to get used to everything. In some ways I'm succeeding almost too well. You see, Katie, I always had more than enough; this wasn't exactly a rags to riches bit. But a million times more than enough—that's something else again."

"You'll make it," said Katie and added thoughtfully, "I wonder if I would. Oh, sure . . . I'd eat it up. And Whit's a dream. Most girls wouldn't get *Mrs. Calabash* except as some snaggle-toothed, pot-bellied, fish-faced old playboy's third wife. . . . Hey, tell me about Joe Meeker. What does he do?"

"A little of everything for Whit. There isn't much to tell except that he's Whit's closest friend; they were in the Navy together."

"Is he married?"

"No."

"Nice guy," said Katie, happily bouncing off the bed. "A little on the serious side perhaps."

"Oh, I don't know," said Janice.

Katie looked at her sharply. She said, "Maybe he'll loosen up on this my, so to speak, maiden voyage. I'm talking about yachts."

Janice was laughing when she rang to have her tray removed.

Later she went to the afterdeck where she found Katie hanging over the polished rail talking to Joe. Whit had disappeared.

"Where's Whit?" she asked Joe after their greetings.

"On the bridge with the Skipper," said Joe, and Janice remarked that he'd come all over nautical.

Until the end of the cruise, the *Mrs. Calabash* lived up to advance billing. Whit and Joe were transferred in Boston into Mortimer's care; they joined the yacht on the Cape. There was time for sight-seeing and swimming ashore. When Katie and Janice went touristing by themselves, Cecil came too, and a couple of the crew evidenced an intense interest in things like Portuguese bread, sea shells, driftwood, miniature lighthouses, bayberry candles and beach-plum jelly. They (Hank and Rusty) never missed an opportunity to follow the owner's wife, and guest and maid into whatever shops took their fancy. They even bought a thing or two (Rusty, for the wife, Hank for whomever next turned up in his vagabond life).

Richey came ashore a number of times during their cruise explorations, but his interest was strictly in live lobsters.

Often Whit and Joe came along; other times not, when they were busy in the big salon with whatever had taken them to Boston.

The same routine was followed in Nantucket and on Martha's Vineyard, and in Maine. Everyone grew brown, except Janice whose pigmentation caused her to turn a very attractive apricot gold. Katie put on weight and complained bitterly to Joe. They had become friendly. Janice observed to Whit that she had never seen Joe laugh as much. "Trust Katie to break the ice," she said.

"Not ice, just reserve."

"Whatever you say. But, it proves he doesn't like all gals to be stupid and beautiful. Katie's neither."

"There are always exceptions. But don't start the old married-woman ploy?"

"Which is?"

"Matchmaking, Mrs. D."

It was a lovely lazy life. In any of the towns if they wished to go into the country, not on the throughways, and drift along winding back roads, and look at the sea or a beach or cove from a quiet place or on a high rise of land, Mortimer drove them. On numerous occasions they dined or lunched in an uncrowded inn. And Janice was able to forget for stretches of time that when she and Katie wandered around, Cecil wasn't along just to carry packages or advise on sun hats, and that Rusty and Hank were anything but sightseers off a yacht.

On the way home no one had anything unpleasant to remember, except Katie, who had been embarrassed by one small go of mal de mer; she insisted that it was not, it was either something she'd eaten—"No offense," she told Richey as he and Cecil ministered to her—or a touch of that creepy virus you could get anywhere.

To appreciate making love off an island or a Cape or the beautiful Maine coast with water all around, you don't have to be a mermaid, Janice discovered.

There'd been some fog in Maine, everyone was therefore a little browner or more golden. Rocks and little islands, curving coves and shingled beaches—Katie fell violently in love with Maine. She told Joe, "I'm coming up here some summer, marry one of those lean hawk-eyed lobster men and live happily forever after!"

No actual date had been set for their return in two weeks, or three, give or take a couple of days. On the way back, they made no sight-seeing or business stops, and everyone would be briefed by telephone as to when they'd disembark; which included the Foundation, the Corporation, the Smiths and Katie's Mr. Raoul.

On their last night they lay at anchor off the yacht club on the Sound, and Whit and Joe went ashore in the launch because Whit wanted to make some calls of a very private nature.

It was past the dinner hour when he returned alone. As members of the crew made ready to take him aboard, he called from the launch to Katie and Janice at the rail: "Did someone bring Joe back?"

They answered, "No." Whit came aboard, telling the man who ran the launch, "I'm going back ashore in a few minutes."

He looked anxious, and Janice had never seen him look anxous. He leaned against the rail on the afterdeck and said, "He's vanished."

"How could he?" Janice asked.

"I don't know. I went to make the calls and I left him reading this morning's *Times* in the bar. When I got back, he'd gone and no one remembered seeing him leave. I'm going back and look for him; Mortimer's waiting."

They were to dine and sleep aboard and head for home in the early morning.

Whit patted Janice's shoulder. He said, "I hope I'll be back shortly. But if not, don't worry. You and Katie have dinner, and if I'm late don't stay up." And was gone, in the launch.

"He's worried," said Janice, "and told me not to——"

"But why on earth," asked Katie, bewildered.

"I don't know."

Richey came and she told him that Mr. Dennis would not be back for dinner; she didn't know when he'd return. Meantime could she and Miss Evans have drinks on the afterdeck?

"Would you care for dinner there as well?"

"No, we'll dine below," she said absently. "You've set the table and there's no use in making things more complicated, Richey."

Richey went below to tell his assistant, "I must say I dreaded the day the Skipper got himself hitched but . . ." All the crew, except the Captain, referred to Whit as the Skipper; and he rated it, often taking his turn at the wheel when it pleased him to do so.

Katie did most of the talking at dinner.

"Nothing can have happened to Joe," she said stoutly; "he probably left the club on some errand of his own."

"He didn't take the car."

"Well he's a big boy, he might have walked; any accident would have been reported by now," Katie said reasonably. And after dinner to which they didn't do justice, to The Chef's sorrow—he preferred to be known as The Chef—Katie suggested, "Let's go upstairs—oops I forgot where we are—let's go topside or whatever the hell you call it and wait on the afterdeck."

It was after eleven before Janice heard the launch. Katie was half asleep curled up on the big cushion-heaped structure which she persisted in calling a couch.

Janice went to the rail, and crew members materialized there for the launch. There were four men; Whit, the man at the wheel, Mortimer, and someone, unstirring.

Between them, Mortimer and Whit carried Joe Meeker, a not particularly easy task, up to where others were waiting to help and below to his stateroom. Janice followed, Katie at her heels, crying, "Was there an accident?"

"No. . . . Richey, stay here with Mr. Meeker . . . Janice, ask Cecil to lend a hand . . . Mort, go on back to the club in the launch; we'll see you in the morning; I'll phone if anything's altered. First get hold of a doctor and have him come out in the launch and wait till he does."

He glanced again at his wife, "You go to bed," he said, "and Katie too. You can't be of help here. Send Cecil," he said again. "Step on it."

"But," Janice whispered, "not an accident?"

"He's very drunk," Whit said.

Katie said, "I can help, I'm used to—at least I was—my father used to go on periodic binges."

"Thanks," said Whit, "we'll manage, but I'll yell if you're needed."

Janice had gone to fetch Cecil, explaining the emergency briefly. Cecil nodded, and went off to Joe's stateroom.

Lying alone in bed, telling herself the truth, which was that she would only be a hindrance in this situation, Janice thought: But why—what happened?

It seemed a long time before she heard the launch again, and the doctor come aboard . . . and longer before she heard him leave.

Cecil knocked and came in. She said, "He'll be all right, Mrs. Dennis. Mr. Dennis said to tell you. They won't need me any longer now; Richey will stay with him."

When Whit came in, very late, his face was drawn. He said sitting down wearily, "I've seen drunks before, but never one quite like this, even on shore leave; blind, fighting, crazy drunk. I had to knock him out so Mort and I could get him into the launch."

"Where did you find him?"

"In a dingy little bar; every bar we'd been to—well, he'd been there and just left. When we found him, he'd done considerable damage and they'd called the police. I know them; I've been coming to the club for years. I persuaded them that the damage would be paid for and that we could handle the matter of getting him back aboard. The bar owner didn't prefer charges." He put his head in his hand and said, "It was pretty damned discouraging to see him out of control after all these years. This time was worse; he hadn't had a drink since God knows when."

"Here, let me help you," Janice got on her knees and pulled off Whit's shoes; she unbuckled his belt, took off his tie. "But what brought it on?" she asked wonderingly.

"His wife. She was in a plane accident, with her husband, yesterday. They released the passenger list today. It was in the paper."

"Poor thing," said Janice. "Poor Joe."

"He'll feel like hell tomorrow and for several tomorrows; also he'll be eaten up with remorse and guilt and grief. I'm going to send you, Katie and Cecil ashore tomorrow, Mort will take you home. I'll stay here with Joe as long as necessary. The doctor will be out again in the morning. He suggested a hospital, but I said no. Joe's had his share of waking up in hospitals. If he needs a male nurse, we'll get one. You keep Mort, it will simplify things. Jenkins can come down for us when we're ready to go back."

He had risen and finished undressing; he went into the bathroom, returned and came to where she was lying and kissed her. He said, "Thanks, darling," and fell into bed.

FIFTEEN

WHIT WENT ASHORE WITH the women in the morning, to see them off, he said, also to do some telephoning—ship-to-shore is often not very private—and to give Mortimer some instructions. He kissed Janice, then Katie, saying, "It was fine to have you aboard; I'm sorry things wound up as they did." He was still anxious, Janice observed, a vertical crease between his eyebrows. She felt a pang of pure compassion, for Whit as well as for Joe, and Katie said, "Well, gosh, the poor guy!"

"He'll be all right," Whit said, and there was that stubborn look about his jaw which Janice had seen on more than one occasion. She thought: He'll be all right if Whit has to kill himself to make it so.

Cecil sat sedately in front with Mortimer. There were of course few confidences to be exchanged, since both Cecil and Mortimer were not only aware, but had been involved in, what Joe had once called his "backsliding."

Neither Katie nor Cecil knew of the plane crash; it was possible Mortimer did. Janice reflected on the closely knit pattern which was Whit, Joe, Foster, Mortimer . . . Captain Adams to a lesser degree, and heaven knew how many others. It certainly wasn't the money he paid them, it went beyond material benefits; as he'd once said, "You can't buy loyalty." She felt another twinge of emotion; it was, this time, pride.

Katie pondered aloud, "I wonder what brought that on? He seemed so relaxed and friendly on the trip. I thought, when I first met him, that he was a stuffed shirt. He isn't, or if so, I like what he's stuffed with." She wanted to ask, "Do you suppose it's woman trouble?" But did not.

Janice said truthfully, "He had a drinking problem years ago; but had been dried out for a long time, Katie."

Katie said. "My old man never dried out; he was always a little damp around the edges. And we didn't have the knowledge or the money to put him in expert hands. My mother and the rest of us just coped. He was always so sorry afterward—oh, he was hospitalized a couple of times." She shivered. "It wasn't exactly pleasant for him or us. Anyway he always got down on his knees and promised never again; he'd tell my mother 'I swear it'—but in a couple of weeks, off to the races."

"I'm sorry."

"He died of it," said Katie after a moment, "and I think, later on my mother did too—I mean, the years of strain and worry and the hanging onto hope; she was always hopeful, and the missing him. Funny how you can miss someone who's always been a millstone around your neck. She never stopped loving him." She shrugged and asked, "What are you going to do with Whit away?"

"Work. Try to get Audrey and Tom for dinner; you too, if you're free."

"You won't forget the fall showing? Raoul will fire me if you back out—not that his usual designs would turn you on," said Katie. "He's really pretty far out. But I can take my Leader by the hand and do a little guiding. After all, he'd give his eyeteeth to include you among his clientele. And they've been capped at horrendous expense."

"What has?" asked Janice, off on a journey of her own, thinking about the cruise, about Whit and Joe.

"His teeth, silly. Gosh, I didn't thank Whit nor Richey nor the Captain to say nothing of the crew. Best time I've ever had, but so bad for me."

"How come?" asked Janice, laughing. "You look like a million dollars, brown, rested, more attractive than ever."

"That's what I mean, a million dollars—which was a cliché if ever I heard one—but it's more or less what I meant. A million dollars," said Katie dreamily, "which of course is a drop in Whit's bucket. But I'd settle for it."

"You've always been conservative," Janice remarked.

"Unfortunately," said Katie, "there isn't another *Mrs. Calabash* lying around loose—not even a junior version; and there certainly isn't another Whit, not even a carbon copy." She looked at Janice a moment, and added, "As I'm sure, you agree."

"Of course."

In town, work, lunch sent in, and back to the apartment. On the second evening Audrey and Tom came to hear all about the cruise, and did, in an expurgated version. Katie couldn't come; she said she had to catch up with a couple of her more or less steady dates, otherwise she wouldn't be eating as well, "not that I need to," she told Janice over the telephone, "I've put on five pounds. This doesn't distress Raoul, since I'm not a model, but I don't want to grow out of my employee-discount wardrobe!"

Whit was away for almost a week. He telephoned every night—at first from the Club, later ship to shore, as *Mrs. Calabash* was under way again, going nowhere in particular. He did not say anything, except from the Club. From *Mrs. Calabash* he simply reported their whereabouts, and that everything was all right, "If you need anything special," he said, "call Bill Foster."

She didn't. She found that she greatly missed Whit, which both troubled and astonished her. On an impulse, toward the end of the week, she looked up the Felicity address and had Mortimer take her and Cecil there one afternoon. The shop was in an office-type building eight stories up and there was a crawling elevator. On the door of the shop the sprawling name in gold lettering. There appeared to be just one languid blonde woman back of a showcase and Janice said, "Good afternoon, are you"—she smiled—"Felicity?"

"No," said the girl, without interest.

"May I see her please?"

The blonde tapped a long blazing-red finger nail against her blazing-red mouth. She asked doubtfully, "What name, please?"

"Mrs. Whitney Dennis."

The saleswoman flashed into instant vivacity. "Well, in that case, Mrs. Dennis," she said and whisked off to what was evidently a private office. Cecil permitted herself a small smile. Janice was momentarily disappointed. She hadn't for a moment believed that this was the owner, too indifferent, too—to her mind—unattractive. She couldn't imagine Whit running around town with her. So why was she disappointed?

Felicity came quietly from the office. Née Sadie she had from somewhere . . . Berlitz? . . . acquired a slight, undefinable accent. She was a small redheaded woman, with beautiful eyes, a rather uncompromising mouth and fine skin. She wore black, despite the season, and very well, as she was beautifully put together.

"How nice," she said, holding out a ringless hand—evidently she didn't believe in wearing her own merchandise—"How nice to meet Whit's wife, Mrs. Dennis."

"I came by," said Janice "to tell you how much I'm enjoying my egg cup."

"Indeed. Do tell Whit that I'm still looking for a spoon."

"Spoon?"

"Oh, I'm desolate. It was to be a surprise, I suppose. Please don't tell him I have—how do you say it?—spilled the beans."

I bet she knew how to say it before she took over her present role, thought Janice grimly—that and a lot more. She had a wild impulse to say, "Well, not to worry, Sadie," but didn't.

She said instead, "Of course I won't."

"Ah, well," said Felicity. "It takes a time to find the special rare things."

"You design too, do you not?" Janice asked.

"But of course," said Felicity wide-eyed. "That is my real metier, the designing. May I show you some of my little trinkets?"

Janice looked as trinkets were produced and laid reverently upon velvet: necklaces, bracelets, rings, cuff links. They were lovely, Janice acknowledged. She thought: But I'm glad she didn't make my bird cage.

Slowly turning over the glitter, thoughtful, she said, "Whit has a birthday in September."

"Ah yes, I well remember," said Felicity, looking remote. "Virgo."

"I was wondering about cuff links," Janice said. "He has a good many pairs but, something unusual?"

Felicity went to a price-tagged inlaid desk in the far corner, opened a drawer and produced a book. She said, "The original birthstones have changed, or been added to —as some of the stones are not very interesting. . . . Mid-September," she went on, turning pages, "as I recall it. He once gave a small birthday party . . ." She shrugged. "However, many people prefer to have their sign in jewelry. It would take longer than setting stones and in this case"—she raised lightly penciled eyebrows—"the sign of the Virgin?" she asked. "I think not."

"What about a stone?" Janice asked, ignoring that.

"Sapphire," said Felicity, "but I daresay, he already has sapphire cuff links. They're not unusual."

Janice said, "I don't know if he has or not."

"Then do not take a chance," advised Felicity . . . "Sardonyx Carnelian—not too exciting. But some of the jewelers have also allotted to the birth month peridot."

She put the book aside, came over, pulled out a tray, and showed Janice a ring. "That's peridot," she told her.

Janice looked at the clear green, turning the ring over in her hand. "Very good quality," said Felicity with just a touch of Sadie; and went off on a short lecture tour of the crystalites and chrysoberyls.

Janice said, "I would like cuff links with this stone, but small," she said hastily, "and simple."

"Oh, quite," said Felicity, suddenly British, "I'll make you a design and mail it to you. If you approve, I'll have the links ready in plenty of time—I do many of my own settings. This will have my personal attention."

Janice said, "That will be fine," and was aware of the green eyes—not as green as peridots nor olivines nor emeralds, but nevertheless, green—taking an inventory; the pearls, the engagement ring. "Now," Felicity said carelessly, "you wish it charged to Whit's account?"

Janice suppressed a ripple of rage. She said, "No—to my own—if that's all right with you."

"Perfectly satisfactory," said Felicity. She came from behind the counter and extended her hand. "I do hope to see you again," she said kindly, "and not, of course, just on business."

That'll be the day, thought Janice, saying something pleasant in return and went with Cecil—whom Felicity had eyed thoughtfully several times—to the door and the creeping elevator. The ripple became a surge, but this time the anger was not directed at the woman she'd just left but, as was often the case, at herself. She could have gone to Yard's, Cartier's, Tiffany's—anywhere, but no, she'd had to go to this obscure little shop out of idle—was it idle?—curiosity. She had an impulse to approve the design, buy the cuff links, throw them in the East River or give them to a passer-by. But she wouldn't. She might be—indeed, she was Mrs. Whitney Dennis—but she hadn't quite lost her mind.

She wondered if, in September, Whit would be pleased, annoyed or amused at the name on the little box and told herself candidly, "If the situations were reversed, I'd be furious."

In the shop Felicity was talking to her clerk, assistant or whatever. They were alone, and she was saying, "Well, you could have knocked me over with a planter's punch."

The assistant, who was Felicity's second cousin, said, "She's really too much, Sadie."

"Someday you'll forget when customers are here," said Felicity sharply. "I've told you again and again, Nella."

"Sorry about that. Anyway she's a dream, and," said Nella, "a natural blonde too."

"If you like the type," Felicity conceded. "Anyway," she added with satisfaction, "they're not at all suited, Gemini and Virgo."

At one time she had known a male astrologer intimately.

Nella said, "Suited or not, I'd like to be married to that guy for even a few weeks. Not that I've ever seen him. He could be cross-eyed, bandy-legged and three feet high for all I care."

"He's a very charming man," Felicity said sadly.

And Nella remarked as others had before her, and would after her, that some women have all the luck.

"The stars help," said Felicity, thinking of her vanished astrologer now living it up in California—he had been good about and under the stars—"but in this case, I think not; anyway, sometimes you make your own luck."

"How did you know she was born under, what's the sign?"

"Gemini . . . Whit told me, when he bought the Russian egg cup. You weren't here when he came in."

"Well," said Nella, "it wouldn't have done me any good if I had been. You really looking for a spoon?"

"Egg spoon, gold, emeralds in handle if possible. At those prices I'd look for a slice of the moon."

"How about it!" Nella said, having reentered Felicity's life only within the last year or so. "Did you know him pretty well?" and Felicity replied in a rare moment of candor, "Not nearly as well as I'd have liked to."

Time passed slowly. It was hot outside, wiltingly so. Janice worked, and once Bill Foster came to see her at the Foundation. He had papers for her to sign. He asked, horrified, "You didn't even read them!"

"I trust you and Whit, and maybe I wouldn't understand them anyway," Janice said, smiling.

Lunch at the desk, and coffee or milk, and home to put herself in the capable hands waiting to serve her. She looked at television—not having asked anyone to dine since Audrey and Tom; she talked to Edna Norton and to her parents by telephone. She read a book; there were always books around, the latest. Whit probably had a standing order at Brentano's, but when did he read novels?

Then, he called from the yacht club, and came home in time for dinner.

When the bells chimed and Smith opened the door with, she thought, undue ceremony and Whit came in, she saw instantly that he looked tired but less anxious. She said, as he put his arms around her in a crushing careless bear hug, "I'm glad to see you."

"Good." He asked as he'd done before, walking into the wide hall with an arm about her, "Did you miss me dreadfully?"

She was almost tricked into saying yes. She thought: Oh, no, you don't. It's against the rules, and said instead, as before, "No . . . not dreadfully, but I missed you."

"Fair enough."

"How are things?"

"Tell you all about it later," he said and followed Smith and the luggage upstairs.

At dinner he told her where they'd been on the short trip, making no comment except, "Restful," and asked what she'd been doing.

"I tell you every night; work——"

"And you saw Bill and signed the papers?"

"I told you that too. By the way, what was in them?"

"I'll never make a businesswoman of you. It was a confession, in triplicate."

"Of what?" she asked, startled and a little apprehensive.

"Never mind. Or perhaps a consent."

"To what?" She was relieved. He was, as usual, putting her on. When would she ever learn?

"Top secret," he said gravely. "Wait and see. No one's been here, have they?"

"Just Audrey and Tom. Oh, your mother called here this afternoon. Smith told me. Wants you to call her——"

"Did she ask for you?"

"She did," said Janice.

"Fine, you'll make the grade yet. She generally calls Joe or Bill. Sure you've told me everything?"

"I did go on a slight shopping spree."

"For what?"

"Top secret," said Janice.

"Cecil go along, I hope."

"She did, and if you ask her, I'll kill you."

"I won't ask her. I've already told you you're entitled to some privacy."

After dinner, she said, when Smith had left them, "Now, tell me about Joe."

"He was pretty shook up as you can imagine—no, I guess you can't. But I think he'll be all right. It was sort of a lunatic kind of release, I think, grief and guilt, all mixed up. Our little boat ride did him good. He didn't talk much—Richey gradually coaxed him back to eating—and I slept in the stateroom next to his, door open, also eyes and ears." He yawned, "I didn't get much sleep. Cruising around, he soaked up wind and sun, and there were long periods of silence. It hurts like hell to fail yourself and your friends," said Whit, "and to be so ashamed. I've persuaded him to take time off and go into the country by himself, except for Jenkins who will look after him."

"When's he going?"

"Perhaps the day after tomorrow. He wants to see you first."

"Me? Why?"

"He likes you, Janice, and he feels he owes you an apology."

"But he doesn't."

"Maybe he thinks so, or maybe he just wants to talk to you."

"Why me? Why not you?"

"I don't know. All he said was, 'I have to talk to Janice. Do you mind?' I said I didn't. Anyway he'll join us—I hope—in North Carolina, later."

"Are we going to North Carolina?"

"Yes m'am, as they say down there. I have to see people, relative to the Foundation work, in Tennessee and other places. Thought you'd like to go along. We'll take Cecil and establish her at the Lodge with the current Smiths. Actually the man Thad is by way of being kin to Martha's invaluable Jasper, and his Mary is kissing kin also. I thought you might want to see how the offices thereabouts are run. This has to do with clinics mainly, child care, and nutrition."

"I'd like it very much."

"All settled then."

They went upstairs, and she said, "Tonight you'll get a good sleep. Want to take anything?"

"Nothing in tablet or capsule form anyway," he told her, laughing, "and I don't need a great deal of sleep."

Joe called her next day at the Foundation. Would she see him that afternoon, and at what time?

She said, "Of course. Do come for dinner, Joe."

He said, "I'm going away for a little while. . . . New Hampshire. Didn't Whit tell you?"

"Yes, but you have to eat."

He said simply, "I only want to talk to you, Janice."

She was home by a little after four, and he came before the half hour. She offered him tea, but he shook his head, and she suggested, "Suppose we go up to my sitting room, and you can say hello to Herman. She's hardly spoken to me since I came home."

It was quiet there, cool, and more intimate. Herman greeted their guest with enthusiasm and romped about until Janice rang. Cecil appeared and Janice said, "Would someone have time to take Herman out for a little while?"

Cecil reflected that the Smiths and the maids were in the house, and also Mr. Meeker, who was like one of the family. She had greeted him with her usual impersonal courtesy, but he had said instantly, "I didn't have a chance to thank you, Mrs. Cecil, but I do now," and Cecil said, "It was nothing, Mr. Meeker."

"There goes a treasure," Joe told Janice as Cecil went out with Herman on the leash. Herman was looking two ways at once, forward, as she was going for a stroll, and backward as Janice wasn't. She had decided to forgive Janice for having been away, and for returning minus Herman's special deity. Herman had been as upset as if Janice had buried Whit like a bone; but he'd come home, last night.

When the door was closed, Joe said, "I told Whit I owe you an apology; but an apology isn't adequate."

She was embarrassed and distressed for him. She said, "Joe, please don't humiliate yourself. Whit's your best friend, and I believe you and I are friends too. I certainly hope so. Suppose we forget it?"

"I won't," he told her, a white line around his mouth. "If that ever happens again . . ." He stopped, brooding, his clear but haunted eyes on Janice; and Janice said, "I'm sure it won't, Joe."

"That's what I thought a long time ago. Alcohol's a sneaky enemy. You think you have it licked and then—well—there it is, snipe-shooting from ambush. Did Whit tell you why I went off my rocker?"

"Yes. I hope you don't think him disloyal?"

"Whit disloyal? Never in a thousand years. You had a right to know why . . . perhaps you'll understand as much as anyone can. Whit does, with his mind and reasoning powers, but this isn't something you can reason about."

She said, trying to lighten the heavy atmosphere, "Women don't—or can't—reason."

"Some think with their hearts."

He couldn't be more right about me, she thought, and

it flashed through her mind: How much does Joe know about Dave and me? She remembered Whit telling her on the beach at Montego Bay when he'd given her a thumbnail sketch of her relationship with Dave that he had his sources. . . . What better, discreet investigator than Joe Meeker? No, she thought, not Joe; someone else, someone who was a really hired hand.

Joe walked across the room and stood by the windows with his back to her. He said, "I want you to understand that I wished her dead. My God, how I wished her dead. I'm not a religious man, but I knew enough not to pray for her death. I don't suppose such prayers are answered. Whit's a religious man," he said suddenly.

"Whit!"

"Oh, sure . . . not much of a churchgoer, but—well —I guess you can call him a believer; he believes in people and in himself; I think maybe in order to believe in people and yourself, you have to believe in God."

He swung around and faced her and she cried involuntarily, "Joe, don't torment yourself."

"I won't tell you I thought I was over her; I knew I wasn't and I wished her dead. So then she was dead, and," he said in anguish, "I wasn't there to help, even a little"—his voice broke—"to see her through. So I failed myself and Whit."

"Only yourself," she said steadily.

He said humbly, "I'll try never to fail again."

When he left, she went downstairs with him and said at the door, "We'll expect to see you in North Carolina; we'll count on it."

He took her hand and held it hard. He said, "I'll be there come hell or high water. Whit thinks I need a little time away, and by myself. Maybe he's right."

She noticed that Smith had remained in the background; the people who looked after Whit knew when to appear and when to disappear. Now he came to open the door and Joe said, "See you, Janice—and give my best to Katie, will you? Sometime I'll thank her myself. I didn't know that she was there or Cecil for that matter until after you'd gone back to town."

Going upstairs again, Janice had the curious feeling that Whit hadn't known that Joe had wished his wife dead. And she thought: Perhaps he thinks he killed her, just by wishing. But he's too sane for that; it was all a long time ago.

When Whit came home, he asked, "Joe turn up?"

"Yes. I'm sorry he thought he had to."

"He respects you, Janice."

After a while she said, pouring his second demitasse, "You were right of course, as you know. He was still in love with her; but I think he hated her too, just the same. The love-hate relationship isn't uncommon."

"I know, but I couldn't hate anyone," said Whit promptly.

"I'm not so sure. What makes you think so?"

"It's a waste of energy; besides, I never get that involved."

She thought: I wonder if I could hate as well as love him and was instantly scarlet. And Whit said lazily, "Your skin is giving you away again. What were you thinking?"

She was thinking—no, she was experiencing—something that she hadn't admitted to herself before. She was dizzy with it; and also frightened.

She said, "I was wondering if I could ever hate you."

"It's a big word and used, as it—its opposite—too often and too lightly. . . . Well, did you come to any conclusion?"

"Yes."

"Yes, you could?"

"Yes, I came to a conclusion. I couldn't, of course."

"Why not? A volatile little character like you?"

"Oh," she said, smiling, "I like you too much; for as I've told you before, you're a very nice person."

"Good, you take a load off my mind. . . . There's a program I'd like to catch on channel 13. Care to join me, Mrs. D?"

SIXTEEN

❀❀❀

LONG AFTER he was asleep Janice lay quietly in the darkness. Why had this happened and when? Tomorrow—or so he had informed after they'd watched television—they were going to Dunewalk. "Just you, me and Herman," he said. "We'll get an early start and be there for lunch; we'll come back in time for the office Monday morning. Unless, of course, you were planning a trip around the world."

She thought: I'll have to be careful at Dunewalk . . . Dunewalk had a special meaning for her . . . the big ungainly, undistinguished, elderly house by the ocean. It was a house without pretensions. Over the years it had absorbed the searching winds, the beneficent sun, the stinging therapeutic salt, the patterned stars, the limitless sea and sky. Even with the shutters closed, blinds drawn and doors locked, Dunewalk would be a house open to elemental things . . . and if you were at all sensitive to these, the basics, it would make an honest woman of you.

She knew very little of the people who had lived there; the ones no longer terrestrial were rumors and hearsay; those she did know revealed little of themselves. Martha, her son had said, had been happy at Dunewalk. Hilda and Heloise created their own contentment wherever they were. And Lily, or so it seemed to Janice, was singularly unaffected by the world around her. Whit had said Dunewalk bored Lily; boredom is a heavy but tepid state of mind. As for Ned Turner, amiable man, he had his own world—the children, art, books and various excursions into other matters such as archeology, music, philosophy; to him Dunewalk was probably only a pleasant and peaceful place.

Whit loved it.

I love it too, thought Janice.

They drove down next morning with Herman, already sensing sand between her paws, and arrived in time for lobster salad, greens from the nearby farm, berries and cream and quantities of iced, strong coffee. Whit said when she proposed a beach walk that she and Herman could suit themselves; he wasn't stirring, but would keep an eye on them. So Herman and Janice went walking within sight of the house. Herman had an ecstatic time and Janice, wretched. The salt stung, the sand clogged her feet, the blue sky and the sun's radiance darkened.

She asked herself: How could I be so stupid?

She'd been exposed to Whitney Dennis for half a year before she'd married him, on the terms of a bargain as firm and unemotional as a handshake. She had kept the seemingly easy commandments, affection, honesty—up until now, honesty—and responsive sex.

"When did it begin?" she asked herself, walking along the beach, her hair free and her heart in bondage, and shied away from questions as Herman shied at a dead fish, and then went to investigate . . . Janice looked up, ran and rescued. Herman was crushed. That lovely smell . . . she'd been about to roll in it.

No. Janice didn't want to know when it had happened, or perhaps it would be closer to the truth to say, when it had begun to happen, without her awareness.

Nearing the house, she saw Whit uncoiling from a long chair and coming down the steps to meet them. Herman cut a caper and Whit took Janice's hand and swung it, as he often did.

"Nice contemplation of the infinite?" he inquired. "I could see you, head bent, stalking along, wholly preoccupied."

"Just with the beach," she said, smiling.

Little mermaid, walk on knives.

"Bored?"

"Of course not."

Somehow the time passed, the time which might have been a *déjà-vu* of Eden, and which should have gone with the speed of light, but instead, stuttered along, dragging its heel.

Early Monday morning, to Rhoda's and Eric's regret and Herman's dismay, they left for town. "When will you be back, Whit?" asked Rhoda and he told her, "Not for a while. There's no season which isn't good . . . September, October, Rhoda."

They were heading, it seemed, for the apartment rather than the office. He'd had a telephone call just before they left, and took it downstairs while Janice throwing her few things in a bag had been in their bedroom, remembering the two nights she'd been there.

"Is anything the matter, Janice?" he'd asked.

"No, nothing."

"You're tense," he'd said, smoothing her hair. "You just don't want to let go. Is it anything I've said or done?"

"No, Whit—I'm fine."

He said, "And you haven't been sleeping . . . last night I woke and there you were owl-eyed."

"I didn't mean to disturb you."

"You didn't. You didn't move or speak; you breathed evenly, trying to pretend sleep. Why?"

She had fallen back on the old excuse, he must forgive her, perhaps she was a little nervous.

"You'll sleep at the Lodge," he said.

She doubted it.

Most women can simulate ardor, it is a special talent; to dissemble is more difficult.

He explained as they neared the apartment, "It's just something I have to see to; we can go along to the office later, after lunch, that is if you feel up to it."

"I feel wonderful," she said, and did not avoid his direct almost impaling regard.

She went on upstairs when they reached home; she was bone-tired; she ached as if she carried a burden. She had a desire to lie down on her bed and stay there for a long time. She looked about the room and was suddenly homesick for her own bits and pieces of furniture, bought at auctions, in little dusty shops, or shipped from her parents' house. She'd given away everything she'd owned in her original apartment and the one she'd shared with Katie and Audrey—a desk and a blanket chest to Audrey and Tom, the rest to Katie. That had been furniture you could throw yourself on, or at—the bed, the couch, the two big chairs—and cry until you drowned; but not here, not with Dennis furniture looming correct, beautiful and impersonal all around her.

She went downstairs and into the library; she would tell Whit that he was right, she didn't feel well; she wouldn't go to the office.

He was standing by the great desk, with a letter in his hand. Cecil was here too, and he was saying something to her.

He stopped when Janice erupted into the room and nodded at Cecil who melted away. But Janice had seen the envelope. She said, astonished, "But that's a letter for me!"

Whit sat down. Cecil had closed the door. They looked at each other and he turned the envelope in his hand, "Yes, it's for you," he agreed.

Anger is a release also.

"What right have you to open it? You and Cecil standing there, a couple of conspirators," she said furiously.

Standing by the desk, leaning forward, she could see the illiterate penciled writing: "Mrs. Whitney Dennis."

"Give it to me."

He said, "I'd rather you didn't read it, Janice. It's a filthy letter."

"Give it to me. I'm not a child!"

He gave it to her, she took the single sheet of paper from the envelope, and read the first lines. She crumpled it in her hand, and sat down blindly in the nearest chair. She felt very sick.

Whit leaned forward and took it from her; he tore it up, put the bits of paper in an enormous ashtray and held the flame of his lighter to them.

He said, "There's no way to trace anything like this, you know."

"I suppose not," she said.

"It came by special delivery yesterday afternoon. Cecil was out. It was late evening when she opened it, so she called me this morning."

"Cecil opened it!"

He said gently, "Janice, she screens your mail; she has to; it's one of her jobs."

Now she remembered that Cecil always brought her her mail or gave it to Smith or it was left on the hall table. She swallowed hard.

"How does she know what to open?"

"Postmarks sometimes, or handwriting; she also knows

what not to open. There are a great many sick minds in this world, Janice; also greedy people."

"This isn't the first time, Whit?"

"No. It is, I think, the third. But not from the same person."

"You said greedy people—what did you mean?"

"Begging letters. I get a great many at home, or they go through the Corporation mailroom, or the Foundation's. All are read. Bill Foster reads those that may have been written out of honest desperation. He has those people investigated. One in a thousand rates help. You get such letters too. Cecil gives them to me, I give them to Bill."

She said blankly, "It's so hard to believe."

"It happens, all the time. Obscene letters, begging letters, threatening letters. You haven't been Mrs. D. very long, but you've had your share."

Guards, strong-armed men, Cecil, the watchful eyes. . . .

She said after a while, "I'm sorry, Whit. But you should have told me in the beginning."

"I would rather have kept it from you. I know all this protective custody bit irritates you, but I didn't want you frightened. I knew you could be, ever since the purse-snatcher episode."

Janice drew a long breath. She said, "All right. I won't make things any harder for you."

They had lunch, and she decided to go to the office, after all. Maybe she could forget the few penciled words she'd read.

She thought she knew all the words. Heaven knew they were in many books published today. But a book is very different; you can pick up a book, and put it down; you can throw it in the garbage; a book is not addressed to you. It isn't personal.

He said, in the car—Mortimer was driving—"I had hoped very much not to upset you."

She answered, because she knew by now that Mortimer was privy to the family problems. "Do you have many threatening letters? Do I?"

He touched her shoulder in reassurance and the casual comforting gesture hurt her as if it had been a blow. "You haven't had, as yet. My grandmother, mother, the aunts and Lily have had their share. You will, in time."

"But why?"

"Oh," he said lightly, "you have the misfortune to be married to me."

Fear was a cold tide washing over her, but not for herself.

"But why?" she asked, "for heaven's sake why?"

He said, "There are many disaffected people; people who believe that money is the root of all evil, and some of them are passionately honest in their belief; others believe it because they have no money or very little themselves. There are also people, sincere and dedicated, who do not like the way the Corporation makes money or the way the Foundation spends it. Everyone has his own idea about spending, you know. Those who attack the Foundation openly, those who write to me—and most of these sign their names—have causes of their own which they consider more worthy. Some do not like a race or a religion—it's as simple as that—which makes it complicated for us. I could do without it; I don't like complications."

She thought, with a twinge of wry humor: And now you have one you're not aware of on your hands.

"You said threatening letters," she reminded him.

"So I did. They're not written because of the Foundation except in the rare case of a fanatic of one kind or another. They come addressed to me at home or at the Corporation. Sometimes they can be traced—but most of these pen pals are anonymous, and the police department is always cooperative. But we avoid publicity if we can." He added casually, "Don't we, Mort?"

She could see Mortimer's face in the mirror; it was grim, but there was a certain spark in his eyes, as if he enjoyed being in battle.

"That's right," said Mortimer.

Whit said, "You'll find guards, dogs and various electronic devices around the Lodge; they are meant to reassure, not terrify, anyone who's living there. Disaffected people are there also, Janice—a very small minority; they don't like what the Foundation's doing in their bailiwick."

"I give up," said Janice.

"Scared?"

"No," and thought: Except for you.

That evening after dinner, he said, when they were alone. "I should have told you during my lecture earlier that there are also blackmailing letters."

"Blackmail?" Janice repeated as if she'd never heard the word.

"You are becoming a parrot, a very pretty one I may add. Yes, blackmail."

"From whom?"

"In my salad days," he said, "some used to be from irate parents, accusing me of having seduced their innocent daughters. Maybe fifty or a hundred thousand dollars would do as reward to restoring the unrestorable."

She said, horrified, "But that's crazy."

"Thanks for the vote of confidence. There have been times when I've been seen in public but never with untouched innocence unless chaperoned." He laughed. "But there were often spectators; let's say, some of the furious fathers were innocent themselves, when their daughters would come home at dawn and say guess who I was out with last night. And while we're on this unsavory subject you had a blackmailing missive a while ago."

"Now you are putting me on again."

"No."

"But who in the world——"

"A little waiter. He works at The Special Spot where you and Dave had lunch. He was very glad to see you again; he'd waited on you before and he hadn't forgotten you or Dave. He saw your picture, when we were married . . . and when you came back to him, with Dave, he was of course overjoyed."

She was turning scarlet and he watched her with amusement and also compassion. "But what did you do?" she asked.

"Oh, he was found and severely spoken to—all he needed was a warning. He has a police record in another state. So, the next time Dave wants to see you minus the Little Woman, have him come here to the apartment."

"He won't want to see me, Whit."

"I doubt that. Anyway, if he does, and you consent, have him here. Smith will double as male duenna, equipped with tea, drinks, or what have you."

"I don't intend to see him, Whit, so you needn't issue orders. I take it that was an order?"

"Why, yes," he said easily.

Quick anger struggled with slower curiosity and as usual curiosity was victor. She asked exasperated, "What in heaven's name makes you think he'll try to see me again? Are you psychic or something?"

"Occasionally, but not in this instance. One, you are spectacularly seeable, and two, he's in New York."

"At this time of year—and how do you know?"

"Your father phoned me, Luv—on quite a different matter."

"Oh, that? The new client, who's loaded, who wanted to charter *Mrs. Calabash?* To which you said no, but made suggestions about other boats. I was here when he called and later talked to him."

"Correct, but he also added, before you came on the wire, that Dave was leaving for New York—on business. This reached your father via the grapevine."

"Well, he won't bother me," said Janice loftily.

On the following day they went to the office together, and on the way, she said, "I forgot to tell you, I'm lunching with Uncle Howard."

"All your old loves," he said, "first Dave then the boss."

"Oh, keep quiet," she said crossly, "I haven't seen Uncle Howard since they came to dinner."

"They've been away."

"I thought lunch would be pleasant—like the old days."

"Did he often take you to lunch?"

"As a matter of fact not after I started working for him. Out of the office I saw him and Aunt Edna at their house; sometimes they came to my apartment."

"Have fun," said Whit. "Give the old this and that my love. We'll certainly see them when we get back from North Carolina."

Mortimer took her to meet Howard Norton at one of his stately clubs; all dark furniture, high ceilings, gloomy paintings, soft-footed, antique service and good food. He was there waiting for her and when she was ushered in, with great ceremony, he rose and kissed her heartily. "I'm so glad to see you," he said. "How's Whit?"

"He's fine. I'm glad to see you too. I wanted to, which is why I phoned. Whit sends love and everything to you and Aunt Edna."

"You," said Howard Norton as they were escorted with solemnity to a corner table, "are looking very attractive but not, I think, blooming. Why?"

"Oh working at the Foundation, rushing around—you knew we'd be on a cruise?"

"Yes. But that should have been restful."

"Most of it was and we're just back from Dunewalk."

"Edna and I were there with Whit, some years ago; it's a very restorative place. I hope you like this table. I bring unhappy clients here, as it's practically private. One reason I like this tomb is because no one table is very close to another."

She said, "I'm not an unhappy client."

"No, just unhappy. You've forgotten I've known you a long time. What's bothering you? Is it Dave Peters?"

"No, it isn't. What gave you that idea?"

"He's in town."

"So Whit informed me; my father told him. What is this, a sort of espionage cell or something?"

He said smiling, "He's here on business, and this morning, half an hour ago, right here, I met the man he came to town to see. He was having a drink; he's gone now. Suppose you tell me about your work at the Foundation? I'll see Whit at the Board meeting, come autumn, and he'll tell me. But you first."

"I didn't come to talk about the Foundation."

"I know. But let's get some cold soup and a little food into you, and hot coffee. You look undernourished."

Later, over the coffee, he said, "All right, speak your piece."

"Remember," she asked slowly, "I told you the terms under which Whit and I were married?"

"I do—who could forget such lunacy?"

"I did," she said miserably.

"What exactly are you trying to tell me?"

"Just what I told you before we were married. Whit wanted the kind of wife I promised I'd be; intelligent—and that's pretty funny—responsive, capable of, and willing to bear children; affectionate, but not in love with him."

"I remember that too."

"So," she said, looking at him from her dark eyes, "I've failed him."

He said, "You weren't in love with him when you were married, but you are now, is that it?"

Janice nodded.

"I don't find that a cause for quiet desperation but rather for rejoicing."

"You don't understand. This is something I'll have to keep from him the rest of my life." She dropped her spoon on the saucer and thereby created an unseemly clatter in the quiet room where everyone seemed to speak in hushed whispers. "If you are thinking of breaking it to him gently," she said, "I'll never speak to you again."

"I wasn't. This is your problem. It isn't for a lawyer to solve unless you're thinking of leaving him."

"How can I? That was part of the bargain too . . . the 'til death do us part.' Oh, I knew you couldn't help me, but I had to talk to someone . . . not to anyone; just you."

He put his big hand over hers. He said, "I've heard a lot of strange marital complaints in my practice of the law but none stranger than this; and there's nothing in the books which covers it."

"I don't even know when it began," she said, keeping her voice down to an angry whisper. "Or maybe I do; I don't know. I don't want to examine it further."

"What are you going to do, Janice?"

"I'm going to be Mrs. Whitney Dennis," she said. "A

good, overprotected wife; a charming hostess; interested in her husband's business, his thinking, even in his family; and I'll have a family of my own. If I'm jealous, he'll never know it. I'll go to my grave without scenes or embarrassing displays of emotion—except, now and then I do lose my temper."

"You've always lost your temper, now and then."

"Vanessa's hair was red," said Janice.

"Have you lost your mind? Who's Vanessa? Has Whit——?"

"Oh, a—just my grandmother," said Janice, "and no, Whit hasn't. Not yet, anyway. And if he does—he wouldn't release me; that till death do us part is a one-way street; we both walk on it."

A little later, he took her to the waiting car.

"I'm sorry not to be able to help you," he said. "If you were my own child, I couldn't love you more."

"I know. You have helped. Just admitting it aloud helped. How could I be such a . . . ?" She shrugged. "Well, there it is," she said. "Thank you, Uncle Howard. As you said, it's my problem."

He watched Mortimer drive away and thought: Here's something I can't even tell Edna, and informed himself, not for the first time, that he would never understand Whitney Dennis.

SEVENTEEN

JANICE WENT BACK TO the office. She had succeeded in convincing Public Relations that a few minor changes in the brochure annually sent to board members and other interested individuals as well as the communications media, would infuse its conservative dullness with the hint of a spark. It gave her a sense of accomplishment. Whit had approved her suggestions when she discussed them with him, "Except for its now updated concern for what we're doing," he'd said, "the Foundation is still in the good old days."

She returned home at her usual time. The sidewalks were considering melting and she was glad to achieve the cool, even temperature of the apartment. She wondered if she'd ever use her gold key, as Smith always materialized before she could take it from her purse. There was mail on the hall table. She picked it up, aware that it must be harmless, and looked through it. An invitation to a cocktail party from people she knew slightly, and Whit not at all; a letter from her mother, another from a school friend. Remarkable how school friends suddenly remembered you were alive.

She was thinking: I'll answer these, when Smith said, "Mr. Peters telephoned half an hour ago. I told him when you'd be expected home and he said he'd call then, Mrs. Dennis."

Oh, damn Whit and his ESP! she thought wearily. Or was it merely the reasoning powers to which Joe had referred? She thought: I can tell Smith to say I'm still out and won't be back until late. Instead, she said, "If he calls, Smith, I'll take it upstairs."

"Very well, Mrs. Dennis."

One, among many virtues exhibited by the entourages attached to the Dennis families—well, she wasn't sure about Lily's—was their avoidance of the third person. Sometimes Cecil, whom Janice herself had instructed, slipped, but always corrected herself at once.

She had spoken to Cecil, she had commandeered Vera or Hattie to take Herman out and was writing her mother when the telephone rang. She thought: Here we go again, and found she did not really mind. She was in much better position than once she had been.

Dave said, "I have to see you. It's vital, Jan."

What could be vital? . . Madge is dying or I'm too wretched to go on; forget Madge and the children, fly with me to South America? She found herself suppressing laughter. Such absurdities were not in Dave's character or the cards.

"I hardly think that anything you could have to tell me would be so important," she said.

"It is, I swear it." She thought: In another moment he'll say, "It's a matter of life or death" and I shall burst into howls of merriment. "When can you meet me and where?"

"I can't," said Janice coolly, "but if it means so much to you, come here, as soon as you can."

"There?"

"That's what I said. I'm alone," she hastened to assure him, "except for the staff. Whit won't get home until after six, but when he does, he'll be delighted to see you."

There was a slight pause. Then Dave said, "I'll grab a taxi and be right up."

Going downstairs again, she told Smith, "Mr. Peters is stopping by. I think he might like a drink. I'll have tea."

Smith said solemnly, "There's nothing like hot tea on a warm day, Mrs. Dennis."

In this house you wouldn't believe it's a warm day. "Iced, please Smith."

She went into one of the two powder rooms downstairs and regarded herself. She could do with a brush of powder, a little lipstick and a smoothing of her hair. She had not changed, she did not intend to—the cool, simple dress and jacket were right for the Foundation. She'd discarded the jacket, when she went upstairs, but the dress had sleeves.

Evidently Dave had been fortunate in cab grabbing. Smith admitted him shortly and Janice waited serenely in the big room. She said cordially, "This is a surprise. Come in and relax; you look hot and bothered, to coin a phrase."

"I am," Dave admitted. "You, on the contrary, look cool and unruffled." He regarded her with a shadow of the old intimacy.

"Thank you, even if I doubt it. I've been working all morning. Do tell Smith what you'd like to drink. I'm having iced tea."

Dave preferred vodka and tonic.

"And how are Madge and the children?" Janice asked brightly.

He told her, accepting the fact that Smith would at any moment return bearing a tray. Madge and the kids were at the lake; the heat was unbearable otherwise; unseasonable, really. "How come that you're still here, Jan?"

"We aren't always, we've been off sailing," she said,

trying to give it a modest thirty-foot-cruiser sound, "in the Hamptons and are going soon to North Carolina."

The drinks arrived. Smith retired. Dave took a long swallow of his. Smith had closed the door. And Janice continued doggedly with another social gambit.

"What brings you here, in this weather, and so soon again?" she inquired. The ice tinkled in her glass and the mint smelled delicious.

He said, "I'm in a jam."

"Oh?" Madge had left him, she thought, unmoved. One of his extra-marital indiscretions had caught up with him and his slip slowed.

"I'm sorry," she said sincerely. She thought: I suppose I'll have to be sorry if, and when, he's in trouble. It's a sort of unimportant hangover, but there just the same. She'd worried about him, whether he'd really been hurt or just knocked out on the football field. Or what had possessed him to drink so much, out with his particular male gang and would his father find out? Or would he pass his examinations? Would he get a good job? And then after his marriage, despite her despair and humiliation, was he happy? After that, the anxieties multiplied. Worrying about an individual who was for a long time the center of your life becomes a habit even when he's no longer of importance; and he wasn't now. She supposed that Joe had felt that way—not that she'd ever wished Davidson Peters dead—or maybe, at the time he married, she had.

"What kind of a jam?"

"Financial."

"Financial?" she repeated and thought: I'm really a parrot. But what else can you say. "Really?" Or "How frightful." But the pieces fell into place or at least one of them; her father, Whit, Howard Norton, all had said Dave was in town, on business.

"It's hard to explain," he said slowly.

"Well, try."

Condensed it amounted to this: the small industry in which he had begun as a minor executive was in trouble, competition, a lessening demand for the product, and it didn't have the capital to modernize the plant and the product.

"But I thought that Madge's father——" she began, genuinely bewildered.

"The hell with Madge's father. . . . Oh sure, he was interested because he owned stock; he put money into the company before old man Wilson died—he was a cousin, you know. It's a privately owned concern and Madge's father, as the president of the bank, could get the company loans when needed. But he sold out when he saw how things were going. He lost money, but found a patsy. Other people sold out too before there was no market."

"But the bank?"

"The bank of which my father-in-law is still president does not consider us a good risk."

Janice leaned forward. She said, "Dave, you're young, experienced and clever. There must be a dozen better jobs."

"Several dozen, but everything I have is tied up in the company—all I inherited from my father and also at the time we were married I persuaded Madge to put the money her parents gave her as a wedding present into the business. They thought, at the time, that was fine. I'm executive vice president now, but Wilson's successor is a washout, goes around wringing his hands. I want to put our house on the market. I've told Madge the kids must go to public school after nursery, kindergarten. She had hysterics. She said we wouldn't be in this position if I'd saved money instead of throwing it around—I'd just said we should resign from the country club—and keeping other women. I threw it around all right," he added, "on her safaris to Palm Springs and other places; clothes, jewelry, furs, and the clubs, but I've never kept a woman nor have I had to."

Which was undoubtedly the truth, Janice reflected.

He went on, "I came to New York to see a man who is principal owner of the Harris outfit. You wouldn't remember it; anyway he bought it a couple of years ago. He has other interests here in the East. He came out shortly after his deal went through, I met him and went through the usual motions, entertaining and all that bit. He was out again recently, and I approached him about a merger. That would have saved us; oh, he'd have had all the say of course, but he can afford the modernizations, and I wouldn't have to——" He broke off and after a moment said heavily, "Well, he had thought it over. I've seen him and his answer is no."

"I'm so sorry," said Janice again, inadequately.

Dave had pride—maybe it was vanity; he'd always had it; it had been well nourished in high school and at the university. Born to succeed, the high-school annual had said. It had been fed by admiring young males and of course females; herself included and then by Madge. Vanity or pride, it hurts when you find yourself looking at an empty plate.

He said, "You could help me?"

Completely astonished she asked, "How? In what way?"

"There's Whit," he reminded her, and her spirit shriveled. "The Corporation . . . oh I don't mean that the Corporation would consider coming to the rescue of a two-bit outfit, but he has influence—banks, his own money, tons of it. I thought if you'd put in a word for me, and, after that, if I could talk to him?"

She said quietly, "I won't consider it, Dave."

"Okay, okay." His face was a little ugly with disappointment. After a moment he said, "Well there's one more forlorn hope. You, yourself. You have money of your own, haven't you? I heard he'd made a hell of a big settlement on you."

"Where did you hear that?" she asked stonily.

"Oh, around." She thought: He's asked and pried and —well—I suppose everyone would consider it routine.

Aloud, she said quietly, "That's right, Dave."

He asked, with strained eagerness. "Do you have to account for it?"

"No, except to the Income Tax Bureau."

"Then, can't you make a legitimate investment? The tax bureau wouldn't be interested except so far as it affects them."

Janice got to her feet. She said, "No, I can't. It's Whit's money." She tugged at a petit-point bell pull and Dave, also on his feet, his hands in his empty pockets, looking at her with something close to hatred, said, "After all we've——"

Smith was there. "You rang, Mrs. Dennis?" and Janice said, "Yes, Smith, Mr. Peters has to leave."

You don't make scenes; you shake hands; you say, "How nice of you to come; give my love to Madge and the children," and you don't mean a word of it.

Dave said something, anything. The door closed behind him and Janice went upstairs and summoned Cecil. She said, "My head aches, Cecil."

"Aspirin, Mrs. Dennis?"

"No. I'll just take a warm bath and lie down."

Cecil ministered: massage, bath, the cool bed in a darkened room. But Janice didn't sleep. She lay still, in humiliation.

If Dave had felt humiliation . . . he hadn't shown it until those last moments. He'd also started to crash into a cliché: "After all we've meant to each other."

Just what had they meant to each other?

Springtime, love time, dreams—on her part anyway—and, of course sex, a fragile blossoming. She had one thing to be grateful for—Dave not inexperienced, had not taken her, nor himself, into the hothouse where the blossom is forced. Not until later, and what had it meant? Recklessness, quarrels, unhappiness, jealousy, anger and adult sex?

Someday she would be able to mourn the girl, and the woman she had been; someday she would be able to mourn Davidson Peters without pain, without anger or shame . . . but, not yet.

Whit came in just as Cecil had completed the hair brushing. "Rapunzel," said Whit, admiring the shining silver gilt fall. "If you ever cut it, I'll divorce you."

"You can't," she said promptly, forgetting Cecil and he agreed. "That's right. . . . You're late."

"I know, I'm sorry. I had a caller, Dave Peters."

"So?" he raised an eyebrow. "It figures," he said and went out saying, "I'll brief the Smiths to hold back dinner." He regarded her from the doorway. "You look as if you could use a moderate drink," he suggested, "or have you had one?"

"Just iced tea. I'll be down presently."

They would be alone as they often were. She came downstairs in dinner pajamas. "Very fetching," said Whit, "although as a rule, as an old-fashioned guy, I don't like pants suits or pajamas . . . but you can wear 'em. Don't, however, order all Raoul's stock."

"I won't."

They had their drinks, and he said, "Care to tell me about Dave?"

"Of course, but later."

She thought: Let me enjoy this, the beautiful room, the quiet, and you, sitting opposite me.

"Permission granted," he said graciously. "We have all the time in the world," and smiled at her, twisting her heart, but the tight, shrinking, shriveling feeling was gone.

Later always comes. After dinner he talked about their plans for North Carolina and it wasn't until Cecil had left and he'd come into Janice's bedroom and cast himself on the chaise that she told him, turning from the dressing table. He had just remarked, "I'm always smitten with gratitude and delight that you don't go to bed with a lot of junk on your face."

"Now how would you know that some women do?"

He said, shrugging, "Peeping Tom. . . . But what about Dave? Why did he come—except of course from a desire to see you?"

"For money."

"I can't say I'm exactly astonished," he admitted after a moment, "but whose money—mine, yours?"

"Yours first and when I told him I wouldn't approach you on the subject, mine."

"It's all yours," he reminded her, "to do with as you wish. If you want to dangle a rope down the well——"

"I don't. Besides, I told him that I've always considered that it's yours really and not mine."

Whit said sharply, "Forget it. If you want to endow a home for frustrated cats, or set Herman up in her own establishment, with a housemother, a chef, and patio—giving me visiting privileges of course——"

"Please be serious, Whit."

"Never more so than when I appear not to be, or," he went on, "finance a Guru—without undue publicity—a beauty salon, a dress boutique, soda fountain or an antique shop, go ahead. Or if you wish to invest in an old friend by all means, send out the lifeboat—into the sea of bankruptcy—you have my blessing."

He was serious. She said, unsmiling, "Thank you Whit. No, I don't wish to make any investments."

"Of which our brokers might not approve? Look here, Janice, what I'm trying to say is the money's yours; you must do what you want with it; you account to no one but the Treasury department."

"I told Dave that."

"You did? How did he take it?"

"Badly."

"You're sorry for him, aren't you?"

"In a way. I suppose it's habit . . . but, not that sorry."

"Are you being practical? You could lose quite a bit of change, Mrs. D., yet never feel it."

"I'm not being practical." She looked at him, her remarkable eyes, astonishing with her pale hair, very grave. "I don't want to help him, Whit."

"Would you like me to? It could be arranged, I believe, so that he wouldn't know where the money came from; at least," he amended, "not at first. He's not stupid really, Janice. But by the time he discovered the source of salvation, he'd accept it—as fast he would have accepted my help when he asked you to ask me, or yours, when he directly approached you."

"I don't want you to help him, either."

He said, diffidently for him, "This isn't a sort of 'the back of my hand to you' impulse, is it?"

"There are words for that, satisfaction or revenge. No, never at any time."

"I thought not." He got up, pulled her off the dressing table bench and held her. She was quiet in his arms; she wished she need never leave them.

He said, "Well, then, we won't talk about it any more. Don't worry. I have a feeling he'll find his way out of this somehow—I doubt Madge's father will let her starve. He'll come up with something. I'm sure he dotes on Madge and the grandchildren. Of course, it will mean a hardship on Dave, and whatever business he goes into next, it will mean the whip hand, two whip hands in fact; I don't seem to know anything about Madge's mother. . . . But, don't worry, Janice."

"I'm not worrying; I was just sorry. As for Madge's mother, she's a pleasant Hokinson type, but not nearly as alive."

"We're alive," he said. "And now that that's all settled, how about coming to bed? Tomorrow we'll talk more about our trip south. Actually it's all arranged. You, Cecil and I fly—oh yes, and Mortimer. Cars will meet us. We'll settle Cecil in the Lodge and take off, by car, with Mortimer."

"Herman?"

"Herman stays home; she wouldn't like the larger canines roaming the Lodge grounds—Alsatians——"

"Cecil won't be alone?"

"I told you who was there. Also, there's an engaging house dog, a beagle; and television, radio and a pool in which to swim, or the lake if she prefers. Also boats and someone to run them, a canoe for sightseeing, rowboats for idle fishing, if you care to move off the dock, and a little speedboat."

"Dear me," said Janice, "you do think of everything!"

"My father thought of it all. He built the Lodge for hunting, fishing and relaxation. It isn't Dunewalk, but you'll like it. And don't fret. Herman will be spoiled; Cecil will have a breather. I can zip and unzip, even," he added, "brush hair and——"

"Don't leer," Janice reproached him, smiling.

"Was I leering? I thought I'd lost the knack when I was rising fourteen. I'm afraid we'll have to put up in some rather unlikely motels and such."

"Just like ordinary people," said Janice, and looking at him, couldn't remember a single motel, likely or unlikely.

Waking, early next morning, she thought of Dave. I suppose he hates me, she told herself and felt nothing except a brush of sorrow. It was inevitable that in a situation such as theirs he would hate her. Whit had said that he couldn't hate anyone; but many must hate him, she'd thought, foreboding—the blackmailers, the beggars, the fanatics, the disaffected. And then she remembered Joe Meeker and how she had explained the love-hate relationship to Whit who'd said, "I know." Recalling this she was taken back to a sunny beach and Whit, speaking of Dave, saying she hated him because she still loved him. She hoped he didn't remember that.

Whit woke and peered at her in the light filtering in and said, "You must have had an erotic dream, Mrs. D."

"Don't be absurd. I didn't dream, at all."

"Then why, at this hour, are you blushing?"

EIGHTEEN

❀❀❀

A YOUNG MAN Janice had never seen drove her, Whit, Mortimer and Cecil to the plane. Whit introduced him as Jimmy and he touched his hat. "Who on earth is he?" she asked, going to the car, and Whit said, "One of the mechanics . . . sharp kid, goes to night school."

On the way to the plane, "I've never asked you if Fred and Harry are married."

"To each other?"

"Of course not. But they didn't bring wives when they were with us for dinner."

"None to bring. Fred lives in New Jersey with his parents and is wary of marriage. More fun not, he says. Harry is separated from his wife—no divorce possible—and lives alone also in Jersey. Scotty on the other hand, has a wife who looks rather like a robin, a couple of kids and a flat in New York, uptown, west side."

Someday, if she lived long enough, she'd see the Dennis picture whole, not in bits and pieces like snapshots.

Fred, Harry and Scotty greeted her as if they hadn't seen her in a long time, which was comparatively true. They'd been flying around the stacked sky yonder, Whit explained, bearing Corporation people on various errands and also a Foundation group or two on missions, he said gravely, of mercy. Cecil was made known to the crew and they took off, Cecil in a seat at one end of the lounge, with a book and a knitting bag. It occurred to Janice that Cecil melted unobtrusively into any setting. She would be as composed and at home in a dog cart, a helicopter, a battleship, a Rolls Royce, a model A, afoot or horseback as she was in the Corporation's executive jet.

At the airport nearest the Lodge they were met by two cars: one, a big comfortable job; the other, smaller. They were driven by two men, both young, both dark and with enchanting smiles. They were twins and, Whit explained, the progeny of Thad and his wife; one was W. Dennis Jones, the other Dennis W. Jones.

"My father was their sponsor in baptism. I wanted to be but was considered too young as well as frivolous."

"Really Jones? Not Smith?"

"Really Jones. . . . The smaller car's for Cecil to tool around in while we're away or on her time off when we're there. She can drive and has licenses to prove it, New York, Great Britain and International, of course."

"Naturally," said Janice. If he'd told her that Cecil could fly their plane, she would not be astonished; she was past that.

"When she doesn't want to drive, Dennis, known as Denny, will take her. Good kids, the twins, they're in college; this is vacation."

Entering the Lodge gates, electronically controlled, in the car Mortimer drove—Denny drove the other, with his brother and Cecil as passengers—they seemed to proceed for miles before they reached the house. As it was daylight, Janice saw the shapes of mountains, misty blue, and the clearer blue waters of the lake. The Lodge was built of native stone—long, low, and seemed to grow from the ground. Dogs barked from the kennels; the Alsatians; and they'd passed a stable with the smell and sound of horses and Janice said, "I bet Cecil can ride."

"Can't you?"

"Oh, a little, but I'd never take any blues."

"Practically no one uses the saddle horses now—the work horses are used, of course—except the twins, who exercise them and when they're off at school, someone else sees to that. There were quite a few in my father's time; he rode a lot. Since then some have been sold, some put out to pasture, and one, my mother's favorite, was destroyed; he broke a leg taking a fence; she wasn't hurt."

"Your mother rides?"

"Brilliantly, but she hasn't since then. Lily is frightened of horses. It's funny. She's a terror on skis, any kind of skis, addicted to racing cars—not that Ned lets her race—and an amateur pilot—she has a small plane in California. She's good at almost any form of activity, but horses give her goose bumps."

More snapshots.

The Lodge was a one-story building; the central part contained the big living room, with an enormous fireplace. The chairs and couches were in leather, the tables of native wood, there were antlers on the walls, mounted fish, and some hunting prints. Off it there was a gun room full of guns and fishing rods, and beyond that, dining room, pantry and kitchen. One wing contained the master bedroom and bath, a small study, the walls lined with books, and a single bedroom and bath where Whit explained Cecil would sleep. The guest rooms were in the other wing, where Mortimer would stay, and Joe, when he came. The swimming pool and patio was on the guest-wing side of the house. As for the resident Joneses they had, a little distance away, their own stone house, two stories high. Farther away were the stables, also stone with quarters for unmarried male employees. "It's mammoth," Whit had said as they passed it. "I'd like to make it over into a day camp for kids

—it has showers and a recreation room—and build a smaller stable for the horses, and more modern quarters for the men."

"Are there many?"

"An old gardener," he said; "a general maintenance man—we sometimes have trouble here with the power—and of course," he added, smiling, "our protective custody. The rest of the yard men come by the day from the village."

The kennels were impressive too; the man who looked after the dogs had his quarters there, Whit told her.

Thad and Mary were at the door to meet them. In Thad, a tall man, Janice recognized a faint resemblance to Martha Dennis' Jasper—younger, but the same aquiline nose and strikingly set eyes. "They had a Cherokee grandfather," Whit explained when Janice spoke of it. Mary, Thad's wife and the mother of the twins was darker, shorter and pretty.

They went to their room to change. "After your oration on girls in pants," Janice asked, "do you mind my slacks?"

"No, they're right for here and Dunewalk; what I can't abide are blinding pajamas, sequined trouser suits or velvet hoopla, for evening wear."

Slacks and a pullover then, and Whit—for the mountain air was chilly as the sun went down—also in slacks and flannel shirt. "Like mint juleps?" he inquired.

She said, "I've not had many."

"I hope not. Thad is a genius. Everyone who comes here gets into a grave discussion with him. 'What school do you follow?' they ask. 'Do you crush the mint or not?' "

"Well, does he?"

"He compromises, he bruises it gently."

She asked, "Will Cecil take her meals with Thad and Mary?"

"I asked her if she'd like trays," said Whit, "while you're busy shuddering away from the guns. She said she'd rather eat with the Joneses—they have a dining area in the kitchen—if I didn't mind. I didn't. I silently applauded her decision. Not once in a dukedom will she meet as fine a gentleman as Thad. All will be desegregated as Mort and Thad are old friends."

Harry, Fred and Scotty were staying near the airport and Whit said idly, "North Carolina is noted for its pretty girls."

After the mint juleps, which were spectacular, and dinner which was simple, good and beautifully served, they left their coffee and wandered out to the patio to look at the view.

"It's beautiful."

"Like it better than Dunewalk?"

"No. It's just different."

The pool, magnificent shrubbery, good lawns . . . the mountains not too far, the lake a long way down. It was reached by a path through the trees. The air was as intoxicating and stimulating as the juleps.

"Does your mother come here often?"

"She hasn't been here since my father died. She never liked it much anyway. Too many guns and hunting and fishing took him away from her on their holidays here, when she did go along. She doesn't shoot; sometimes, she'd fish. She's a water person, my mother. She likes Dunewalk, her house in San Francisco, the smaller place on the Big Sur; mountains oppress her, also thinner air. She likes the informality here, the native stone, wood and leather, but the dogs scare her. They don't Aunt Hilda of course; she offers them her hand to eat, but so far they never have." He put his arm round her narrow waist. He said, "If you're not too tired, we can start off with Mortimer tomorrow morning and pry into a little Foundation business."

"Where?"

"Tennessee, and Kentucky; and I have a couple of inquiries to make for the Corporation, also."

"It's here too? As if I had to ask."

"Textiles, tobacco, brick yards—yes, it's here. Sure you're not too tired? I can leave you with Cecil, Thad, Mary, and the twins."

"Also the guards."

"Of course; you won't be bothered by them, they just lurk behind the bigger trees," he said, laughing.

"I'm not tired," Janice said.

But she was, in a curious falling-apart sort of way.

In the morning at a breakfast from which she shrank because there was so much of it, Mary came from the kitchen to ask if Miss Janice wanted anything she didn't see.

Watching Whit consume eggs, bacon, ham, waffles and other comestibles, the names of which he didn't know she knew, she didn't even want anything she could see.

"You'll eat eggs yet," Whit promised cheerfully, "but first, I have to get you a proper spoon."

She thought of Felicity and said firmly, "Spoon or no spoon, I hate eggs."

"No one's perfect," said Whit and presently they left. They were gone for almost a week, putting up as Whit had promised at motels in strange towns. Janice went to Foundation offices with him, she talked with the people there, she went to clinics, and to one partly finished medical center; and on Corporation business went into more offices, and also tobacco sheds, mills and brick yards. At night she collapsed into whatever strange bed was offered and slept without moving.

Whit said, "Well, a few days in which to rest and relax at the Lodge and we'll be on our way home. Someday I'll bring you to North Carolina and its coastline and rivers; South Carolina too." But she did not hear him. He smiled, got up, adjusted the air-conditioning and pulled down the shades against a red neon sign across the street.

Back at the Lodge, Janice was glad to put herself into Cecil's hands and to ask how she occupied herself. Cecil had driven, with Denny, about the area; she had made friends with Sloppy, the endearing beagle; gone fishing in the lake, also with Denny. She said, "It's such beautiful country, Mrs. Dennis."

On the second night, they left the Lodge and the big living room, which was full of flowers, and went walking, out through the obedient electronic gates and into the woods. Mortimer tagged behind with Denny. Later, Janice would remember that Mortimer was smoking a pipe.

The sky was star-silvered and there was a full moon sailing over the massed tree tops, red gold, a summer moon.

Walking on a path thick with fallen pine needles, she asked idly, "Your father called the house just the Lodge?"

"No, we do. It has a long Indian name which I can't pronounce, much less spell; longer than the name of that minute fish in Hawaii. . . . By the way have you ever been to Hawaii?"

"No," she said dreamily, looking up at the tall trees, the moon, at remote stars and smelling pine and pipe smoke.

"We'll take you there, *Mrs. Calabash* and I, someday."

"Not tonight. I don't want to go tonight," said Janice.

She didn't want to go anywhere, just to keep on walking slowly, her hand in Whit's.

He heard the small sound, she did not; the next thing she knew he had thrown her to the ground and himself upon her, and the first shot went harmlessly over them, and the second and third. And men were running and dogs were running, and there was a vast but ordered confusion; Mortimer, Denny, the unknown men she'd not once glimpsed, and the man who had loosed the dogs. . . .

She wasn't frightened, not then; she was indignant, face down on the pine needles, and hurting a little.

There were no more shots.

Whit got up. He said, "I'm sorry, I had to do that, Janice."

He helped her up and Mortimer appeared, his pipe burning a hole in his pocket.

"You're on fire," Janice told him, shaking needles from her hair and Mort asked, inattentive, "You hurt, Whit?"

"Sprained my shoulder a little, I think—nothing serious."

Mort said, "They'll get them—or him—the dogs are out and the men."

"Where's Denny?"

"Off with the others. That was a near thing, Whit."

Janice began to shake. She said incredulously, "Someone shot at us?"

"At me, most likely," Whit said. "You just happened to be around. . . . Let's get back to the Lodge."

Mort said, "Going out of the gates at night, damned fool thing to do." He removed the pipe from the pocket in which he had thrust it and beat out sparks. His jacket was pushed back and Janice saw the gun.

Whit said, "Are you all right, Janice?"

"Yes." She walked beside him, in silence, then she asked, "Why? Why now?"

"I daresay I created a little rumble of disapproval when I went to discuss another clinic. Word gets around among the diehards."

They were silent, walking faster than they'd come, to the Lodge, Mortimer on one side of her, Whit on the other. Once in the big quiet room, Cecil appeared with Thad and Mary, and Mortimer took off Whit's coat. "Just a sprain," he said, wincing.

"X rays," said Cecil firmly.

"In the morning; we'll go to Asheville. Meantime it hurts, but it's better than a bullet."

Janice turned and ran through the living room wing to her bedroom, and Cecil asked, "Shall I go after her, Mr. Dennis?"

"Do that," said Whit. "There's a scarf in my dresser, it will make an improvised sling. Mary, will you go with Mrs. Cecil; she'll find it for you."

Cecil knocked, and Janice muttered something. She was shaking. Cecil came in and said, "Mr. Dennis asked me to find a scarf for him, Mrs. Dennis."

"Find it," said Janice, "and go away."

Cecil found it, although only one light burned. She took it to the door, gave it to Mary and came back, closed the door and approached the bed where Janice was lying face down. She asked, momentarily jolted into the third person, "If Mrs. Dennis would let me help her to undress. . . ?"

Janice sat up. Her face was cream white, her eyes blazing brown.

"I'm fine," she said, "just go away."

"You've had a shock," Cecil informed her soothingly, "I'll get you something——"

"Just go away," said Janice, "and leave me alone."

"Very well, Mrs. Dennis," said Cecil as she went out and shut the door. On her way back, she met Whit, sling and all, and he asked, "How is she, Cecil?"

"Somewhat disturbed, Mr. Dennis. She wouldn't let me do anything for her." She smiled at him, a bright, open smile, and added, "If you could persuade Mrs. Dennis to take something for her nerves. . . ? I couldn't."

She went kitchenward to discuss the events of the evening with the Joneses. Mortimer had gone off to look for Denny—his mother was nervous about him—and also for his twin, and to talk with the guards. The big dogs barked in the distance and Sloppy, the beagle, gave voice in the kitchen.

Whit went into the bedroom and Janice, still sitting up, felt herself coming to a fast, rolling boil.

He said conversationally, "They fixed me up with a sling."

"So I see. Cecil came in here and went trotting through your things as if she were looking for——"

"Truffles?" Whit inquired. "You haven't asked me if my shoulders hurts," he said pathetically.

"I couldn't care less. Does it?"

"A trifle. How do you feel?"

"As if I'd been tackled," she said shortly.

"And so you were; there wasn't time to ask your permission."

"I feel dandy," said Janice, "I feel great. There's nothing like being thrown on your face on pine needles——" Her voice wavered and broke. She was crying, she was laughing, she was having her first attack of hysterics. "You," she managed to say, "you're a damned fool, you might have been killed!"

"So I might." He went over to the bed and slapped her hard. "So what else is new?" he asked.

She was stunned into silence. And then she said, "That tears it——"

Whit said, as Cecil had, "You've had a shock."

"Get away from me," said Janice, red flags flying. "Sure I've had a shock. Cecil said so; she's always right; so are you." She reached for a hunk of polished stone on a night table, and threw it at him.

He ducked. "I wish I never had to see you again," she said.

Tears ran down her face, tears of anger, of reaction, of something close to despair.

Whit sat down on the bed, "If that had connected," he told her, "you might have been a very pretty, very rich widow."

"Please just go away."

"Not until you tell me when you fell in love with me, Mrs. D."

"I didn't. I haven't. I don't *know* . . . I feel sick," said Janice and, for the first time in her life, fainted.

She heard Whit shouting, "Cecil" as she swam up through the dark but springless buzzing waters, and then Cecil was there, making her smell something and drink something else. And she swallowed and sputtered and remembered what Whit had asked and what she'd said.

Then Cecil was gone and Whit's good arm was around her. He said, "There, lean back. Why didn't you tell me you're pregnant?"

"I'm not sure . . ." She looked at him, eyes widening. "How did you——"

"Cecil thinks so."

"Oh, Cecil!"

"There's nothing left around to throw, Janice. Lean back, catch your breath. If you suspected this, why didn't you go to a doctor?"

"Because you would have known. I was going to tell

you what I thought when we got home and then I could go to the doctor, with permission. You have to know where I go all the time."

"Do you mind very much?"

"Not really. I just don't seem to care any more. I'm sorry, Whit," she told him. "We'll work this out somehow."

"Work what out? Babies usually take nine months—longer if you're an elephant, of course."

"Oh stop it," she said. "Will you never be serious? I mean"—now she was flushed again—"I mean this stupid complication. I was so sure I wouldn't——"

"Wouldn't what?"

She did not answer. He held her fast, he kissed her. He said, "But I so hoped you would, darling."

"You're crazy," said Janice. "You're just trying to make the best of it . . . and I can't even leave you," she said mournfully.

"No."

"It will be dreadful for you."

"What?"

"Being tied to a woman who loves you."

"I'll bite on the bullet."

"Don't say that word; don't say bullet!" She was shaking again. He put both arms around her.

"Your shoulder——"

"To hell with my shoulder."

She began to laugh and Whit said, "More hysterics?"

"No, I was thinking about the party."

"You're still in shock. What party?"

"The one we're to give in the autumn, all your old girl friends and their kinfolk. Is it proper to give an elegant party for an expectant mother—that is, if I am."

"Quite. Raoul will run you up some beautiful gold

lamé shifts. Everyone looks pregnant nowadays, debutantes, dowagers, grannies. Don't worry. It's just sooner than we planned, but the Pill isn't infallible."

She said in a small voice, "I stopped taking the Pill, Whit."

"When?"

"After—after I had lunch with Dave."

"I suppose I'd better ask why?"

She said, with an effort, because whatever Cecil had given her was making her drowsy, "I was furious at you for making me keep that appointment. Then later I thought: How marvelous of you, even though you didn't love me—and I thought I'd do something for you. That's what you wanted most, a child, children——"

He said, "I think we'll call the plane 'Vanessa.' "

He removed the arm which hurt, but held her with the other and Janice asked sleepily, "Suppose it's a boy?"

"In that case we'll still call the plane Vanessa, a promise of things to come. Remind me to tell you what the Lodge is really called."

"Tell me now."

"Translated it means, 'Beautiful squaw, above lake and under blue mountains, loves handsome brave who loves her.' "

"I don't believe it——"

"Don't go to sleep yet. I fell in love with you—oh not the first day in Howard's office, and maybe not even when you wouldn't go to dinner with me, but, when you did. The Spanish place, remember?"

She shook her head to clear it. "I don't believe that either," she told him.

"It's true. You weren't in love with me, darling; you made it abundantly clear. But I thought perhaps, in time, you might be."

"You made it all up—that elaborate business about not wanting a wife who was in love with you?"

"Naturally. Nothing would have frightened you off faster than my telling you, 'I love you, I'm insane about you.' You would have run like a rabbit. So I thought perhaps on my stated terms, you'd marry me. That was the chance I took."

"How do I know you're not putting me on again?"

"That's the chance *you* take. You don't know, and perhaps you never will."

He saw her eyelids close. She was trying to say something. She managed, "When we're sure, will you let me call Martha? You can tell Joe." And then very slowly, with half a chuckle, "To think I bought you cuff links for your birthday . . ."

He laid her back on the pillows. He'd have to call Cecil. It would take two good arms to get Janice out of her clothes. He thought: Well, my luck's held so far and now it will be Vanessa or young Whit—all that and heaven too, as the man said.

Before he rang, he leaned over to kiss his wife and—a supremely happy man—to watch her for a little while, as she slept.